INCITE
INSIGHT

by

Robert New

Tale Publishing

National Library of Australia Cataloguing-in-Publication entry:
Creator: New, Robert, author.
Title: Incite insight / Robert New.
ISBN: 9780994439901 (paperback)
Subjects: Detective and mystery stories.
Dewey Number: A823.4

Tale Publishing
Melbourne Victoria

Books by Robert New

Incite Insight
The Conversationist

Dedication

This novel is dedicated to Genevieve, Michael, Rachel, my family and my friends. It is also dedicated to the teachers who have inspired me throughout my life and people who daydream.

Prologue

The Professor was buying breakfast when the reaction started. Intuitively, he knew he didn't have much time. Habit made him start taping his voice.

"I know I am about to die, I cannot control what is happening to me."

Even as he spoke the first sentence he was aware of the magnitude of what was occurring. If only he could explain what had done this to him so that others might understand. People wandered by, blissfully unaware that the man they were passing was answering the great questions of life. By the time the first thin trickle of blood ran out of his ear, the Professor had already answered Who am I?, proved mankind's existence and outlined a utopian society where everyone was an 'elite' and there were no lower classes. His mind was flooded with information; he could access every memory, every piece of information stored in his brain. Soon he found himself generating new knowledge. As he proved a theory that unified all physical actions, blood began to flow out of his ears, nostrils and eyes. His mouth remained free of blood and he continued to speak. As he spoke the words which unlocked the mysteries of life and the universe, the chemicals in his mind reacted so violently his brain was liquefied. For a fleeting second before he died, he had become a god: able to create, control and exist in all the dimensions of time, awareness and reality.

The people around him would later describe the way he died as looking like his brain had melted.

Act One: Chapter One

It was a grey and dreary morning when Detective Brad Thomas took a call at his desk from his boss, Sergeant Wendy Pan, even though her office was just ten metres away. Brad sighed and reminded himself that he had wanted to be transferred to this city station as it was his dream to be a Metro homicide detective. The reality was that during the two months he'd been here, he had struggled to cope with the hectic pace of the department. He had even begun thinking about moving back to his old station in Northam. Here they called him *country boy* and made him feel worthless.

"Detective Thomas?" Sergeant Pan snapped. The strength of her tone created an intimidation that her physical stature could not.

"Yes?" Brad replied.

"Time to go to work. A possible homicide. Food court, Lakeside Shopping Centre. Detective Summers will meet you there."

Wendy hung up on him, once again giving Brad the impression that he wasn't worth her time. As Brad left the police station in his unmarked car, he reminded himself of what it had taken to get here - a seven year placement in a rural town, four attempts to pass his detective exam and much hard work. Whilst at the rural station of Northam, he had developed a reputation for chasing down every lead and a strong work ethic. He wasn't the brightest, his previous Sergeant had told Sergeant Pan when the transfer was complete, but he was honest and dedicated. His Sergeant had also added that he worked better with women than men. Brad had hoped that this new placement would be the making of him and the chance to improve himself. Instead, he felt constantly out of his depth and worried that he'd be lucky to last the year as a detective.

It took Brad a while to arrive at the crime scene. On the way he had driven around the lake that was beside the shopping centre. Brad often stopped by the lake to find a moment of stillness. As he drove past, a strong breeze was blowing across the water, the ripples made Brad shudder. *Today is not going to be a good day,* he thought. He was the first detective to arrive at the taped off food court. In amongst neon signs, bright lights and billboards advertising food, a crowd had gathered. Many were straining their necks to see what had happened. Some people were being interviewed by the first Constable to arrive. As Brad ducked under the tape he overheard a witness say that "the old guy just froze and then collapsed."

It certainly was a surreal sight: In front of signs proclaiming the health benefits of eating well was a supine body in a small pool of blood. An overweight security guard, dressed from head to toe in black, walked over to Brad.

"It probably took ten or fifteen minutes to get all the witnesses to clear the area. I don't think anyone touched the body, but I can't say for sure," the guard said without introducing himself.

"Oh, ok… Can I get a copy of the security footage?" Brad asked.

"Sure," the security guard stated with uncertainty. Brad recognised the 'out of my depth' tone of the guard's voice and felt an immediate kinship with him. Brad smiled and nodded to the security guard, then returned his gaze to the body. Even from a few paces away he could tell the victim's suit was expensive and tailored. His face was covered in what looked like a mixture of blood and snot, forming a mask over the lower half of his face. From this perspective there were no obvious signs of trauma.

The trauma must be on the other side of his head, Brad thought. As the photographer finished taking some photos, Detective Sally Summers arrived. Brad smiled as he saw her approach, her blond ponytail bobbing as she ducked under the tape. She was the only officer in the department who was friendly with him. Brad greeted her as she entered the crime scene.

"Hi Detective."

"Hi. So what's the story?" Detective Summers asked.

"I'm not sure yet, there's nothing on this side of the body. Can you give me a hand turning him over?"

"Sure."

Together they turned the body over. It was immediately clear that the cause of death wasn't physical trauma as there were no visible wounds or injuries.

"Poison?" queried Detective Summers, mostly to herself.

"Probably." Brad tried to remember which drugs might cause haemorrhaging and made a note to look it up when he was back at the station. Carefully squatting by the body, Brad inhaled deeply. His nostrils filled with the metallic scent of blood and a hint of musky deodorant, but nothing else. *Nothing with a smell anyway.*

After more photos were taken, Brad arranged for the body to be sent to the Medical Examiner's office for an autopsy. Brad examined the scene for any evidence or clues that might help establish the cause of death, but was mystified as to what it could be. There were no weapons on the ground, or tell-tale signs of defensive wounds on the body's hands. Brad could only hope that the whole thing was a suicide and that the toxicology report would reveal something. None of the witnesses described any attack or even anyone near the man, just that he was standing still and seemed to be talking to himself. He hadn't called out or appeared distressed as he started to bleed and collapse. The story was remarkably consistent amongst the observers, which seemed odd to Brad. Normally if a lot of people had witnessed a crime, there were multiple interpretations of what happened. But this was different. All the witnesses said that they felt compelled to turn and look at the man while everything was going on. It was as though they were witnessing a rapture. One observer even said that the man's head was glowing, almost like a halo.

With gloved hands, Brad searched the body, hoping for a clue to the man's identity. All he found was some change to go with the phone that was on the ground nearby. The items were carefully catalogued and bagged, along with the food the man had purchased. The man wasn't carrying a wallet or any identification. Brad sighed and scratched his head. He looked over to Detective Summers, hoping that she would have some great insight, but she just shrugged. There was no likely cause of death, no identity of the victim and all the witnesses said the guy just stood still for a while, then collapsed. It was almost like a conspiracy, except that there were no obvious connections between the witnesses – who consisted of fast food employees, shoppers and a security guard and no obvious reason for anyone to have conspired together.

The lab better turn up something 'cos I'm stumped, Brad thought to himself.

By the time they had wrapped up their onsite investigation, and arrived back at the station it was mid-afternoon. The victim's possessions had been analysed by the lab and were now in sealed envelopes that Brad retrieved from evidence storage. The keycard and phone from the body, yielded fingerprints belonging to the same person, but when they were run through the police database no match was found. There was no criminal record for the deceased. Brad called the Medical Examiner's office to see how long it would take for the autopsy and toxicology report. He groaned inwardly when he was told that he might have to wait a week for the results.

At least I have the man's phone to work with, Brad thought. He turned it back on and went straight to the contacts list. He was amazed to discover that there were no contacts. He tried the call log – there were no missed or received calls and only one dialled number. Brad gave it a call from his desk.

"Hello, West East Restaurant. Lily speaking," a female voice answered.

"Uhh, hello?" Brad said.

"Yes, can I take your order please?" Lily continued sharply.

Brad was surprised and disappointed at the same time. This was likely to be a dead end.

"Uh, hi. Umm. I found your number in a mobile phone."

"So?" Lily queried.

"Sorry, I was just hoping you could tell me who the phone belonged to."

"Well what is the phone's number?"

"Umm, I don't know. I'll call you back." Brad cursed himself for not having thought to get the number. He hung up and looked up the phone's number which he wrote on a piece of paper before redialling.

"Hello, West East Restaurant," Lily answered again.

"Hi, it's me again. Detective Thomas," Brad began and then realised that he had not given his name last time.

"Hello Detective. So what's the number?"

Brad read out the number.

"Yes, yes. That is the Professor's number," Lily said matter-of-factly.

Brad felt a surge of excitement.

"Professor?"

"Yes that is what we call him. He orders almost every week - always the Westlake duck and steamed rice."

"So where does he live?" Brad asked.

"No idea, he always comes and picks up his order himself."

"What about a credit card receipt?" Brad asked, thinking that he could track him that way.

"No, he always pays cash."

Damn, Brad thought, *I just can't catch a break.* He thanked Lily, then leaned back in his chair, thinking about what to do next.

Brad entered the phone's number into the police database, which ran slowly, giving Brad time for two thoughts – one that he should have thought of this earlier, and two that it would reveal nothing. Unfortunately for Brad his premonition was accurate. The computer pinged and revealed that the number was an anonymous prepaid phone. Brad was frustrated; this case was not progressing in the usual way. Normally there would be obvious leads to follow, but at this point he was stuck. He found this annoying and at odds with his work ethic.

Give me a lead and I will follow it, he thought, *so where are they?* He let out a groan just as Detective Summers approached. She heard him and said "hang on, I haven't even given you the news yet. Cause comes before effect, not after."

"Huh?" Brad grunted.

"Boss wants to see you."

"Oh, ok." He unconsciously groaned again.

"That's better," chuckled Detective Summers.

Oh no, is Sally going to start teasing me now too? he thought.

"What?" he said aloud.

"Don't worry, just go see the Boss," She replied good-naturedly. "I'm off to court to give evidence in the Prensky trial, so you're on your own."

Brad walked to his Sergeant's office and knocked on the door.

"Come in," barked Sergeant Pan.

"You wanted to see me Sarge?" Brad asked.

"That's Sergeant, Detective," she said icily.

"What progress have you made on the Lakeside shopping centre case? Does it need to go on the investigations board?"

"Umm," Brad mumbled.

"What's 'umm'? Yes or no?" Sergeant Pan was starting to regret Brad being placed in her department, not that she'd had any say in the matter.

"Maybe…" Brad said.

"What do you mean 'maybe'? It's either a murder or it isn't. What does the evidence say?" Brad slowly explained the frustrations of the day with its lack of clear leads and evidence of how the man died.

"I'm not even sure it was a murder," Brad said.

"Hmm," Sergeant Pan murmured, "There is one lead you haven't followed yet."

Sergeant Pan typed the address into an online satellite based mapping program. The police found this free resource immensely useful. She then added the address of the West East Restaurant. They were within a few kilometres of each other.

"People are lazy and creatures of habit. The closeness of these two places and the fact that your professor always picked up his food suggests that he probably also lived in the area. That should narrow down your search area."

Brad frowned like he was trying to process how this connection was made.

"Hmmm," Sergeant Pan murmured again, "Look at what's here."

She pointed to the top of the screen.

"So?" Sergeant Pan couldn't help but think that for all his determination and hard work, Brad would never make a great detective. He just couldn't make enough links between pieces of evidence. He would still be a good detective and useful for the ninety percent of cases where the perpetrator was known to the victim, but not for those where the links were less obvious and the case less linear.

"Well, the person at the restaurant called the victim 'professor.' What if that was not just a nickname, but his actual profession?" The Sergeant felt like she would have to make the connection for Brad. "What if he worked here?" she said pointing to Western University, a large, world renowned university and looking at Brad's face.

Brad's eyes shone with sudden insight.

"Yes, that would fit," he replied.

"You don't need Detective Summers for this, so what are you waiting for – go!" Sergeant Wendy Pan commanded.

"I'll get right on it," said Brad, as he bounded out of his Sergeant's office. Wendy smiled to herself as he left;

he was just like a puppy.

###

The university was on the bank of the river that separated the north and south sides of the city. Brad parked in an emergency services bay in front of an old sandstone building near the front of the campus which Brad assumed would have a receptionist for him to ask where to go. Unfortunately, Brad had to wander around reading the signs on the front of each building. He saw display boards everywhere advertising the university graduates' achievements. Several posters mentioned that there was a Nobel Prize winner on staff who was famous for curing ulcers. Brad couldn't help but be reminded of how little he had achieved with his life. He had not had a girlfriend for two years, was failing at his job and not living up to his father's expectations. Deep in thought Brad suddenly realised he was lost. All of the buildings were numbered but with no obvious order.

He knew he needed building five for human resources, but it was not located anywhere near building four or six. He walked past the Library, momentarily distracted by it being surrounded by a real moat. Eventually he asked people for directions and after two had shrugged and said they didn't know, the third person was able to point him in the right direction. Once he was at the right building, he noticed the clear room numbers on the ground floor – necessary due to the identical dark brown doors. A short elevator ride took him to Human Resources which occupied half of the top floor of the building. Behind a front desk was an expansive, open plan office. The view of the campus from the continuous windows was spectacular.

It's like being in a command centre, Brad thought. The view was like a prison design he had studied at the police academy, where the prisoners roamed free in a courtyard and were observed from a central tower. The thought was that by being under a constant 'gaze' the prisoners would learn to control or modify their behaviour and that after a period of time this would become conditioned in them and they could be released.

Brad approached the front desk where an administration assistant in her mid-twenties, with long, dark brown hair and a name tag that said "Amy" smiled in welcome.

"Hi Amy, I'm Detective Thomas. I phoned earlier," Brad said, trying to sound confident.

"Yes, hi, we were expecting you a little while ago," she said pleasantly.

"I got a little lost," Brad admitted, smiling sheepishly.

"That happens here."

"The building numbers don't seem right, they aren't sequential." Given Amy's attractiveness, Brad tried to sound intelligent.

"Well they are, but not in the sense of building one being next to building two – they are numbered in the order they were built in," Amy said with a smile that lit up her face.

"I guess that sort of makes sense," Brad said with a slight grin, "By the way you have an amazing view from up here."

"We do. You can see nearly the whole campus from up here."

"I bet there is nothing that goes on here that you don't know about,"

"Well, we do know all the comings and goings of personnel and all the scandals." Amy lowered her voice and giggled. "This one time a student and his professor were caught…"

The intercom buzzed. "Amy, is that Detective Thomas?"

"Um, yes it is," she replied.

"Well send him in, it's late."

"Ok." Amy turned off the intercom. "Mr Horace will see you now, Officer," Amy said with a flirtatious smile. Brad made a mental note to stop by her desk again on the way out. He hoped to hear the end of her story and maybe to get her phone number.

The Director of Human Resources was the only one in the department with his own office, everyone else worked in partitioned sections. His room was filled with filing cabinets and shelves containing folders of law, guidelines and policies. Everywhere Brad looked there were documents or document storage. The one exception was the desk which only had a laptop computer, a photo of the director and his family at a theme park, a stained, empty cup and a small notebook and pen.

"Hello Mr Horace," Brad said, suddenly losing the confident tone he had managed a moment ago.

"Call me Tim," he replied firmly as they shook hands over the desk. Tim motioned for Brad to sit in the chair opposite.

"Hi Tim, thanks for meeting with me. As I mentioned to you on the phone I was called to a crime scene this morning where there was an unidentified male body that we think might be a staff member of this university."

Tim nodded, "Yes, I've had a look into it for you,

even though that sort of enquiry is normally handled by the Director of Professional Services." Tim paused, "And yes, we do have two staff members who have not turned up for work today and not called to say why. One is a research assistant and one is a tenured professor."

Brad's heart rate quickened.

"I have a police sketch of the deceased man's face, minus all the blood."

Brad slid a copy of the picture over the desk to Tim.

"Does it look like either of the two missing staff members?"

Please, Brad thought.

"Yes, that is Professor Episteme. He's a professor in our Philosophy Department... Or should I say was?" Tim asked dispassionately.

"Yes, unfortunately he's dead," Brad replied. Tim frowned.

"We're not sure how he died yet. Witnesses say he just collapsed. So we're unsure if the death is suspicious or not. Is there anyone who would want him dead?" Brad asked.

"Not that I know of, but then I don't know him well. You might want to talk to his colleague Jane De Silva. She has, I mean had, worked with him for a long time," Tim said.

"What was he like?" Brad asked.

"Again, you're asking the wrong person, but I do know his publication history was exemplary, except for the last two years. He was an engaging and successful lecturer and his students seemed to like him. Although there are fewer and fewer students studying philosophy around the country these days, the reputation he and his team had built meant that our numbers are healthy enough to sustain the department and even have a degree of growth. We even had to hire a new sessional lecturer." Tim said as though the achievement was through his personnel management alone.

"Ok. I realise it's late, but would Jane be available to speak to now?" Brad asked.

"No everyone has gone home."

Brad turned to look back at the front desk and saw it was empty. He was disappointed that Amy had left too.

"What's your number in case I think of anything else that may help you?" said Tim.

Brad gave Tim his card.

"Do you have an address for the Professor?" Brad asked.

"Yes, but due to privacy laws I'll need some form of legal authority to release it to you," Tim replied.

Damn, Brad thought, *I should have thought to bring that with me* but then he realised that he would now have an excuse to return and speak to Amy again. Brad smiled to himself.

"Ok, I'll get that and come back tomorrow. Thank you for your time." Brad shook Tim's hand, noting the strength of his grip. On his way out he took in another look at the panoramic view and mentally mapped out the path back to the carpark. *Time to go home*, he sighed, *even if it's just to puzzle over this case in a different location.*

Chapter Two

The next morning, Brad groaned as he realised that Detective Summers was still in court and he'd have to make progress without her help. He sat at his desk and called the university, hoping the Professor's colleague Jane was a punctual sort of person. The receptionist transferred him to her direct line which went through to voicemail. Brad hung up without leaving a message.

Brad paused to contemplate his next move. He decided to arrange for the warrant to get the Professor's address officially released by the university and give him permission to access the home. Ninety minutes later, Brad had the authorisation he required and made his way to the university.

This time it was a short trip to the Human Resources Department. As he stepped out of the elevator, Brad smiled to himself when he saw Amy at the front desk again.

"Hello Amy," he said lightly.

"Hello Officer," Amy responded with a smile Brad took as encouragement. "The boss is expecting you. As always he has somewhere else to be, so make it quick."

"Thanks, I will." Brad walked as confidently as he could into the Director's room.

"Hi Tim," Brad said.

"Hi, have you got the warrant?" Tim gave the impression that he didn't have time for interruptions.

"Yes, here it is." Brad handed Tim the warrant. He glanced at it and handed it back to Brad along with another piece of paper.

"Excellent. Here is the address. Is there anything else I can help you with?" he asked without sincerity.

"Actually, while I'm here, I wouldn't mind talking to Professor De Silva, if it's possible?"

"Sure, hang on a minute … Amy, can you come in here please?" Tim called out. As Amy walked over, Brad noticed the lightness of her step and the way her lithe body moved. He normally preferred more curvaceous women, but there was something about her grace and femininity that he found irresistible. Amy noticed him admiring her and smiled. Brad blushed.

"Yes Boss?" Amy said breezily.

"Can you please take Detective Thomas to the Philosophy Department to see Professor De Silva?" Tim asked, softening his voice, it seemed that he had a soft spot for his assistant.

"Sure thing Boss," Amy said lightly.

Brad tried to conceal his delight. "Follow me" she said to Brad. *I'd follow you anywhere,* Brad thought to himself.

"So, ummm, have you worked here long?" Brad

asked, regretting how his voice changed pitch as he spoke.

"Only for a couple of years, although I did study here before that," Amy said, amused by Brad's effort.

"What did you study?"

"Arts and commerce," Amy replied.

"What sort of arts?"

"Human movement," Amy said with a smile.

"That seems like an odd combination to go with commerce." Brad responded, trying to imagine the diverse subjects working together.

"Yeah, but throughout my teenage years I trained in ballet."

So that's why you move the way you do, thought Brad.

"But then I broke my tibia – my shinbone – and couldn't train for a while, which made me want to do other things. I still have an interest in physical activity and health, which is why I studied it here, but I also want to move up in the corporate world, which is why I am still here now. In another year or two, I will have enough experience and knowledge to move up a pay bracket and from there it's only a few more years until I could head up an HR department or maybe do an MBA and start my own company. We'll see…" Amy said with a surety that made Brad envious.

"Wow, sounds like you have it all mapped out," he replied, while mentally dissecting the acronyms.

"Kind of, but I'm open to other opportunities that may come up," Amy said with a laugh and a wicked grin.

Brad wasn't sure if she was referring to him now or her future. Brad had learnt a lot about body language at the Police Academy. Her body language was certainly open to him, she'd maintained a lot of eye contact throughout their walk, seemingly able to move around the university without the need to focus on where she was going and she had a constant smile. These were sure signs of interest.

But how can I be certain she is interested in me? he thought.

Brad was about to ask Amy if she had a boyfriend and then if she would like to go out for a coffee sometime, when she announced that they were at Jane's office. Brad hadn't even noticed them entering a building. He tried to conceal his disappointment as Amy said goodbye, and then his delight when she added "hopefully I'll get to see you again soon."

He managed to reply "I'd like that" with more confidence than he felt. Brad watched as she walked away and thought about his last girlfriend. She had also been ambitious and that had been the stumbling block for their relationship. She had grown tired of waiting for Brad to be promoted and for them to move to the city. Eventually she'd left him for someone who could get her to where she felt she needed to be more quickly. *But I'm here now*, he thought. *Maybe this time things will be different?*

Brad worked to bring his focus back to his task. He noticed the number of doors all the way along the corridor. *The offices must be tiny*, he thought. This was the oldest part of the university and it was easy to imagine that behind each door was a professor toiling away writing articles that few would ever read, and even fewer would care about. He was glad he had a job that

20

made a difference to the world, even if there were times when he felt he wasn't all that successful. Brad raised his hand and knocked on the solid wood door.

"Come in," a bright voice called out. The cast iron hinge creaked as Brad opened the door to the small office. There was just enough room for an extra chair opposite the professor's desk, the rest of the room was crammed with bookshelves and two large filing cabinets.

"Good morning Professor, my name is Detective Brad Thomas."

"Call me Jane," she replied automatically. "What can I do for you?"

Her pleasant smile disappeared when Brad didn't reply. He was still wondering whether he would have long term compatibility with Amy.

"Please take a seat as I have some bad news. I'm investigating someone you know," Brad continued.

"Really? Who?" Jane frowned.

"A colleague of yours has died in suspicious circumstances and we are trying to figure out what happened," Brad stated in his official voice.

"And by suspicious circumstances you mean …?" Jane queried.

"He passed away in the middle of a food court while bleeding from his ears, nose and eyes" Brad responded.

"Oh my." Jane was clearly shocked. "Who?"

Brad checked his notes for the Professor's name. In his head he only ever referred to him as the Professor.

"His name was Michael Episteme."

"Oh no," Jane said bursting into tears.

Brad gave Jane a few moments to compose herself.

"I'm sorry, I thought you knew. I didn't mean to be

so blunt," Brad said.

"That's ok. You are just doing your job. How can I help?"

Brad felt admiration for Jane. Opening herself up to questions about her colleague while she was still in shock in order to help catch whoever caused his death (if foul play was involved) was courageous. Either that or she was involved in his death, but there was no evidence of that.

"How well did you know him?" Brad asked after a pause to let Jane recover.

"He was a good friend. I knew him well. We socialised together and worked closely," Jane replied while wiping away a tear.

"What was he like?" asked Brad gently.

"Inquisitive, knowledgeable, witty … friendly," Jane replied with a sob.

"Would anyone want to see him harmed?"

"No," Jane said emphatically. "He was a warm and generous person."

"What about other relationships? Was he married?" Brad asked.

Maybe there could have been marital problems and a wife with ill intent and a knowledge of poisons? He could only hope, it would clear up this case nicely.

"His wife passed away five years ago. He has thrown himself into his work ever since," Jane replied.

There goes that theory, Brad thought.

"What was he working on?" Brad asked.

"A philosophical project. It sounded quite fascinating. He was convinced that there was or is a way to open up people's minds."

Brad frowned in confusion.

"Meaning that he thought he could create a program that would greatly improve people's ability to think – you know, boost their consciousness and general intelligence."

"Wow, sounds interesting," said Brad. *Now that would be something worth killing for.*

"It is or was. If anyone could do it, he could. He became even more motivated after his wife died. She was the love of his life and an inspiration to him and he her for that matter. He threw himself into his work, into this project, as a means of overcoming his grief," Jane said as a fresh wave of emotion rolled over her and tears welled in her eyes again.

"So how far had he gotten?" he asked.

Maybe though there was some form of conspiracy to stop him making his work public?

"I, we, that is my colleagues and I don't know. It was the one thing he was secretive about. He would ask us questions and give us titbits from what he had been putting together, but none of us really knew what stage it was at," said Jane softly.

"Oh. So what was he actually trying to create? I mean how was he going to change people?" Brad asked curiously.

"It wasn't a pill or drug like in the movies or tv – he was a philosopher not a pharmacist. He was developing an actual course of work that would make a person more intelligent. The idea as I understood it was that each level of the program would present some new idea or thought exercise. At the end of the program you would be able to think better due to the corresponding change in your brain and its functioning. As I said he was quite secretive about it, so I'm not really sure."

Jane looked to her left as she spoke monotonously, "Although, now that I think about it he did talk a couple of years ago about how wonderful it would be if the average person could produce more links between pieces of knowledge. He was particularly interested in any method I might know to achieve this, as he was struggling to think of a way to get people to do what came naturally to him," she continued.

Brad realised that he would also love to know this information. It was something that had come up again and again as an issue for him in the police force. Other officers seemed to be able to make links much faster than he could and Brad had assumed that he would always operate at a slower pace.

What if there was a way to make links more easily? That would make my job so much easier. Maybe they would even stop calling me 'Country Boy'. That program would be so useful for me, he thought.

"A method like what?" Brad asked.

"Like an exercise, a thought exercise. A specific activity that could help someone to improve links between the pieces of knowledge they have in their head," Jane replied.

"And could you help him?" Brad questioned, his voice rising.

"Not exactly. I pointed him towards school teachers as a potential resource. My thinking was that they try to help students make links and might have a particular technique that they could pass on to Michael."

Jane burst into a fresh round of tears at her

mentioning of his name. Brad gave her a few moments then continued:

"Do you know where he lived?"

"Not far from here. Unit 7, 7 Minerva Street."

It was the same address that the HR manager had given him. He already had a warrant to enter the home once the address was known, and Brad was hopeful he could at least start piecing together other details of the Professor's life and maybe ask some questions of his neighbours.

"Can you show me his office please?" Brad asked.

"Yes. Come with me." Jane led them down the corridor and to another solid, dark brown door. The sign on it simply said Professor Episteme, but next to the door was a wooden plaque with the words 'The Office of the Philosopher King' burnt into it in an old English typeface. Jane knocked on the door, then blushed and tried the handle. It was unlocked.

"Here you go," she said with another sob.

"Thanks," Brad replied wishing he could comfort her more.

"Is there anything else you need?" asked Jane.

"No I think that's it for now. If there's anything else I'll let you know. Here is my card, please call me if you think of anything else that might help with this case," said Brad.

"Ok," Jane nodded and walked absently down the corridor.

The Professor's office, like Jane's, was absolutely crammed with textbooks, notes and papers. Going through all of these would be a nightmare. Brad hoped that he would make a breakthrough in the case soon, so that this could be avoided. Aside from this, there didn't appear to be any signs of disturbance or anything out of the ordinary. Although, Brad reminded himself, he wasn't sure what was ordinary for a Professor. The only thing that stood out was the lack of a computer, but then again the university staff all had laptops so maybe it was at his home. Another quick look around revealed nothing of further interest, so Brad left the office. On his way out he passed the staffroom where he could see a few people had gathered. Jane was in tears and being comforted by another staff member. It seemed that the official announcement had finally been made.

To Brad's surprise when he walked out of the sandstone philosophy building, Amy was standing there waiting for him. She was leaning against the handrail on the building's wheelchair access ramp. Brad's heart skipped a beat. She looked relaxed and her pose and the slight breeze through her hair made her seem like a model. Brad realised that she had removed her hairband. This caused his heart rate to go up even further, as he remembered something his sister had told him – women will often alter their hair if they liked who they are dating. This was either to present them with their best look or to see if they noticed. Brad concluded that Amy had probably deliberately positioned herself in a way that highlighted her figure and this thought really aroused his senses. She breezed over to him, making the overcast day feel like sunshine.

"Hello again, Officer," she said with a sly smile. Her experience with men was that most were useless at picking up on flirting, unless it was overstated. Brad felt himself blush. The moment felt surreal.

Is this what hallucinations are like? he thought.

"Hello Amy. Call me Brad," he replied with a smile.

"I like Officer better … Brad," she said with a raised eyebrow and wicked grin. "How about I take an early lunch and we go and get something to eat?"

"Sure." Brad couldn't think of what else to say. He was even more lost for words when Amy put her arm through his and guided him across the campus to the Union building. She was clearly a decisive woman and knew what she wanted. Brad was impressed and lost for words. He could never have been so daring.

The next half hour was so pleasant Brad forgot about his troubles with his colleagues and the vexing nature of the case. Conversation flowed easily between them and Brad found himself confiding to Amy that he felt like he was not living up to his father's motto to use each day to make a mark on the world. Amy's sympathetic smile in response was all Brad needed to guarantee that Amy would be occupying his thoughts for some time. Amy told Brad that her parents didn't really understand her career choice.

"Ultimately though all they really want is for me to be happy," Amy said looking Brad directly in the eyes. Brad got the impression that she'd decided that he might be able to help her parents achieve their wish.

As Amy's break came to an end they made plans for a dinner date in two days' time. When Brad arrived back at his car, he realised he had been smiling the whole way there. He laughed to himself and switched his focus back to the case.

Brad made a call to the station and was pleased to hear that Detective Summers had finished in court. He arranged to meet her at the Professor's home in ten minutes.

###

The Professor's home was at the back of a series of small townhouses that formed a horseshoe around a central pool. Each house shared a wall with their neighbour, but otherwise they were private and distinct homes. The Professor's home had a dark green door with a deadbolt and lock. It took Brad only a minute to pick the locks.

"How did you get so good at that?" Detective Summers laughed.

"They showed us at the police academy, but mostly through repetition, repetition, repetition," said Brad. It was how he became good at nearly all of the things he was good at – sheer hard work and practice. There were only two things that he felt naturally good at: cooking and swimming.

The small entryway, led into an open plan kitchen, dining and living room, off which there was a bedroom with ensuite bathroom, a second bedroom, laundry and second toilet. The second bedroom was being used as a study and was lined with books. Brad started to look at them and was interested in the odd selection and titles such as *Self Your For Think*, *Mental Floss* and *Revolutionise Your Mind*. As he wandered through the rest of the home Brad was struck by the lack of material possessions. The walls were bare, save for several neatly organised bookcases and a large photographic print of an attractive woman, upon which was written in small letters, *My Angel*. Brad guessed that this was the Professor's wife.

In the living area on a white entertainment unit there was a large flat screen TV with a webcam attached and an old leather 'Chesterfield' armchair, but nothing else – no coffee table, no dining table, not even a footstool. The bedroom was similar: just a double bed, one bedside table with a lamp and clock radio, but nothing else. Detective Summers lay on the bed for a moment, explaining to Brad that she was trying to get a feel for what the Professor experienced in his home. She then helped Brad look through the Professor's wardrobe which was neat and organised. Both were surprised at the small amount of clothing – four shirts, two suits, three pairs of pants, four t-shirts, three pairs of shorts and two pairs of shoes. As they looked through the cupboards in the kitchen, it was more of the same: two saucepans, a frypan, minimal food and an uncluttered cutlery drawer.

"So Detective Summers, what do you think?"

"Brad, we've been working together for a couple of months now, you can call me Sally you know."

"Ok Sally … I don't think I have ever seen such a neat home," Brad said admiringly, thinking of his own untidy and disorganised apartment.

"Well that's easy to explain – there isn't enough stuff for it to get messy."

"When I think of how full my closet is compared to this, I realise I really don't need twenty t-shirts," Brad said with a small smile.

"Or eight pairs of shoes in my case," replied Sally. They both laughed. Brad was grateful for the moment of levity.

"Why do you think he lived like this? I mean he was a

professor and living alone, shouldn't he have had money?" Brad asked.

"Well everything here is expensive – those suits must have cost thousands and the kitchen appliances and TV are all top of the range. Even those saucepans are super pricy. And that mattress! It's so luxurious. It's the first time I have lain on a mattress and just wanted to go to sleep. I want one. Even that clock radio would be worth close to a thousand dollars," Sally exclaimed.

"A grand for a clock radio?" Brad raised his eyebrows.

"I know but they sound great."

It was tuned to a classical radio station and when Sally turned it on the room was filled with a deep resonant sound. Brad could hardly believe that such a small device could produce the depth he could hear. It was as though the orchestra was in front of him.

"Wow," said Brad.

"Yeah, I know. My Dad got one for his retirement. His company joked that he had worked so hard that he would need it now that he had some time on his hands. They were right too. He quite enjoys lazy mornings in bed listening to the thing, particularly now Mum's passed away," Sally said nostalgically.

"Ok, so the Professor is well off, and not lacking things. It seems unlikely that he would have got into financial trouble and this was payback. His wife died from natural causes and it seems unlikely that he would have had lovers fighting over him, so no foul play there. His work at the university was considered very good, and he was well liked, so no jealous rivals. There's no inheritance issue which is why this case is really frustrating me and to top it off I can't say for sure he was murdered. There are no obvious motives for killing him, yet he appears to have been the victim of foul play of some description, although we can't be sure until we get the autopsy and blood work results. Otherwise healthy people don't just bleed spontaneously and die like he did, I have no idea how or why he died," said Brad.

"Glad it's not my case," said Sally with a wry grin.

"Ahh, but you are assigned to help me on it," Brad countered, also smiling. He liked Sally and was grateful that she didn't give him a hard time like some of the other people at the station.

"Yes, but for today only, and besides, it's not my name signing off on all the forms," Sally said with a small laugh.

"True," replied Brad. "Any ideas to help me out then?"

Sally nodded and suggested trying to get a feel for who the Professor was by imagining living here. Brad immediately went and sat in the armchair and turned on the TV.

"Hey Sally, come and look at this," Brad called.

Brad pointed to the blank screen on the TV when Sally came into the room.

"Is it turned on?" Sally asked.

"Yes. Here's the remote, try changing the channel," Brad responded.

Sally pressed a few buttons, but other than numbers briefly appearing on screen nothing changed: "There are no stations tuned in!"

"So what's the point of having such a large TV if you're not going to use it?" Brad was frowning.

"Well there is that webcam. Maybe he connected his computer to it?" Sally thought aloud.

"So where's the computer?" They asked in unison.

"No idea," said Brad answering for them both. "It wasn't in his office or on him when he died."

"So where else could it be?" Sally asked.

"No idea… wait, I am so stupid," Brad said angrily, mostly to himself. It was obvious once he'd made the connection.

"What?" Sally asked.

"Well, have you seen a car here? We never looked at how he got to the shopping centre – I guess I was thinking that he lived so close to it and to his work that he had walked, but he must have been on his way to work when he stopped for breakfast. If he was walking, why wasn't he carrying a bag – because he wasn't walking he was driving! I'm guessing his computer is in his car," Brad said. He called the station and asked them to run a licence search for the Professor. They quickly responded with licence and registration numbers for a charcoal hardtop convertible. Brad thanked them and hung up. For the second time that day he smiled broadly.

"Finally we're getting somewhere," he said. "We've got the car rego, and make. It should be easy to spot. I'll give the security team at Lakeside a call and see if they can locate it for us."

Brad made the call and gave the security team a brief description of what they were looking for and instructions not to touch anything if they located the car.

Sally looked around the room. "What's wrong with this picture?" she asked.

"What do you mean?"

"It's just something I always ask myself at a crime scene. It helps me to notice things I otherwise wouldn't have. Here though I'm struggling to find anything. The home is consistent, impeccably neat, no obvious things missing, no marks on the walls to indicate something has been removed, nothing. What was his office like?" Sally asked.

"Neat. Jam packed with books, but ordered – you know? Nothing on top of other things or books on top of each other, the desk was clear except for a notepad – but nothing was written on that. A lot of papers but they were in sleeves and bundles. Really all very organised given the small size of the room. It was very different to the other professor I interviewed this morning – her room was also packed full of stuff but it was cluttered and messy," said Brad.

"So this fits with what you saw there?"

"Definitely, which just makes everything worse," Brad sighed.

Brad's phone rang and he answered it quickly. Sally watched the colour drain from Brad's face.

"But you said the results would take a week… I see … ok… What might have caused that? ... Anything else? … I'll try… Thanks I'll need it." Brad's voice became quieter and quieter as he spoke.

"Well?" asked Sally.

"It was Will, the Medical Examiner. They managed to do the autopsy on the Professor. He died from massive haemorrhaging, but not simply of the blood vessels in the brain, but the neurons themselves seem to have ruptured too, especially in the frontal lobe. They have no idea what could have caused it, it is trauma that is, and I quote, "unrecorded in the literature." They recommend treating the death as suspicious but really could not give me anything to go on. So now I am officially, utterly at a loss," Brad said despondently.

As if on cue his phone rang again. It was the shopping centre security team. They had found the Professor's car and had a team member stationed near it to make sure no one touched it.

At least that's something, Brad thought. He called the station and asked for a forensics team to meet him at Lakeside Shopping Centre. Sally and Brad did a final sweep of the Professor's home and left, shutting the door behind them.

###

At the shopping centre they found the forensics team had already arrived and the car had been cordoned off. They hadn't waited for Brad and had already been through the car, dusted for prints and gathered several hair and fibre samples. Brad didn't recognise anyone from the team.

"Hi I'm Detective Thomas, I called you here," Brad said trying not to sound annoyed that he hadn't been present when they started.

"Hi. I'm Jim, team leader for this unit. We haven't found much. It looks like a normal car – I mean there was nothing unusual about what we found. There are no signs of any foul play or trauma to an occupant of the car." Jim spoke in a friendly tone of voice.

"Did you happen to find a laptop?" Brad asked.

"Yes," replied Jim.

Thank you, Brad thought with relief.

"It's over there. It's been dusted so you can have a look at it. My understanding is you're trying to work out if this is a murder investigation?" Brad tried not to show how helpless he felt when everyone seemed to know that he hadn't made much progress in the case.

"If you need the tech guys to have a look, you might want to suck up to them as they are really busy at the moment," Jim added helpfully.

"Ok. Thanks," murmured Brad.

The laptop was a sleek unit. It had no disc drive and was thin, light and shiny. Brad took it back to his squad car and showed it to Sally.

"So this is what you've set your hopes on to tell you if anyone had a motive to murder the Professor?" Sally asked.

"Yes I guess so," Brad said while turning on the computer. He was surprised at how quickly it booted up. It was almost instant, unlike the work computers he was used to dealing with, which were mind numbingly slow. A logon screen appeared.

"Damn, of course we need a password." Brad allowed his frustration to show.

"Calm down," Sally said sympathetically. "You know… hmm, I just thought of how you can get around this without having to call in *our* techies."

"How?" asked Brad, frowning.

"Simple…" said Sally with a smile. She liked Brad's honesty and straightforwardness, but understood why her colleagues called him 'country boy'.

"Call the uni and get *their* techies to give you the username and password. Remember this is the uni's computer, not the Professor's own."

"That's brilliant," Brad said, wishing he could think more like Sally.

The technical department agreed to provide the Professor's details once they had checked with HR that a warrant had been issued allowing them to breach the Professor's privacy. Brad and Sally had to wait several minutes while listening to a recording that advertised the University's achievements and credentials as a learning institution. It was recorded in an upbeat tone of voice, but to Brad it sounded cheesy. Eventually the techie came back to them and gave them the details.

Brad typed in the Professor's username: *epismr* followed by his password: *310184126*.

The screened flashed as the login succeeded. Brad gave a little 'whoop' of excitement. The background switched from the University's logo, to a picture of the Professor, his wife and a dog. The desktop was clear of folders and shortcuts save for one link to the Professor's documents folder. Brad clicked on it and up came an organised folder list. Brad thought about how disorganised his own files were. His work computer was organised by case number, but his home one was all over the place. The Professor's folder names appeared to be organised by subject and university course code. A search through a few folders revealed nothing interesting or unusual – other than an extremely high level of organisation, there was no duplication or seemingly unnecessary files.

"Their tech department must have loved the Professor," Brad said in admiration.

"I'm pretty good at file management, but this is bordering on a mental health problem," said Sally softly.

"I know," Brad said.

"Let me try something," Sally said and Brad handed

over the computer. Sally clicked on the menu and found the option for the computer to show hidden files. A new folder called *The Program* appeared on the file list. Brad realised he was holding his breath as Sally clicked on it. The screen showed a list of files named level zero to level six. Sally clicked on level three, but when it opened it asked for a password.

"Damn," Brad said.

"Any ideas?" Sally asked.

"How about 'password'?" Brad said. Sally typed it in but the level three file didn't open.

"Nope," she said confidently.

"What about the other files?"

Sally clicked on 'zero' which opened immediately. Unfortunately all it opened was a blank document. Sally chuckled.

"What?" asked Brad.

"Don't you get it? *Zero*, as in nothing and it's a blank document. The Professor must have had a sense of humour," Sally said with a laugh.

"Yes I suppose so," said Brad without any amusement. "What about the other files?"

Sally tried to open the other files. Only number zero wasn't encrypted.

"Can you email them to me?" Brad asked.

Sally found the Professor's email program. It too was highly organised with all emails sorted into folders. Realising they had no internet connection, Brad pulled out his smartphone and Sally quickly paired them together and copied the files across. They looked through the emails, but once again nothing unusual seemed to show up. Sally tried opening the files a few more times, but they couldn't guess the correct passwords to get into them.

"We could keep doing this all day – how about we just take it to the tech department?" said Sally with frustration.

"Ok. But we will need to make a stop on the way," said Brad with a smile.

"Where? Why?" Sally asked curiously.

"You'll see," Brad was really grinning now.

When he had moved to the city he had misread his Property Manager's address and wound up at a shop that specialised in novel and limited edition lollies.

A short while later they arrived back at the Police Headquarters. Brad took the computer to the tech department and presented it to the head technician along with a bag of caffeinated lollies.

"Wow thanks!" said James, the head technician. "I love these. Where did you get them?"

"I know a place… I know you guys are swamped at the moment, but if there's anything you can do to get this back to me ASAP that would be appreciated," Brad replied. He let out a long sigh to show the pressure he was under.

"I'll say it has been confirmed that you have a murder investigation and mark it urgent. Beyond that, there is nothing more I can do to speed it up," James replied with a wink.

"Thanks, I appreciate it," said Brad. He knew that James's commitment would get him the results more quickly.

Chapter Three

The next day Brad arrived at the station much earlier than usual. Even though it was far from empty the sound of his car door shutting still echoed in the underground car park. Brad found the sound strangely satisfying. As he climbed the stairs to his floor he thought about Amy and wished he didn't have to wait until tomorrow to see her again. The thought of her put a smile on his face and he entered the office feeling as optimistic as he had on his first day here. Brad realised that Amy gave him something that he had been missing – hope. He poured himself a coffee from the communal pot and weaved his way to his desk, only narrowly avoiding the person he liked least in the department – Detective Taupo. Detective Taupo had teased him mercilessly since Brad first arrived at the station and Brad's nervousness around him meant that he made more mistakes when in his presence.

Brad sat at his desk and absent-mindedly spun in his

chair. He spent a few moments pondering the case, before switching on his computer. He paired his phone with the computer, and copied the Professor's files across to a memory stick and the hard drive. He was intrigued that these files could represent the Professor's secret project to raise people's consciousness and capacity to think. After failing to open any of the files with any password he tried, Brad reopened the file marked level zero. A blank document appeared. Brad was about to close the file when he noticed the page number showed one of seven. Brad clicked and dragged down. The first few pages were empty but then on page seven the highlight indicated something was there. Brad made sure he had the whole document selected and then changed the font colour to black. Suddenly words appeared on the screen. Brad felt triumphant and looked around as though he were searching for someone who had witnessed his success.

These are the master files for my program. Hopefully you have received them directly from me, but if not and something untoward has happened, please delete them. If you choose to ignore this advice then you should know the following, which normally accompanies the program when it is sent to participants:

This program is designed to help its audience improve their understanding of the links between aspects of the so called 'human situation.' It aims to increase people's working memory and awareness of what happens around them. It is not simply to make people more intelligent, although that is a side-effect of completing the program. This needs to be an active process which is why the program is divided into levels and why participants need to unlock the next level for themselves.

If you are ready for the next level and participation in this program, please take a teaspoon of the powder, which will help your neurons grow, wait five minutes and then open the next file. The password for the first level is "Nim Chimpsky." The remaining passwords can be derived from a careful study of each preceding document. When you solve the password repeat the powder before viewing the next level. The powder helps you to process the information and should only be taken when you have successfully opened the next level. There is only enough powder for each level, do not waste it. Please figure out each password, open the levels and enjoy the experience of having your consciousness raised.

–Professor Michael Episteme

As Brad opened the file marked number one, he wondered if the mysterious powder might be a lead into the cause of the deaths. Brad was a little disappointed as he read the heading *About Language* at the top of the document. Embedded in the file was a video and when Brad went to play it the Professor appeared on the screen. He was wearing a charcoal suit, white shirt and a bright emerald green tie and was sitting in his living room.

Level One: Language

Language is a universal human quality. When we are born we have an infinite capacity to learn language. We can learn any language, multiple languages. This amazing ability has led us to forget or overlook the fundamental purpose or function of language. Yes, language is used to communicate, but most people do not adequately grasp that language and words enable thought.

We do not store information in our brains in words as such, instead we store it conceptually – semantically. For evidence of this, look no further than people who are fluent in multiple languages. Not only can they use information learnt in one language while speaking another, but if you ask them what language they think in they will usually answer "I don't know", "all of them" or even "I don't think like that." For people who do not speak multiple languages this may not make sense. However, if you consider the idea of synonyms – words that have the same meaning – you can get a sense of what this might be like. The words 'enormous', 'huge' and 'massive' all have roughly the same meaning and can be used interchangeably. This is no different to words with the same meaning from multiple languages such as huge in English, 'enorme' in French or 'ingens' in Latin. Each word represents a concept relating to size and this is how the idea is stored – not as a word but as a meaning.

Understanding the link between words and their conceptual meaning can lead to a second insight into the nature of language that can elevate a person's understanding and intelligence. Languages rarely evolve in isolation. French, Italian, Spanish and Portuguese for example are all Romance languages that are derived from Latin. The English language is derived mostly from German, but has a major contribution from Latin and a notable input from Greek – particularly in sciences. Understanding this fundamental property of language can mean that linking of concepts between words can occur and deeper insight can result.

Early education teaches the meaning of prefixes and suffixes – often rotely and without really exploring what this means for thought. The shame is that they don't take this further and discuss the idea of compound words and how they link existing concepts into new ideas.

An activity you can do to improve your understanding of language is called "word trees." To do this you take a compound word (a word that is a combination of two or more other words) and then split it into its components and think of as many words as you can that include them. For example take the word 'intersection.' This can be split into 'inter', 'sect' and the suffix '-ion'. You find inter in words such as internet, internode, interstitial, interval, intergalactic and intervention. When you think about the meaning of these words you can see that they all contain the concept of being between something. Sect is found in sect, section, sectarian, dissect and sector. When you think of the meaning of these words they all contain the notion of "part" or "apart." When you think of words that had the suffix -ion on the end, they are all nouns, or perhaps more figuratively 'the notion of.' When you combine all this you get 'the thing that is the part between,' but more importantly you get a deeper understanding of all those other words too.

By regularly completing this activity for other compound words you build up a very meaningful and detailed understanding of the links between words, as well as an understanding of things at a conceptually deeper level. Importantly, you also build up the semantic networks – the links between pieces of information or nodes in your brain.

As Brad watched the video he was impressed with the Professor's enthusiasm and the way he spoke rapidly but clearly. The Professor reminded Brad of a Hans Rosling video about world development and population growth that he had watched as part of a police training workshop on intercultural understanding. Rosling managed to make some pretty boring statistics and numbers sound very impressive. The guy was just so alive when presenting the information, just like the professor was in his video.

Semantic networks are like conceptual maps in your brain that organise the storage and retrieval of our long term memory. Another way of describing each linked box or idea is as a node. When one node gets activated the links from it to other nodes are activated, albeit not necessarily to the same extent. Think of the main idea you are thinking of as being lit up and its light spilling over onto the adjoining concepts or nodes. In more scientific words, this is a spreading activation model and more links being activated leads to a stronger memory and recollection of information being recalled. This also improves your ability to process incoming information and make connections between pieces of knowledge that you have.

The tip of the tongue phenomenon is related to and evidence for this – when you know you know something, but just can't say the word. This occurs because the activated semantic network has not highlighted or lit up the node you need. This is also why if you think of many more things around what you are trying to recall, you will eventually trigger that node (as the enough light from the related concepts spills over) and you will be able to state what you're seeking.

The thing that really interests me is the idea that the more developed your semantic network becomes, the more connections you make, the more your knowledge becomes linked. This is more than just an abstract idea, it is a physiological process and one that the powder assists. Your individual neurons – the cells in your brain – sprout new connections to adjoining neurons and become linked. The neurons that you make fire together, wind up wiring together. Taken to its logical conclusion there must be a point at which your networks become so interlinked that when you activate one node, all the others get activated, thereby linking and combining all your knowledge. Just imagine what that would be like – to be able to see how every memory, every piece of knowledge you have is linked. Imagine what you would understand, imagine what you could create!"

The faraway look in the Professor's eyes suggested that he was indeed imaging the possibilities.

Completing the first seven levels of the Program will help you to achieve this; from there you will be able to access the last four levels by other means. Until next time.

The video ended. Brad sat back in his chair, thinking about what he'd just seen. At last he felt that he was beginning to get a sense of what might be motivation for killing the Professor. *If the series did as it claimed and made people more conscious and intelligent then there would be forces that would not want it getting out.*

The thought made Brad sigh with exasperation. He was still not 100% certain that the Professor had actually been murdered. So speculating on motives for murder seemed a little premature. Brad was so frustrated he swore.

"What's that for?" asked Sergeant Pan, appearing unexpectedly from behind him.

"This case is bugging me. I sense that there is a lot more to it but I just can't seem to put my finger on what I'm missing," replied Brad nervously.

"Well this may not be ideal, but I've got another case for you… There has been a death at Ivory Tower, specifically in the Leviathan Enterprises offices. The body was discovered an hour ago and they need a Detective to look it over before they can take the body away. It sounds a little bit similar to your case from yesterday, so maybe you will find a connection that will help you, even though it's more than likely natural causes. The deceased's name is Brentham Hobbs," Sergeant Pan said sounding slightly less stern than usual.

Brad stood up, sighed and took the file from Sergeant Pan. The phrase 'more than likely natural causes' irritated him more than it should.

Brad got into his car and started the short drive over to the Tower. Along the way he thought about the second last case he had worked on in Northam. There had been a series of four burglaries from homes in the town. Brad had thought it was local youths and that the thefts were random, but he couldn't find enough evidence to implicate the teenagers he suspected. It kept nagging at him, partly because it had shattered his confidence right when he had earned his promotion and partly because it seemed like such a straightforward case, the only odd being that some stamps were stolen from the second house.

I must put this behind me. Time to find a new gear and get things back on track, I will make my mark on the world, Brad thought with determination.

When Brad arrived at the Tower complex he was

struck by the sheer size of the building. Although the exterior of the building was mostly glass the thick edges were made of concrete that was coated in a cream coloured render, giving the building its name – the Ivory Tower. The lower floors consisted of a shopping centre, restaurants and a gymnasium. The rest of the building alternated between residential accommodation and corporate offices. Leviathan Enterprises occupied the top floor. As Brad approached the entrance and elevator that were reserved for Leviathan, a security guard stopped him. Brad explained why he was there and once the guard had checked his ID and spoken to Leviathan, he swiped an ID card and pressed a finger to a scanner. The elevator hummed slightly as it whisked Brad skyward. The ride was surprisingly quick for such a tall building. This meant that Brad felt like his stomach was still making its way up from the ground floor when he stepped into the reception area for Leviathan. The view from the windows was enough to give Brad a feeling of vertigo. He reminded himself that he was not afraid of heights, but then he was not usually this high up, nor in a building that seemed to be swaying from side to side. The company was primarily a think tank, with sidelines in data mining and data protection. The decor was modern but somehow futuristic. Brad recognised the furniture from one of the posters he had read while searching for HR at the University. It had won some big design award and was a spin off from a student's PhD in ergonomics. Sitting behind a glass desk Brad could see an administrative assistant who looked like she was born to model business attire. Her long red hair was neatly tied in a ponytail and she wore rimless glasses and a stylish black suit with a white blouse. She looked like she was in her late twenties. She stood up to greet Brad.

"Hello Officer Thomas. Welcome to Leviathan Enterprises, my name is Jenny. Our CEO Dr Engels will be with you shortly. In the meantime can I get you a coffee?" she asked in a formal tone of voice. Brad was confused, he was here to see a body and deal with a possible murder and he was being offered coffee.

"Um, sure. That sounds good."

Unlike the last administration person that he'd met, this one made him feel ill at ease and he began tapping his foot. This thought reminded Brad that he must call Amy and confirm their date for the next evening.

"What would you like? An Espresso? Macchiato? It's after twelve so it's a bit late for a cappuccino," Jenny said in a formal tone of voice. Brad was unaware there was a time frame for drinking cappuccino. He decided to try a macchiato even though he wasn't too sure what that was. Brad found Jenny's formality and lack of concern over why he was there unsettling.

"Excellent." She disappeared into an annex and Brad soon heard the sound of an espresso machine. When he closed his eyes it was almost like he was in an empty café. He opened them as she returned holding an odd looking cup. It was white porcelain at the base, clear double walled glass in the middle and blue porcelain at the top. Inside was a dark chocolate coloured coffee that was stained with a swirl of steamed milk and had a dollop of foam. Brad took a sip, appreciating the caramel coloured *crema* and scent of the coffee – it was one of the best coffees he'd ever had.

He took a moment to savour it and then drank the rest

quickly when Jenny said to him that Dr Engels would see him now. She led Brad down a long, apparently doorless corridor and into a corner office.

The scene that confronted him was startling. The office was immaculate and the plush light brown carpet was contrasted by two white walls and white furniture. In a corner there was something very out of place – a blood stained dead man in a dark suit, slumped against the glass. Around him was a small huddle consisting of the Medical Examiner, her assistant and Dr Engels. The most striking thing about the body was the blood that covered what Brad could see of his face and shoulders. As Brad walked over, he noticed a translucent substance was mixed in with some of the blood. Blood was also smeared on the glass. There was something odd about the smearing, but Brad couldn't quite work out what it was. He looked over at the Medical Examiner and recognised her from his earlier cases in the city. *Her name was Samantha, but she prefers Sam*, Brad said to himself as he admired her diminutive figure. *She gets a little too excited by the different ways people die, but she is pretty thorough. I don't recognise her assistant though.*

As Brad approached the group Dr Engels said a quick hello and walked away from the group making Brad feel uncomfortable.

"Hi Detective Thomas, I know you probably remember me, I'm Sam – we worked together on the Smith and Wiles murders. This is Steve, I don't think you've met him before, this is only his second case with us."

"Hi Sam, hi Steve," Brad replied warmly.

"So take a look around Brad, what do you think?" asked Sam curiously.

"Well, it doesn't look like he was moved as there is only blood in this area and no smears, but I'm not sure. Could you tell me what you think happened?" Brad replied.

"Of course. I have a tendency to focus on small things so I like to see how a scene presents to other people before offering my opinion, in case I've missed something obvious," Sam said brightly. Brad found that, like their previous meetings, he felt comfortable with her right away. He took a moment to take in the scene again.

"Ok, well to me it seems like Mr Hobbs was standing in the corner when something happened to him that made him start bleeding. But that also means that whatever killed him must have been quick because he didn't even move to get help. There's also something odd about the blood on the window, but I can't figure out what." Brad said.

"Good pick-up on the blood, Brad. You're right, the window is surprising. Steve has taken a lot of photos to document it. It took me a while to realise what was odd." Sam paused for effect. "There is no handprint. I mean, imagine you are standing here. Suddenly you start haemorrhaging badly and you feel weak and collapse. Wouldn't you at least put a hand up to brace your fall? Yet there is no evidence of him doing so. Also, if you started bleeding from your nose and ears, wouldn't you put your hands up to try and stop the flow? Yet his hands have no blood on them. It's really odd. The blood smear on the window is from his head falling against it and then his whole body sliding down."

"So whatever killed him must have been either really fast or caused him to lose consciousness really quickly," replied Brad.

"Yes, but I don't know of any poison that is that fast. But what is really odd is that he was clearly bleeding while he was standing, you can tell from the way the blood has spattered onto the floor. Which means that he would have had time to at least put his hands out or even call out for help, yet it seems like this didn't happen," Sam said.

"What is that translucent stuff?" asked Brad.

"We're not sure, we haven't seen anything like it before. It's almost like a water mould, but that makes no sense. We've taken a couple of samples for analysis. Anyway, we'll take him back to the morgue and see if an autopsy can help us."

Sam and Steve went to lift the body into the body bag they had laid out a few feet from the body. As Steve put his hands on Hobbs' shoulders to move him off the wall he stopped, "umm Sam you had better feel this."

"Feel?" Sam replied as she moved over to the body. "Jeepers," she involuntarily cried out, "he's on fire. I thought the heat was coming from the air conditioner. Quick Steve, get the thermometer."

While Steve gathered the thermometer, Brad touched the body and his hand reflexively recoiled. It was like touching a hot stove.

"Wow, what would cause a body to be that hot?" he asked Sam.

"Not a clue," Sam replied, "The most I've seen a body is 43°C in the midst of a fever, but this would have to be more than that."

Steve had found a digital thermometer. When they went to measure Hobb's temperature, the numbers kept climbing up to 43°C before the small LCD screen flashed and displayed the word 'error.'

"Wow," they all said in unison. "Steve grab the analogue one," said Sam with some excitement. They watched as the red column kept rising past 43°C before settling at 47°C.

"And yet when I went to grab his feet, they're cool" Sam shook her head in disbelief.

"Yeah the heat is just coming from his head – wait most of his spine is hot too. Must be in the cerebral spinal fluid. I'll make sure to take a sample of it," Steve said to Sam.

"There's something I need to tell you," said Brad quietly.

"What's that?" Sam and Steve said in unison.

"I've seen a death just like this one already this week."

"Really?" they both replied.

"Yeah, a professor from Western University died like this in the food court at Lakeside Shopping Centre. There were no external signs of trauma and the toxicology was clean. We are still trying to figure out what caused the death."

"You say the toxicology was clean? What did Will say?" asked Sam incredulously. Will was the city's other Medical Examiner. Brad knew that they must work together quite closely.

"Well he said that he'd never seen anything like it. It was as though something had caused every neuron to fire at once. From what he could tell from what was left of

52

his brain there was an unusually large number of, um, glial cells, whatever they are," said Brad.

"You know how the brain is made up of white and grey matter?" said Sam in a friendly tone. It was clear that this case was intriguing her.

"Yeah, kind of. I mean didn't that detective always refer to the grey cells of the brain?" said Brad trying to sound literate.

"Yes, anyway, the white matter contains the long arms of neurons, the cells that fire to process information or create a thought. These arms or axons are covered in a fatty substance called myelin, which is why it looks white. The grey parts of the brain are the cell bodies of the neurons. Anyway, neurons are "nursed" by glial cells. If someone had an unusually large number of them then their brain, theoretically, would function extremely well, I mean at a whole other level… actually, I can only imagine what that would mean…" Sam's voice trailed off. Brad liked the way she just explained things simply and without condescension.

"Yeah, imagine if you could access all your memories and knowledge at once, imagine what you could understand, imagine what you could create," Brad smiled, well aware he was quoting the Professor, but knowing that Sam didn't know that.

"Exactly!" Sam said emphatically, impressed that Brad seemed to understand.

There was a slight cough from the other side of the room, it was Dr Engels who had been standing in the one shadowy part of the room. Brad thought he looked uncomfortable all of a sudden.

"Excuse me, but there is something you should

know," Dr Engels said firmly, as he stepped forward into the light.

"What's that?" asked Sam and Brad simultaneously.

"There is a security camera in this office," said Dr Engels quietly, motioning them to follow him. Steve remained with the body as Sam and Brad followed Dr Engels down the brightly lit hall, Brad asked Dr Engels what it was that they did here.

"People come to us with issues that require inventive solutions or for strategic advice and we help them. In short we solve problems," said Dr Engels with a hint of pride.

"That's it?" asked Brad, sounding surprised.

"That's all you need to know, yes," said Dr Engels coolly.

He stopped in front of what looked like a blank wall. He pulled a keycard out of his pocket and held it against the wall. A beep was heard, but Brad couldn't tell where it was from. Dr Engels then pushed the wall, which then popped out slightly, revealing a hidden door. "Magnetically controlled, push locks. Your discretion on this room's existence is required."

Sam and Brad nodded their agreement. The door opened to reveal a small, dark room. Brad thought it was unlike any security room he had ever seen. It was devoid of monitors and had a narrow bench against the wall. Another swipe of the keycard and the wall shimmered and morphed into a video screen. Brad tried not to look impressed. Dr Engels tapped the screen a few times and that day's video of Brentham's office started. Brad was impressed that the camera was full colour and high resolution, unlike the shopping centre video he'd watched. The darkness of the security room made the image seem very bright and vivid.

"The camera is motion sensitive so the video will start when Brentham arrived this morning," said Dr Engels, sounding a little more relaxed. The video dutifully started with the office door hallway through the process of opening. Brentham walked into his office and booted up his laptop. The camera angle was from opposite the desk, so the computer screen could not be seen. Nevertheless, it was clear from his body language and activity that Brentham was reading emails.

They watched as Brentham took out his keycard and held it next to his desk drawer. He opened the drawer and took out an unlabelled white container. He carefully measured a teaspoonful of the powder and then put it in his mouth. He appeared to hold the substance in his mouth.

"Why isn't he swallowing?" asked Brad quietly.

"Sublingual absorption, the compound must be soluble in saliva. It means it gets absorbed while in the mouth - straight into the bloodstream and bypassing the liver. Whatever that substance is, if it is not showing up on a tox screen it must be very short acting. I mean – look at the time, he dies in less than half an hour. A lot of psychoactive drugs are taken that way," Sam added.

"That's got to be it. I mean that must be what poisoned him." Brad said excitedly.

Finally a definite cause of death. This case might not be so bad after all, he thought to himself. *If it is the powder then all we have to do is track who supplied it and the case is closed.*

"We don't know that for sure. We've bagged the

container with the powder, but there is only a trace amount left, so we may not be able to tell you much about it. It must have been very carefully measured both by Brentham and whoever dispensed it to him," Sam said.

The video continued showing Brentham working on the computer, apparently reading a long email. He then sat back and seemed to gaze at the ceiling for a while. Without warning he stood up and walked over to the corner, but his gaze was not focussed on any particular point. He reached the corner just as the first trickle of blood started coming out of his ears. It wasn't possible to see the front of his face from the camera angle. The blood started flowing more freely but Brentham did nothing to indicate he was aware of it. The sunlight against him made it appear like he was glowing and Brad recalled the statements from the Professor's witnesses that he looked rapturous. After nearly two minutes of just standing there, he collapsed against the glass and slumped to the floor, leaving a smear of blood on the window. He landed in the same position Brad had seen him in when he first arrived.

"Wait, go back a moment," Sam said excitedly.

"What?" asked Brad as Dr Engels dragged the timebar back forty-seven seconds.

"You'll see…Dr Engels, can you zoom in here?" Sam pointed to Brentham's neck.

"Sure," Dr Engels used two fingers to stretch a section of the screen.

"Wow, do you see that?" Everyone looked closely and such was the resolution of the video, that they could clearly see the blood steaming off Brentham's neck.

"Like I said, I tend to focus on small things…" Sam trailed off, shaking her head in disbelief.

"So not murder then," Brad muttered to himself.

"Well that depends. What if someone spiked whatever that was? Or maybe it's a restricted substance that has been provided illegally? Then there are grounds for a least a manslaughter charge," Sam responded as though she weren't sure if she was meant to reply.

Brad was grateful for the idea of the manslaughter charge, but he didn't want Sam to think he wouldn't have realised that possibility for himself, so he kept quiet.

"I'll need a copy of that," said Brad.

"Yes," said Dr Engels reluctantly, "what is your email?"

Brad told him and it took Dr Engels only a few taps of the screen to send Brad an email.

"I have sent you a link to the file. You can download the video by clicking on it. Please note that the link will only work once and that you will need the password *benthic* to open it."

"Can we also have a look at Brentham's computer?"

"Ok," Dr Engels said still sounding very reluctant. He led the group back to the office and booted the laptop that was on the desk.

Must have shut down when it wasn't used for a while, Brad thought. He watched as Dr Engels unplugged the laptop and carried it over to the body and used the Brentham's fingerprint to unlock the computer.

"I cannot let you go through everything on here as we have government and business contracts that are highly sensitive and confidential. I will let you have a quick look at the most recent emails, since it seems like it may be relevant, but after that the computer will remain here and you will need a very specific warrant to take it."

Dr Engels strongly implied that such a warrant would not be likely to be granted. "I am only showing you this, because in regards to Mr Hobbs passing, we have nothing to hide."

Brad recoiled when he opened the email program. The last read email was from Michael Episteme – the Professor! Brad was just able to read that the email was a warning about level twelve and that he feared for the safety of anyone exposed to it. He tried to read more but Dr Engels interrupted him.

"Hmm, that man is not a client of ours," said Dr Engels curiously. He clicked the sort by from button and quickly printed all the emails from the Professor. "Jenny will give you the print outs when you leave. I will also forward them to you."

Brad was impressed when Dr Engels typed in his email address from memory as it was his eleven digit ID number followed by the police domain address. He was a little bit upset that he had not been able to read the whole message, but did not feel confident enough to challenge the authority exuded by Dr Engels.

Sam and Steve said their goodbyes and that they would be in touch and carefully took the body away. Brad thanked Dr Engels for his help, shook hands and made his way towards reception. Jenny dutifully presented him with an envelope containing the emails. Brad once again felt disconcerted by her attitude and behaviour. He was convinced that if anyone was behind the deaths it was Dr Engels and that Jenny was probably in on it too.

As Brad drove back towards the Police station he mulled over the questions that were bugging him about the case. He did not know how significant the link between the Professor and Mr Hobbs was or what was the importance of the powder. *In fact*, he mused to himself, *I'm not even sure exactly how the men died.*

Brad's desk was a mess. The laminated wood surface was barely visible beneath the masses of paper surrounding his computer. Brad was searching for his notepad when his phone rang.

"Hello Brad? It's Sam. We've found something."

Sam's excitement made Brad's heart rate quicken. In the few hours since he'd returned to the office he'd made no progress in the case. He was beginning to think that he never would.

"Great, did you find out anything about the powder?" Brad asked hopefully.

"Err, actually not yet, but hopefully what we have found will help. When we switched on the UV light while examining the body, we discovered a tattoo on his left tragus," said Sam.

"Umm, do men have those?" Brad asked in confusion. Sam unsuccessfully tried to stifle a laugh. "Brad, the tragus is the flap of cartilage on the outer part of your ear. If you stick your finger in your ear and flick towards your eye that thing you flick is your tragus. Anyway there is a small tattoo of a flower and some Greek letters."

"Any idea what the flower is or what the letters say?"

"I'll send you through the image. Steve did a search

and thinks the flower is a pansy and the Greek letters are alpha, theta, epsilon, omicron and sigma. We're not sure what they mean, but they all seem related to physics and mathematics. I mean there is alpha radiation, theta and epsilon are used in math formulas and sigma is what we calculate for statistical significance."

"Hmm," said Brad trying to sound like he knew what Sam was saying, "What about the other one?"

"Omicron, I am not sure of. I haven't heard of that one before," Sam said quietly.

"Thanks for the heads up," Brad said.

"That's ok, I've let the other Medical Examiner, Will, know what Steve and I found, and we'll be back in touch when the rest of the tox stuff comes through." Sam hung up. Brad immediately dialled the Medical Examiner's office and asked for Will.

"Hi Brad," Will started, "I was about to give you a call. Sam told me about the other case and the tattoo. I've had a look at the Professor's ear and yes, he has a similar tattoo. I'll email you some photos, but if you are nearby in the next day or so you should stop in and have a look for yourself."

"Good idea. Thanks."

A few small pleasantries later and Brad hung up the phone. He was sure that the deaths were linked and were most likely homicides. What he couldn't figure out was why anyone would want the men dead. He updated the case notes and packed up for the day. As he left the building he realised that, for a change, he might be able to stop thinking about his active cases. *Amy*, he said softly to himself as his thoughts switched focus and a smile spread across his face.

Interchapter

To: Dr Engels
From: The Professor
Subject: Programming the future.

Greetings Good Doctor,
Thanks for having me round for one of your famous coffees the other day. Here is what I have been working on. It is still not as cohesive as I'd like. There is something missing that I can't quite put my finger on. I have the thought training and ideas done, but it still is not quite working like I want it to. I need to boost the rush the participants get from each level. I have tried giving them a spoonful of sugar to make them think their way into a real biological effect of brain growth but it does not work. I think they guess what it really is, and while that is important, they are not establishing the effect. Dame Rachel Sagan did a fellowship at my university a few years ago and I think she can easily be

persuaded to help us develop a powder that will actually help. I know something about her that she would not want made public, but hopefully, it won't come to that. Besides I think getting her to comply that way would be against the spirit of the program. I'll get in touch and let you know what she says, but since you know her too, maybe you can warm her up to the idea before I approach her.
Cheers,
Michael

Chapter Four

After a restless night during which his thoughts wandered from Amy to melting brains and back again, Brad left earlier than usual for work. He appreciated the planning of the city; the roads flowed as well as could be expected in the morning rush hour and there was a train line down the main freeway with several 'park and ride' centres. Everything was well designed, but he still missed his country town, where the roads would have been empty at that time of morning and people waved as he drove past.

Brad sighed as he arrived at the station. The lack of obvious motive in the investigation, grey rendered walls and reflective glass made the building seem even more impersonal from the outside than usual. At least he could look forward to his date with Amy that night. The thought of Amy put a smile on his face. After Brad entered the office he poured himself a coffee from the communal pot. It was burnt, stale and too strong. He longed for another one like he'd had at Leviathan. He carried the coffee to his desk and began taking sips in between trying passwords for the Professor's files.

Brad watched the video of the second level again, trying to note any stressed words or clues as to what the password to the next file might be. He typed 'compound words' and 'semantic network' into a search engine, but the results didn't give him any new information. It seemed that the Professor had summarised things reasonably well, but had skipped a more lengthy explanation for the sake of brevity. Brad tried a few more combinations of words before trying semantic network and tip of tongue. A phrase caught his eye; "this phenomenon is therefore related to Freudian slips."

Brad had heard of Freud and regarded him, probably unfairly, as an old guy who was obsessed with sex and bowel motions. Brad read on: Freudian slips, also known as a slip of the tongue, are a phenomenon whereby a speaker replaces the word they are trying to say with one that is an unintended expression of what they really think about something. Brad laughed to himself as he recalled his high school principal introducing the new school captain, who was athletic but not academically capable, as "Jock" rather than "Brock." A few people had sniggered and the Principal was clearly embarrassed, but her deathly stare meant she recovered well. Brock on the other hand had earned a new nickname that would stay with him for the next year.

Brad clicked on the third file for the twenty-third time that day and tried typing in another password. Once again he was met with the detestable sound of an error beep. Brad stopped for a moment and began swivelling in circles on his chair. Detective Summers was sitting nearby, watching him. She smiled to herself at Brad's behaviour. Even though he had only been there for a couple of months, she had seen him do this a few times, and always when he was frustrated. He just seemed to regress when he came up against things he could not comprehend. *A nice guy, just a little bit out of his depth,* she thought to herself.

Brad stomped his foot down and stopped spinning. An idea had occurred to him. The Professor went on and on about compound words, so what if the password to the next file was one too? What if it was simply a combination of one of the key phrases in the video?

Brad tried *semanticnetwork* and *tipoftongue* without luck. He was on the verge of giving up when his next attempt did not result in the noise that had been haunting him. He carefully wrote down what he had just typed; *Freudianslip.* The file that opened was a short text.

Level Two: Ideology

A simple definition of ideology is that it is a set of ideas about the world, about how it is or should be organised, and about the place and role of people in it. It is a collection of ideas of the ideal. The importance of ideology stems from it allowing us to define cultural and social practices in terms of their power and political purpose.

Ideology can be held by a person or by a group. A personal ideology is an individual's own set of ideas about the world. It is important to realise that each person has their own particular bundle of ideas and while they may share many of the same ideas, the complete set is their own. A group ideology is a set of ideals that members adhere to or share in common. This is most readily demonstrated with political parties, where members of the party subscribe to a set of beliefs. Importantly, a key part of understanding this is that adherents to a particular ideology attempt to pass on this group of beliefs to others. After all what is the point of having an ideal if you don't believe others should believe it too.

Brad smiled to himself as he realised the Professor was writing the same way he spoke.

Group ideologies can change and even die out, but this can be prevented through repetition and social manipulation. Convincing others to believe the same views is achieved through the dominant ideology being repeated in as many ways as possible. In the end the dominant ideological beliefs become so familiar that people no longer question the basis behind them – they are assumed to be truths and every part of the culture repeats the ideology. At its worst this can be seen as mind control, at its best it can be seen as a uniting common vision. I won't bore you with an extensive discussion of RSAs and ISAs, feel free to look them up, but suffice to say, the ideological viewpoint becomes ingrained and people gain a submissiveness or lack of questioning towards this way of viewing the world. Importantly, people are not usually forced to submit to the dominant ideology; rather they are convinced that this is the way they think anyway and that they are aligned with a common or natural point of view.

Brad was confused. This document did not seem all that consciousness raising. He already knew that people had different political beliefs and points of view. He felt like saying 'well duh'. He spent several minutes trying to come up with some eye opening interpretation of what he'd read, but failed.

"Brad, the boss wants to see you," Detective Summers whispered in Brad's ear. Brad jumped in his seat, smiled sheepishly and replied "great I've been wanting to see her."

Now it was Detective Summer's turn to be surprised. Brad walked slowly over to Sergeant Pan's office. She called him in and shut the door behind him. *Uh oh*, Brad thought, getting the impression he was in trouble.

"Do you have any suspects yet?" Sergeant Pan asked whilst standing behind Brad.

"Yes, I think that Leviathan Enterprises, Dr Engels and his assistant Jenny are most likely behind what's going on. We think that the powder that Brentham took is the actual cause of death."

"Brad we need to talk about something." Sergeant Pan said, without acknowledging his reply. She sat down at her desk and studied Brad intently. Brad felt his heart rate jump and sweat start beading under his arms. He realized why his Sergeant was known as a master interrogator, it was just the way she was.

"What?" he said.

"There has been another death that is similar to the two you have investigated this week. It occurred over in Middleton, which as you know is outside our jurisdiction."

Brad nodded affirmatively.

"But they are very concerned about it since the deceased is Dame Rachel Sagan, who as I've just read about was a world famous philanthropist, biologist and sufferer of Tourette's syndrome. She won the Nobel Prize for medicine and her enthusiastic and tic ridden delivery on a monthly TV show got many people interested in science. Middleton are preparing a press release as we speak."

Even I watched her show, Brad thought.

"Dame Sagan also had the same tattoo that you discovered on our two bodies," said Sergeant Pan.

"Wow," Brad said aloud. He was genuinely shocked.

I am never going to solve this case, it just keeps getting more complicated, he thought mournfully, *I guess this also means that the Sergeant has been reading my files.*

"I am assigning Detective Summers to work with you full time on this case. You need to find out who is killing these people as clearly these deaths are not random. Hand over all your other cases to Detective Taupo. This case is now your sole focus. Do you understand?"

The Sergeant's tone was as serious as Brad had heard it and she looked genuinely worried.

"Yes," Brad responded solemnly.

"Good. Middleton PD can't see you until this afternoon, so do the hand over and then head over there with Detective Summers. By the way, the clock is ticking on this as the Feds have started to show an interest. They'll probably come and try to take over in a week or so if we can't make good progress," Sergeant Pan said assertively.

"But they could be really useful…" Brad began, thinking that it would be great to handball this case to someone else.

"Listen to me Brad. I believe that you are more than capable of solving this case."

Brad felt a surge of confidence. *If the Sergeant believes in me, maybe I can solve it.*

"Please try to solve this case before the Feds have organised their task force and arrive," the Sergeant said.

Brad cleared his throat but could only manage a mumbled 'Ok,' in reply.

"The media are also getting involved and I don't want them solving this or coming up with anything that we have not already discovered. I want a full report from you tomorrow evening outlining your progress. Is that understood?" Sergeant Pan commanded.

"Yes, Sergeant," Brad said as he was ushered out of her office.

As he left Sergeant Pan tried to convince herself that Brad would solve this case before the Federal police arrived. She hoped this case would be the making of him even though her instinct said otherwise.

###

Brad sat at his desk preparing his handover to Detective Taupo, but his mind kept wandering between the Professor and his project, his feelings for Amy and his dislike of Detective Taupo. He was sure the key to understanding the deaths and who was responsible for them was in the Professor's files. Brad decided to take a quick look through Brentham and the Professor's emails to see if they might explain their connection, or hold a clue for the remaining files. Brad started with the oldest and worked his way up. Mostly the emails were an exchange of ideas about how the program should be used when it was completed and there were a few references to test subjects being shown the lower levels. One name appeared several times – Mathew Arnold, who appeared to favour the wide release of the program to people. There was a discussion of how the Professor had developed the powder with a mutual contact referred to as the Commander, but the one email that really caught his eye was from a month ago:

Nearly finished my project. Level Eleven is being distributed through the usual channels. I feel like something is blocking me from creating what I imagine will be the final level. But when I do break through my program will finally be completed! I'm so excited.

The next email from the Professor was from eight days previously and was the second last from him to Brentham:

The other day I made what I think is my final breakthrough – Level Twelve. You should have received it by now. If you have any comments let me know.

The final email, sent five hours later simply read: *Thank goodness I mastered my breath so long ago. You MUST NOT open the last two levels. Since making Level Twelve, I have had the weirdest sensation a couple of times. My whole central nervous system felt like it was on fire. I only just managed to control myself enough to stop it going further and fear that I may not be able to stop it from killing me. I should never have sent Level Eleven or Twelve out. I have 'recalled' the emails I sent with the link, but some got through. If this applies to you and you are still trying to get into either file, please stop and destroy the files, if you have got into them then this email may be too late. Stopping the powder should help you control your progress. Don't seek the final two levels, they may wind up wiping out our network and all the progress we have made. Commit crimestop, it's the only way.*

Brad immediately looked up crimestop in a search

engine, it was a term invented by Orwell for his novel *1984*: "Crimestop means the faculty of stopping short, as though by instinct, at the threshold of any dangerous thought ... crimestop, in short, means protective stupidity."

Brad's first instinct was that thoughtstop would be a better word in this situation. He made a note to try combinations of Orwell's other Newspeak words as passwords for the files. For some reason though the Professor's warning had the opposite effect on Brad and just made him want to work through the program even more.

Imagine being that intelligent, I could finally have success at work, get Detective Taupo off my back and really live my life. I really want to know what's in the rest of the program, Brad thought.

As he felt this urge, Brad wondered if in fact that was the purpose of the last email and if it was not really meant to stop someone from going further, but to give them the drive to make the next jump in consciousness on their own.

Hmm, the first two levels are clearly linked. I mean we have our own personal understanding of meaning and that may or may not align with other people's understanding. Plus people have a shared understanding of the meaning of words. Otherwise how could society function? I suppose this could be scaled up to shared ideas or ideals just as the Professor did in level two. But, Brad mused to himself, *without language how could you express an ideology. I mean, how can you have thoughts without words?*

Brad realised that there had been numerous times in

his life where he had intuitively understood concepts without having the language to communicate them to others. He thought about his police training and how they were trained to shout a sound at someone who was attacking them. Their instructor called it '*kiai*' and it was meant to be a sonic attack that could affect the opponent. Brad had immediately seen with his mind's eye how the attack would work on the body as a whole all the way down to the cellular level, but when he tried to explain it he found that he could not put the knowledge into words. It wasn't until a year later when he was helping his sister revise for a physics exam by reading answers from test questions, that he came across the terminology of 'resonance tones' and was finally able to express his understanding in words. Brad mused that he had experienced thought without language. *What if this explained the idea of speaking in tongues – that concepts were communicated in a way that crossed the barrier of language?*

Brad suddenly felt self-conscious, as though all eyes were on him. In a strange way he felt that people should be looking at him making this thought breakthrough such was the power of the moment. He felt a strong surge of adrenaline. He looked around but everyone was doing their own thing. Brad's thoughts flashed back to the rapture like state that the Professor and Brentham had experienced and wondered whether a breakthrough in thought was behind it.

He got up and made himself another coffee. It was fresh this time, but still not very satisfying. As he walked back to his desk the idea popped into his head that the tattoo might have a deeper meaning than membership of a club. One person might view the flower as a flower, but could it hold another meaning? Brad typed the word pansy into a search engine and after reading about the word being used as a derogatory term for someone who is cowardly, lacking in courage or homosexual, he found a page that gave him a rush of excitement. He read that the name pansy was given to the flower because the scientists who named it thought it looked like a human face that was frowning in thought and the French word for thought was "Penser," which sounded a bit like pansy when spoken. This wasn't what made Brad excited, it was the words: *this flower has long been held as a symbol of freethinking and freedom of thought due to the meaning of the French word from which it gets its name. The flower is the floral emblem used by the Freethinking Society.*

At last Brad knew what the tattoo meant. The victims were all members of a secret society! A few more web searches revealed that the Freethinkers were a not so secret society that had existed for several hundred years, but died out in the late nineteenth century. Brad guessed that a few people must have decided to reinstate it. Brad remembered the sign he had seen next to the door of the Professor's office, "Home of the Philosopher King."

Maybe he was the group's leader?

At least Brad knew the link between the people who had died was membership of a specific group. Now all he had to do was find the group. Brad did a few more searches trying to find a Freethinking group that had the insignia he had seen tattooed, without success. One site had a message on their page that said that their membership was limited to ninety-one people and that they had a waiting list you could join by calling a phone number. Another met every month at a local library, which somehow seemed a little too public. Another was clearly just an anarchist group that used 'freethinking' as a euphemism. Brad felt no closer to finding the group so he returned to completing his handover of cases. After lunch at his desk, he reluctantly started his handover to Detective Taupo.

"So Country Boy what have you got for me?" Detective Taupo asked.

Brad cringed even though the comment made him feel less uncomfortable than usual. Brad realised that instead of viewing the taunts as insults he could 'spin' the comments so that they were constructive criticism and that Detective Taupo, instead of disliking him, was really just trying to help him improve.

Hmm, the program is already helping me think about things differently, Brad mused.

"Well I have a few cases," Brad began, handing over four files, "this one is just pending the court case, this one we have a warrant out for our suspect and these other two are ongoing."

Brad shared the details of the last two cases with the Detective and explained what he had done so far in his investigations.

Detective Taupo grunted, "that's about what I'd expect from you Country Boy, a by the book and plodding job. I hope one day you will learn how to take the evidence further. You know, lead an investigation rather than be led by it." Brad winced at the critique of his work. "Perhaps I can help you with your big case? What do you know so far?"

Brad hesitated but then reminded himself that the more perspectives the case was viewed from the better. He described his progress to Detective Taupo including his thoughts about the powder.

"Yes I agree, it definitely does sound like the powder is the cause of the deaths. I suggest you try to find the source and you'll be all done and then I can hand all this back to you," Detective Taupo said wearily.

Just then, Detective Summers tapped Brad on the shoulder and said that Sergeant Pan had asked her to remind him to visit Middleton Police. Brad sighed, politely thanked Detective Taupo for taking over his cases and left.

"At least he's got manners," Detective Taupo said to Detective Summers.

"Yes he does. You shouldn't give him such a hard time you know. He tries hard and does a good job."

"A good job is not enough in this city, we need inspired work. Our cases are more diverse than those country town cases where everyone knows who did it…" Detective Taupo said as he picked up the files, turned and walked away from his colleague.

Unfortunately for Brad, he gained very little by going over to Middleton other than being able to view the tattoo under a blacklight for himself. Despite wanting to spend some time trying to unlock the next level of the Professor's program, Brad finished promptly at the end of his shift. He raced home and had a quick shower and change, before driving to his date with Amy.

In a city full of restaurants, Brad had struggled to find one that compared to those in Northam. In all of the ones he had tried so far the produce was not as fresh or home grown as he'd enjoyed previously. However, the chefs were world class and he was yet to find a restaurant he would not go back to, even if they were overpriced.

"Hi Amy," Brad practised saying while he waited.

He had arrived fifteen minutes early, which gave him ten minutes to quietly ponder his life and the strange deaths he was investigating. He thought about his Father's motto to "make a mark on the world today."

Brad was unsure how he was going to make a mark on today if he could not figure out why three people who were members of the same group and probably knew each other, had died in such an unusual way within two days of each other. *What have I missed?* he asked himself.

He sensed Amy entering the restaurant before he saw her. Her hair was held off her face by a black headband and her red lipstick drew attention to her lips. Brad was glad he'd found the time to shave and change into a polo shirt. Brad enjoyed watching Amy walk to the table. She just seemed to flow towards him, with continuous movement and a light step.

"Hello Officer Brad," Amy said playfully.

"Hello Amy," he replied.

The rehearsal had worked well, he sounded far more confident than he felt. Amy intimidated Brad with her grace and assured demeanour and yet he found her very attractive. Amy sat down with one movement, leant forward and smiled a wry grin. It was all so smooth and natural that Brad instantly forgot about the case.

"Brad, before we begin there are two things I have to confess," Amy said with a sudden hint of shyness.

76

"What?" he felt his heart thump in his chest.

"I am ..." Brad was sure she was about to say something that would devastate him, "or was..."

Brad's heart was pounding, "... unsure why you were coming to the uni, and that was part of my reason for making this date with you, as I was really curious."

Brad's hands became sweaty.

"But, then I heard about the Professor and put two and two together. But before you get the wrong idea..."

Too late, Brad thought.

"... And just to be clear, this *is* a date."

Amy smiled sweetly and reached over and to give Brad's hand a reassuring squeeze. Her touch did little to help Brad's rapid pulse.

"Which also means that I have to confess that I knew the Professor and a bit over a year ago was one of the guinea pigs for a project of his."

Brad suddenly understood the expression to have the rug pulled from under you. Brad groaned as he realised that he should not continue with the date and that he was now in a compromising situation. He was suddenly uncertain as to whether he should be reading Amy her rights or whether anything she said could be used in evidence.

"Amy, as you know I am investigating a murder and any information you provide may be useful, but I am not sure if I should be reading you your rights? I mean anything you say could be used against you..." Brad began.

"Officer, you may use anything you like against me," said Amy lasciviously. Brad involuntarily muttered "oh God" under his breath as Amy had tapped into his subconscious. This heightened his confusion over the best course of action. He was very attracted to Amy, for reasons he could only partially explain and he really wanted to see if they could have a relationship, but if she was a witness or potential conspirator, Brad knew he should cut off any contact with her outside of his official police duties.

"I'm sorry that was a little inappropriate, but I've had that line in my head since we made this date. Anyway don't worry, I just wanted to be upfront that I knew the Professor, I mean it's not like we were friends or anything, I just met with him a few times for a project and then we haven't seen each other since. If I can help you just ask," Amy said.

"Tell me about the project," Brad asked cautiously.

Please don't let it be the intelligence raising program, he thought.

"Well, I don't know all the details, but basically the Professor felt that people have lost some of their level of consciousness and that as a result we are not thinking as well as we can. He felt that people aren't seeing the links between pieces of information and that building those links would help people see more and think better." Brad groaned to himself as Amy studied his face.

"Like building semantic networks?" Brad he asked after a pause.

"Yes exactly," Amy said enthusiastically, showing recognition that she knew this was the first of the Professor's lessons.

"What do you know about semantic networks?" Brad queried.

At least I can get some answers, Brad thought with

equal parts elation at being able to make some progress and trepidation at what it may mean for their potential relationship.

"Well they are similar to the logic behind the internet, where each node or computer is linked to other computers. Getting information from one to the other can take many, many paths and even if one node is taken out, the information can still be transferred. This was really important as the basis for military communication, if one location were to be wiped out by a nuclear bomb, information could still travel from one point to another and communication between military sites could be maintained. The key idea is that the more links there are the more easily the information *can* be accessed and the more frequently it *will* be accessed. Building your network means that your working memory becomes larger, you will consider more, make better decisions, be more inventive..." Amy trailed off, she had a similar look in her eye to the one Brad had seen from the Professor in his video.

"I think I get it. So that is the first lesson and the second is about seeing the world from other people's perspectives," Brad said hoping to show his knowledge and that he had been able to open the second file.

"Yes and no, I mean that's not only it. It's about seeing that everyone has a particular point of view that may or may not overlap with yours, true. Understanding that everyone has their own bundle of ideas about how the world is or should be run and the place and role of people in it, is important for understanding why people behave the way they do. But, the key thing is that people will behave in accordance with or *to manifest* their ideal.

Really understanding this means that you have more than an appreciation of other people's perspectives, it means that you have *respect* for other people," Amy said earnestly.

"Why such an emphasis on group ideology then?"

"I don't know if I really figured that out, I did wonder about it though and came up with a theory of sorts," said Amy thoughtfully.

"What do you mean?"

"Well if you decide to align yourself with a group's ideology rather than your own, you have to compromise or give up some of your beliefs."

"Yeah, but you're never going to find a group or even person that has exactly the same beliefs as you," Brad said.

"Yes, but that means that compromise is a feature of the human condition, which is a really cool idea," Amy said.

Her enthusiasm for the idea made her seem even more radiant than Brad was already finding her.

"Think about the adolescent who becomes a doctor, marries someone from the 'right kind of family' and does things because that is what is expected of them by their parents. They give up trying to follow their own path and make themselves fit into the one that has been chosen for them."

"I know a few people like that. Believe it or not you actually see it in the police force. There are cops who are third or fourth generation and who feel like they had to keep the family line in place," Brad replied.

His parents had never dictated to him what he should do as a career other than it should be something that made him happy. His motivation for joining the police force was the romanticised notion that he would be able to solve crimes no one else could and really make a difference. What he found after a few years was that he only solved the crimes most police officers could.

"Exactly, and that is one reason why understanding ideology is important. It can make you more aware of who you are. The more you understand your own beliefs and the more you stop and think about what your core beliefs are, the better you will know yourself and the easier it will be for people to get along with you. I mean, if you accept that others have ideals and ideas that are different from your own, then you won't get angry when people disagree with you or at least, not as angry. You will be a better person," Amy said.

"I suppose so," replied Brad in agreement and then realised this was what had happened with him and Detective Taupo.

"I guess also that the Professor wanted people working through the program to use an understanding of ideology as a basis for forming links between nodes of information in the brain," Amy said quietly but confidently.

"The other key thing is understanding that *you cannot escape ideology*. You can never be free of it. Which is why it is so important to have a decent understanding of it," Amy declared.

They both paused as Brad considered what Amy had said.

"So what are the rest of the files about?" Brad asked.

"What level are you on?"

"Level?" Brad queried.

"Yes the Professor referred to each lesson as a level. Back then he planned to have eight or nine levels in the course."

"Well I've only done the ones on semantic networks and ideology…" Brad trailed off.

"Oh wow, I'm so jealous. It's such a rush when you start piecing it all together. But then I was only shown up to level four."

"Well what are the next levels then?" Brad asked.

"The next one is on evolution – it's another video and the one after that is on change," Amy said.

"So what are the passwords?"

"Passwords?" Amy questioned.

"Yes each level's file has a password to open it," Brad said.

"The ones he gave me didn't have passwords on them. Hmm, I guess he wanted to make you work for them."

Amy laughed, realising that Brad had not been given the files by the Professor. "I mean, um, he must have wanted people to have to work to reach the next level rather than just handing them out. I guess it makes it more meaningful if that is the case. Although each file I had was made so you could only view it once. I guess that was just something he was trying."

"Do you know about the powder?" Brad asked.

"Do you have some?" Amy asked curiously, "I would love to get some more, I felt like it really helped me make connections, almost as though it was making my brain grow."

"We have a small sample, but can't work out what it is," Brad replied.

"Maybe you can ask the Dame," Amy said matter-of-factly.

Brad's heart skipped a beat.

"Dame?" he asked incredulously.

"Yes, Dame Sagan. Man I love her TV show. She's hilarious…"

Amy imitated some of her better known tics.

"The Professor worked with her to develop it. Is it still that swampy green colour? The Professor asked me if they should find a way to make it white, but I told him that the green colour made it seem more medical. Besides, if it was white it would just look like caster sugar and that…"

Amy finally noticed the look on Brad's face.

"What?" she asked.

"Dame Sagan died this morning," Brad said sombrely.

"How?" Amy asked.

"The same way as the Professor."

"Shit…" Amy said, genuinely shocked.

"Amy, I'm not sure how to say this, but so far everyone I've come across who knows about this has died," Brad said quietly.

"And you think I'm at risk," Amy said swiftly.

"Yes."

"Nope," Amy said with a wry grin.

"How can you be sure?" Brad asked.

"The Professor was ethical, I was only ever referred to as a number when he documented my experience with the program or interviewed me. We only met on my lunch breaks and I was recruited by contacting him in person after he put a small flier up in the Union building.

There is no paper trail leading to me and the only one who knows I was involved is, well, you."

"Ok," Brad said with relief. "So what else can you tell me?"

"Well, I am not sure why I was never shown the higher levels, but I think the Professor was trying to work out how far to take it. He mentioned that some people he knew wanted him to release the program to them so that they could control its distribution. But I got the impression that he wanted to develop the complete program and then draw a line as to how much he would release to the general public, I think he also had some other group he was sharing it with."

Brad eyes opened widely and he leant further forward.

"He seemed to think that there probably needed to be a line, otherwise it would change society a bit too much. I mean he wanted to open people's minds, and was intending to make the program free, but was just not sure what impact it would have. He mumbled something about people needing their caves at one point," said Amy.

Brad wondered if maybe that could be a motive to wipe out the people who knew about the course. Maybe change the powder to one that was stronger and would cause an overdose, get the program in its entirety and sell it for a profit? At least with Amy's information he had something more to go on, but he was still unsure who he should be targeting.

"That's useful. What else?" asked Brad.

"Well, the Professor once asked me a question, that I didn't and still don't understand. He asked me what

Athena's gift was. I think it had to do with one of the higher levels he was working on and he wanted to know if his version of the answer was well known. I don't know if that will help you, but it was something that stuck in my mind."

"Sounds like a clue to me, so yes it will be useful."

Brad then thought about the tattoo and the Greek letters in it.

Athena was a Greek Goddess, maybe there is a connection? He made a mental note to follow-up on that tomorrow.

"That's all I have though. If I think of anything else I will let you know," Amy said.

Amy and Brad spent the next hour talking about everything other than the case and enjoying a pleasant meal. Brad told Amy about his sister, who was the success story of the family. At twenty five, she was the youngest Senior Engineer at her firm. She had been with her boyfriend for seventeen months and their parents treated him like he was already their son-in-law.

"I'm jealous of her success," Brad admitted, saying it aloud for the first time.

"Don't worry, you will be a success too," Amy touched his hand making Brad believe it too. The sensation made him feel like it would be worth dating her even if it meant being sanctioned or fired.

How can I not keep seeing her when she makes me feel so special? he thought.

Amy told him more about when she broke her leg.

"I spent over a week in hospital. The time I spent recovering and away from ballet training, gave me long periods of time without anyone around me. It made me really stop and think. I became really worried that I mightn't be successful at ballet. I guess I'm quite ambitious and want to be the best at something…"

Brad nodded.

"That was when I decided that a career in ballet was too risky and could end too easily, so I decided to study Arts/Commerce. My parents were actually upset at first because they liked being the supportive parents who let their daughter pursue her art. They would brag that I was going to be a *prima ballerina*. Now, they are proud that I have two degrees and work at a prestigious sandstone university. Me, I'm just happy with the path I'm on."

They both smiled sheepishly at each other. Brad liked that they were already comfortable sharing personal information with each other. At the end of the evening they made plans for another date in a few nights time despite Brad's nagging reservations.

Amy smiled as Brad walked her to her car arm in arm and only just managed to resist kissing him when they said goodnight.

Interchapter

To: Michael Episteme
From: The Commander
Subject: Should I be Angry?

Good morning Professor,
I have thought more about our chat the other day and your intriguing program. I thank you for being upfront that you know my secret and that you did not want me to feel pressured into helping you. I am keen to be involved and have a solution that I am willing to contribute. There is a neurotransmitter that will produce the effects you are after and it is readily obtainable in powder form. The person consuming it will feel it stimulating them, as it will make them feel paraesthesia and breathlessness. But it is diminishing returns with the doses, so it would be a good idea to restrict it to one dose for each of your levels. Let's take this even further though, how about we

put my stamp on the tubs? Consider it my 'token of a better age'. Also, have you thought about how you will distribute the powder? I have a few industry contacts who could help us set up a discreet factory to manufacture and distribute it. I can set up a shelf company to sort out payments. Let me know what you think.

Warm Regards,

The Commander

Chapter Five

After a night of intermittent sleep, Brad was awoken by the sound of the paper being dropped at his door. He sleepily put on his dressing gown and made himself a coffee before sitting down to read the paper. The lead article was about the death of Dame Rachel Sagan and emblazoned with the headline 'Dame Sagan: Victim of the Melting Brain.'

Dame Rachel Sagan was found dead in her home yesterday. She was apparently one of several victims of the melting brain phenomenon that has also claimed the life of Professor Michael Episteme, a known friend of the Dame. Dame Rachel Sagan will be best remembered for her monthly science show that was credited with bringing science to the people and her long fought battle with Tourette's syndrome. Rachel was appointed as a Dame Commander in the Most Distinguished Order of St. Michael and St. George for her services to the Commonwealth in developing global health programs and policy. She was also a Nobel Prize recipient in Medicine for her research into neuroplasticity. Rachel was a patron of several mental health organisations and they have released tributes for her and her work. For more on her achievements and the melting brain affair, turn to page 3...

Brad read the article three times before going in to the Police Station. Yet again, he was struck by the impersonal nature of the building.

But I guess that serves a purpose to say that the law and police are impartial, Brad thought for the first time.

Once at his desk he decided to try applying what he had learnt from the Professor and Amy to the Greek letters in the tattoo. *One person might view the letters for their scientific meaning, like Sam had because of her science background, but how might someone with a different perspective view them?* Brad asked himself.

He searched for the individual letters in a search engine and found that they also were all Greek numbers.

Who knew the Greeks had their own number system that was like the more well-known Roman numerals?

Alpha was one, Theta was nine, Epsilon was five, Omicron was seventy and Sigma was two hundred. So the letters represented the numbers one, nine, five, seventy and two hundred. Brad was surprised that they were out of order and made a note to try number sequences as passwords for the remaining files. He also wondered if their total of two hundred and eighty five was significant. He realised that a Greek person may have a different point of view so he sent an all department email asking if anyone could read Greek. Seven minutes later he had a response from Constable

Paul Stavropolous who was a recent graduate of the Police Academy and, like Brad, new to the station. As the most junior officer in the department, Paul's job was to man the front desk. Brad realised that he'd walked past him nearly every day since he arrived a month ago without even introducing himself, although he had said a passing 'hello'. Brad walked briskly across the room and through the mirrored door that led to the front desk. He quickly introduced himself to Paul and after a few pleasantries Brad gave Paul a quick overview of the case and why the letters may be important. He showed Paul a piece of paper with alpha, theta, epsilon, omicron and sigma written on it.

"Were the letters written as words in the tattoo?" Paul asked.

"What do you mean?" replied Brad.

"Well you have written the pronunciations down, not the actual letters."

"Oh," Brad said mentally kicking himself, "the tattoo definitely has them as letters."

Brad pulled up a copy of the tattoo that had been sent to his phone and showed Paul.

"Oh, ok then. Well there are a few things to say about that then. First that version of the last letter, sigma, is used only when it's the last letter of the word and the word is not all capitalised, so whoever wrote it knew their Greek," said Paul.

Brad felt his nerves tingle at the idea that these letters were a *word*.

"And the word itself is interesting, it's 'atheos' which means 'those without God' or 'godless' which is why it sounds a lot like atheism," Paul continued.

"That fits. All the dead people were members of a group that were big on free thinking and rejecting the received wisdom. And they are also numbers right?" Brad asked.

"Yes, one, nine, five, seventy, six," replied Paul.

"You mean two hundred for the last one don't you?" Brad questioned.

"No, sigma is two hundred, yes, but that symbol is six."

"I thought it was sigma, so shouldn't it be two hundred? Why is it six?" Brad asked.

"Yes it's a form of sigma but when sigma is written that way rather than the usual symbols that look similar to a capital E or a small o, it has a value of six. As for why, I guess I don't really know, but I do remember studying a Greek philosopher who came up with a calculation of how many grains of sand could fit into the universe and he invented a bunch of new numbers. So maybe it just evolved out of necessity?" Paul replied.

Amy's words about the next level of the program echoed in Brad's mind. He wrote down what Paul had told him, including his mentioning of the sand. He thanked Paul and walked slowly back to his desk. Sally saw him approaching and asked him how he was going and what he would like her to do now that she was assigned to him.

"I don't know, help me research organisations for freethinkers?" Brad suggested.

"How have you researched them to date?" Sally asked.

"Just online, what other ways are there these days?" said Brad.

"Well, you could try the phone directory or ask people. I mean the dead people were all well connected, maybe ask their friends what they know about such a group?"

"Yeah, that might work. How about I start with the University and you try Dame Sagan's people?" Brad said, finally finding the confidence to be directive.

"Ok," Sally replied obediently. "Anything else?"

"Yes, see what you can find out about Leviathan Enterprises, especially Dr Engels. I'm sure that they are behind this somehow and that the link between them and the Freethinking group is the key to solving this," Brad responded.

"Ok. Will do," Sally turned to face her computer as Brad returned to his desk.

Brad picked up the phone and called the University. He resisted his urge to call Amy by reminding himself that they already had another date planned. The receptionist put Brad on hold while they transferred his call to Professor De Silva. While he was waiting Brad started absently doodling on his notepad. He found himself writing down the numbers Paul had told him and almost unconsciously added them up. He noted that they totalled ninety-one.

It took Brad a few moments to place why that number was so familiar. With the certainty only an epiphany can bring, Brad knew he had found the right group to investigate. He could not help but reflect that their waiting list had become shorter recently. He hung up the phone just as a voice said "Hello."

"Sally, come here," Brad called out across the room.

"Sally, I know which group we should be looking at,"

he said as she came over.

Brad opened up his browser and brought up the history. A few clicks of the mouse later and he had found the website he was looking for.

"This is the one," he said triumphantly.

"How do you know?" Sally asked.

"Their waiting list is the same number as the total of the Greek numbers in the tattoo on the bodies," Brad replied.

"Huh?" Sally responded.

Brad smiled to himself as he recognised the confusion in her that he often felt.

"It just is. This is the group. Help me find out more about them. I'll call the number on their website, you see if you or the techies can find out who owns the website and where it's hosted," Brad said, feeling like he was on a roll.

"Sure thing, Boss," Sally said with just a hint of condescension as she walked back to her desk.

Brad immediately picked up the phone and called the number on the website. It was answered on the fourth ring.

"Greetings, you have reached The Network of Freethinkers. This is Eliza speaking." A feminine voice answered.

Brad wrote down the group's name, noting that its initials spelt *font* backwards.

"Hi, my name is Brad," he said.

"Hello Brad, my name is Eliza."

You said that already, Brad thought to himself.

"How may I help you?" Eliza continued.

"I'd like to join your organisation."

"We are full at the moment. Our network is limited to ninety-one members," Eliza replied. Brad stopped for a moment to think about what he wanted to know.

"What do members gain by joining your network?" he asked.

"They get the chance to improve their thought processes and raise their consciousness. In short they get the gift of Athena." Brad's pulse shot up.

This was it, he thought.

"I need to join your network, now," Brad said.

"Would you like to join the waiting list?" Eliza's tone did not change.

"No I would like to join now," Brad said urgently as he felt a tickling sensation in his nose.

"That is not possible," Eliza replied maintaining her neutral tone.

"But I know that the number ninety-one is what you get when you add up the Greek letters for atheism." Brad fought the urge to sneeze.

"That is interesting." Eliza's tone of voice was beginning to annoy him.

Brad couldn't resist any longer and sneezed violently.

"That is interesting," Eliza repeated. The repetition and neutral tone made Brad suddenly feel like he was talking to a machine.

"Amy, Professor, Dame," he said rapidly.

"Can you repeat that?" Eliza questioned.

"Gobbledygook, French wine, abuzz," Brad said.

"Can you repeat that?" Eliza repeated.

"Miranda, copper, frozen," Brad said.

"Can you repeat that?" Eliza repeated again.

"Are you a computer?" Brad asked triumphantly.

"Yes," Eliza responded.

Brad was shocked. Up until his sneeze he was sure he was talking to a human.

"How can I get more information from you?" he asked.

"State the password," Eliza said.

"Godless." Brad guessed.

"Congratulations you have been moved up the waiting list. To move further up the list state the first passphrase."

"Atheism?" Brad queried.

"That is not the passphrase." Eliza's monotone replied.

"Tell me about the passphrase?"

"Which one?"

"How many are there?" asked Brad.

"How many of what?" Eliza responded.

"How many passphrases are there?"

"There are a total of two," replied Eliza.

"Tell me about the first passphrase," demanded Brad.

"It's related to the password."

"Tell me about the second passphrase."

"It's related to the first passphrase." Eliza replied.

Brad wasn't sure how to respond to this so he hung up the phone. He figured that he would not get any further with guesses. He returned to the Professor's levels and the third level that he was trying to crack. He thought about the Professor's suggestion to look up RSAs and ISAs and decided that was the place to start. A quick review of some websites revealed that these acronyms stood for Repressive State Apparatus and Ideological State Apparatus. The person who had coined these terms was named Althusser. When Brad tried that on the Level Three file it dutifully opened and revealed another video of the Professor. He was at his home and sitting in the old chesterfield armchair. The Professor appeared relaxed and was leaning forward conspiratorially.

Level Three: Evolution

Evolution is a crucial part of why humans behave the way they do and an awareness of this is vital for us to improve our thinking. As Richard Dawkins argues in the introduction to his book *The God Delusion*, an understanding of evolution by natural selection is consciousness raising in and of itself. At its core, evolution is about the movement of genes. Genes are what make each of us who we are and they are the units that measure inheritance. The important understanding is that genes seek to reproduce themselves. Ideally, they bestow some trait or physical appearance that confers some advantage to a person that will enable more successful reproduction and survival. Human behaviour seems diverse and chaotic, but when you start looking at it from an evolutionary perspective, it makes a lot more sense.

So much of human behaviour is explainable through evolution: a mother's morning sickness means that she is less likely to ingest something that will harm her baby; a large vocabulary is seen as a sign of intelligence, so when meeting a potential mate, men use longer words to try and impress the woman, making them more likely to be selected as a partner; gossip is akin to a form of verbal grooming and helps build and maintain social relationships. Any behaviour that relates to social status, social norms and biological health all confer advantage from an evolutionary point of view. But this understanding of the importance of evolution is just the beginning…

The brightness in the Professor's eyes and raw enthusiasm once again struck Brad. The Professor was genuinely excited by what he was doing and the program he had created.

The next bit is something that takes our understanding of evolution to the next level. After all genetics is more than just predispositions and protein coding. There was an interesting study done in 2013 at Emory University, where researchers trained mice to fear the smell of cherry blossom using electric shocks. They let them reproduce and this is where it gets eye opening; the offspring showed a fear response to the odour of cherry blossom despite never having smelt cherry blossoms before! But wait there's more… The following generation also showed the same behaviour. The researchers found the fear conditioned mice and their offspring and their offspring's offspring had structural changes in their brains in the areas associated with odour detection. Now here is the really crucial part of this study, the DNA of the rats also carried chemical changes on the gene responsible for odour detection. The researchers concluded that life experiences are somehow transferred from the brain into DNA, allowing them to be passed on to later generations.

The reason why I like this study is that the conclusion also explains instinctual behaviours and how they could be bred into a species. What's also really fascinating is that this field of biology, known as epigenetics, is revealing even more about how this process works and that we now have the technology to measure the impact of the environment upon gene expression. You can expose a rat to a traumatic event and measure the change in expression of its genes for things like depression and anxiety. Think about that for a moment, we can now measure the impact of the environment on a person at a genetic level and then confirm that the change in DNA is inheritable! We can measure how and what genes are switched on and off through experience. Why is this important for our consciousness? Well, think about it!

The video stopped and Brad dutifully followed the Professor's advice and stopped to think about what he had just watched. Understanding that the environment can play a role in determining how your body functions wasn't new, but the detail that it does so at the genetic level was eye opening and the fact that this information could then be passed on to children was unbelievable.

Wow that is amazing, Brad thought. *But it also means that we have the moral imperative to behave in a manner that sets the example for our children or potential children, as they may very well inherit our behaviours and experience. This really explains the idea of cultural knowledge and the development of instinctive behaviour.*

Brad realised that this could not only explain family traits but also how those traits could fade away.

We really do have a lot to thank our ancestors for, he thought.

Although this wasn't much of an epiphany when you added it to the other levels of the Professor's program, Brad could see how considering all the aspects the Professor had spoken about: the nature of language and memory, ideology, and evolution, when viewing the world would really open your eyes to how society functions and the human condition. Brad had the image of a microscope with a rotating dial of lenses and that each lens was one of these ideas. He envisioned turning the dial the opposite way and realised that ideologies and language evolve, and that the two were in fact related processes. Not for the first time while working through the program Brad felt like there was a spotlight on him.

He called Sally over.

"Gee it's been what, five minutes?" Sally said in exasperation.

Brad smiled and then had the thought that her tone of voice was a verbal clue as to her emotional state, and that his understanding of this meant he was able to interact with her in a more positive way; one that would build a social bond between them.

Evolution in action, he thought quietly to himself, and then he smiled again.

"Yes, I'm a puppet, stop grinning and tell me what you want," Sally said with a mix of humour and frustration.

"I have just cracked the next file in the Professor's program," he said proudly.

"Great, so you've solved the case?" Sally asked sarcastically.

"No, but it does mean that I am beginning to see the power of it and why someone would want to see it hushed up."

"Is that all?" Sally asked with mock derision.

"Hey, that's actually quite significant," said Brad.

"Yes, I know, but I was really interested in what I was doing. I was actually getting somewhere myself you know."

"Wow that was quick. What did you find out?" Brad

asked.

"Well I wasn't able to find out much about Leviathan Enterprises. They seem quite secretive. I did find a tender document where they were granted the job of creating a program to reduce the cost of aged care to the government but that was about all. However, I did find out a few things about Dr Engels. His PhD thesis was titled *From Atoms to Adam to Automatons* and he was a bioengineer who became wealthy through several patents relating to neural implants that the government bought off him for a small fortune. It seems that with Leviathan he has moved on to social engineering. His business dealings have been a bit shady though – there are three different people who have tried to sue him: one was for wrongful termination and the other two were for patent infringement. Here's the kicker, none of the cases ever reached court," said Sally.

"So, are we assuming they were murdered?"

"Yes and no. I've tried to track them down and one of the litigants who was suing for patent infringement died the week before the court date."

"Well that's suspicious," Brad said.

"Yes."

"So he's not above murder then?" Brad thought aloud.

"Well I don't know how the person died, just that they did," responded Sally.

"But with his background Dr Engels could make it look like pretty much whatever he wanted," Brad thought aloud once again.

"Well if that is the case and he's responsible for the deaths we're investigating, why wouldn't he kill them in a less public way?" Sally questioned.

"Well… maybe he wants to send a message?"

"That's an idea."

"Yes," Brad paused, "So what about the other two?"

"I'm yet to locate them, that's what I was trying to do when you called me over," replied Sally.

"Well back to it then," said Brad with a cheeky grin. Sally tried to maintain her irritation, but could not stop herself laughing.

"Fine," Sally turned and walked back to her desk. Brad mused that he had just used humour to change someone's attitude. Another evolutionary adaptation.

"Brad, my office. Now," Sergeant Pan's voice suddenly appeared in Brad's ear. He jumped and felt his pulse shoot up – the fight or flight response they had called it when he was at school, yet another quirk of evolution affecting his behaviour. As he walked with the Sergeant to her office, he mused that he was suddenly hyper-conscious of evolution. The Professor must have wanted it to be another means of forming links between pieces of knowledge.

As soon as they were in the Sergeant's office and the door was shut, Sergeant Pan said that there had been another two deaths that had been reported to her as a result of publicity about Dame Sagan.

"Both had the tattoo and according to their spouses both had received it several months ago. In both cases the victims had said that they had been stung by a bee and their partners believed them. This group you have discovered is clearly being targeted. What do you know about them?"

"Only that they have ninety-one members and there is

a kind of screening process as a barrier to joining them. I have gotten through a couple of phases of the process but probably have another couple to go," Brad replied.

"Great, well keep on that." Sergeant Pan looked suitably impressed. *Brad might just be capable of solving this after all, she thought.*

"Unfortunately, these deaths mean that the Feds are on their way and will be here tomorrow. We are going to have to make more of the case public as well. Now, you say that there is a program and powder that could be causing the deaths?"

"Yes."

"Well we don't know who else might be using it so we will have to release a statement urging anyone in possession of the program or powder to come forward."

"Ok." Brad replied.

"I'll have our media liaison draft a release and send it off. What additional resources do you need to make more progress?" asked Sergeant Pan abruptly.

"Time?" Brad responded.

"That is one thing we don't have. You'd better get cracking then," Sergeant Pan said.

Brad dutifully turned and left the office while trying not to sigh.

Interchapter

To: Mathew Arnold
From: The Professor
Subject: Greetings

Greetings Old Friend,
Dr Engels passed on your new contact details. I have a project that I'd like to share with you. I have developed a program that raises people's intelligence and social awareness and I was wondering if you would like to help us test it. Dr Engels and I are hoping that you would be able to use your position as deputy chairman of RTI to help sell it to the members. The program may provide a way of helping us create that social change we discussed but had different opinions over.
I look forward to hearing from you, it has been too long.
Cheers,
Michael

Chapter Six

Brad walked over to Sally's desk. He could not help but contrast her with Amy in both appearance and demeanour. His mind drifted to evolution and how the two women were examples of different features being selected for and inherited. For Brad, their different genetic mixes were great examples of how the whole package of genes a person presented with was what was important. Brad decided that he did not like the Professor's emphasis on individual genes.

But, he mused, *if the Professor is right, then their cultural and familial background were also important in shaping who they were and how they viewed the world.*

As he started to relate this to ideology, Brad suddenly realised who he needed to speak to. He walked straight past Sally, barely looking where he was going and bumped into Detective Taupo, who grunted "Watch it, Country Boy."

Brad ignored him and carried on to Paul at the front

desk. Paul seemed grateful for the interruption. His job seemed to consist of mostly signing statutory declarations or helping people fill in paperwork for minor thefts that were then passed on to a Senior Constable.

"Hi Constable," Brad said with a quick smile.

"Hi Detective," Paul replied warmly.

"Small favour to ask, by any chance do you know what Athena's gift is?" Brad asked hopefully.

"No. Unless you mean wisdom. That's what she is the goddess of," replied Paul.

"I've considered that but it didn't work. Oh well, it was worth a try," said Brad.

"What about Athens? It's named after her," said Paul.

"I've tried that too. But it doesn't really fit either."

"What about olives?"

"What?"

"Yeah, you're testing my knowledge here, but I think I remember something about the reason Athens was named after her was about olives. Two gods, Athena and Poseidon were competing to name the city and Poseidon gave the people a salt water spring and Athena gave them an olive tree. The Athenians thought that this was a better gift because olive trees could be used for wood, oil and food whereas the salt spring, while good for trade was not good for drinking," said Paul.

"Give me a moment…" Brad raced back to his desk, this time Detective Taupo saw him coming and got out of his way. *At least the Country Boy is doing something,* he thought.

Brad redialled Eliza and tried olives as the second password but was told "I'm sorry that is not the password."

This time Eliza's neutral tone wasn't so annoying. Brad went back to Paul's desk. He had to wait while Paul certified some documents for a member of the public. As soon as Paul was free Brad asked him if he knew of anything else that could be thought of as Athena's gift.

Paul frowned in thought, "I can't think of anything else that could be interpreted as her gift… but she did have a mark."

Brad's ears pricked up like Border Collie hearing a whistle.

"Yes?" he asked eagerly.

"Yeah, obviously she gives her name to Athens and in Greek Athens is written *Αθήνα*." Paul drew the letters on a sheet of paper. "But the first three Greek letters for Athena are *ΑΘΕ* and this sounds like 'Athe' and historically that was a nickname of Athens. ΑΘΕ used to be on some coins that also featured owls which were another symbol of hers. So ΑΘΕ is Athena's mark," Paul said.

"Great. That sounds really useful. Thanks," Brad replied.

"Don't thank me, thank the internet. When you raced off before, I searched for Athena and found a page about her owl coins," Paul admitted.

"Really, I had searched for her but didn't come across that?" Brad said.

Paul smiled "Yeah, but I probably used a different search engine to you and maybe a few different search terms. Anyway let me know how you go."

Paul turned towards a person who had just come in. It

was yet another request for a document to be certified. Brad went back to his desk and called The Network of Freethinkers. Brad was getting used to Eliza now and quickly reached the request for the second password.

"A.O.E." Brad said reading the letters Paul had written down. He was not surprised when Eliza said that wasn't the password as he had read out their English equivalents.

"Alpha, theta, epsilon," said Brad.

"And what is the significance of that?" Eliza replied.

"It's the mark of Athena," Brad replied confidently.

"Congratulations you have been moved up the queue. For immediate access to the Network, please state the second passphrase in the form of the answer to the question, what is Athena's gift?" Eliza said.

Brad thought hard.

"What is Athena's gift?" he said softly after a pause.

"That is not the correct passphrase," Eliza said monotonously. Brad started daydreaming about Amy's warm and compassionate voice and comparing it to the slightly sterile one of Eliza's.

"Why is it not correct?" Brad asked absently, before realising that he had not answered the question, but then he did not have an answer to give.

"That is not the correct passphrase," Eliza repeated.

Brad reminded himself he was talking to a machine and gave up. He was so close, but he knew that he probably needed to understand more before he would crack the third passphrase and gain access to the Network.

He decided to try to access the next level of the Professor's program. He watched the last video again and decided that there were two things he should read, one was the research paper on cherry blossoms and genetic inheritance and the other was *The God Delusion*. He downloaded the e-book to his computer. He did a few searches for the research paper but all the sites that had the article required membership or payment. Brad decided to call Amy. He tried to convince himself that calling her would also satisfy his desire to talk to her so that he could concentrate on the case.

"Hi Amy," he said cheerily, aware that his voice rose when her talked to her.

"Hello Officer, I'm looking forward to seeing you tomorrow." Amy responded brightly. Brad was amused that he did not need to introduce himself.

"I have a favour to ask," Brad admitted.

"I'm not coming over there just to kiss you," Amy said as though she'd been thinking of nothing else.

Brad felt himself blush.

"You will have to at least buy me dinner first."

"That's not what I …" Brad blustered.

Amy giggled, "I'm just messing with you. How can I help?"

Brad tried to regain his composure, "Can you get your library to locate a document for me?"

"Sure."

Brad told her the details.

"Is that all you wanted? Or was that just an excuse to call me?" asked Amy, the smile evident in her voice.

Brad had to admit to himself that he was using the document as a reason to call Amy, but there was no way he was going to say that to her even though she probably knew exactly what he was up to.

"No that was all, but while I have you here, can I confirm tomorrow?"

"Sure. Kissing of you at 6.59pm, dinner at H-Bar, 7pm. Ooh, I have to go, the Boss is coming. See you tomorrow Brad,"

Amy hung up the phone as Brad blushed again. He tried to remember the last time that had happened, but could only think of an occasion from primary school. Blushing was an interesting quirk of evolution that Brad felt existed for no useful reason. Five minutes later his inbox flashed with an email with the article as an attachment. It was signed off with *hugs and forthcoming kisses, Amy.* Brad smiled and thought, *You're not helping me focus on my case.*

As Brad reached for the phone to call Amy to say thanks, it rang. He answered, hoping it would be Amy calling to check if the email had been received.

"Hello, Detective Thomas speaking," Brad stated in his formal voice.

"Hello Detective Thomas. This is Sam, the Medical Examiner," came the reply.

"Hi Sam," Brad said trying not to sound disappointed.

"I just had a very interesting email and call from the M.E. over in Middleton," Sam said conspiratorially.

"Yes?" Brad replied quickly.

"He had just completed the autopsy on Dame Sagan and he gave me the details. Now, as you know her brain was pretty messed up by the whole melting thing, but he was still able to find that she had an abnormally high number of glial cells like our victims, but that is not the interesting bit," Sam whispered into the phone.

"No? So what was?" Brad queried.

"Well, he was also given access to her medical records. You know how she was famous for her Tourette's?" Sam queried.

"Yeah."

Brad imitated a few of her famous tics, just like Amy had and then felt guilty, as he knew it was inappropriate behaviour, even though the Dame had embraced her tics and made them a feature of her delivery on her show.

"Well, get this… she didn't actually have Tourette's!" Sam exclaimed.

"What?" Brad replied.

"Yes, the M.E. emailed me some old scans and when someone has Tourette's their brain's white matter connections are unusually high in the thalamus, basal ganglia and frontal cortex but hers were all normal. I mean wow, she was so known for her condition. It's the reason many people watched her show."

"So it was just a … an affectation?" Brad replied incredulously.

"Yup!" Sam responded excitedly.

"That's incredible, I mean, who would … Why?" Brad's mind was reeling.

"I know! Anyway, I thought you should know," Sam said, making it seem more like she had to tell someone and he was the only one she could.

"Thanks."

"Oh yeah, any chance you have found any more of the powder? We are stumped as to what it is, but we've run out of it. Middleton PD didn't find any with the Dame," said Sam.

"But she created it and was providing it to people," replied Brad.

"Hmm, Middleton PD mentioned that they were looking into her business dealings and that they'd found that some funds had been diverted into a secret account. I'm guessing that was what it was for," said Sam absently.

Brad scribbled down what he had been told.

"Must be. My department is putting out a press release today. Maybe it will make someone bring in some of the powder." Brad said.

"Maybe. I can only hope. I really want to know what it is. We know it's an organic compound and reacts with chlorates and nitrates but beyond that…" Sam stopped.

"I think I might know what it is, but I will have to do some more tests and look at the ones we have already done again. Which means that I need another sample. If you get some, can you send it my way?"

"Sure. In fact we have just had another two cases reported to us and both were new to the group."

Brad quickly explained what he had found out about The Network of Freethinkers and that they were responsible for the tattoos and that the powder was part of a program to raise consciousness. Brad promised that he would try to get a sample of the powder from the new cases and pass it on to her.

"Thanks, bye." Sam hung up.

It was clear to Brad she wanted to investigate her idea further.

Brad clicked open the document Amy had sent him. He read through the journal article slowly, looking for new terminology or something that stood out as a possible password for the next of the Professor's levels. After nearly three quarters of an hour, Brad gave up and switched to Dawkins' book. As he read the introduction he was sure this book was where he would find what he was looking for since it spoke of four consciousness raising ideas. Brad wrote down two of them on his notepad:

1.   Evolution by natural selection is an idea that can elevate your thinking.

2.   Atheist pride.

Brad wondered if the Professor had stolen the idea about evolution from Dawkins since he was clearly aware of his book.

However, Brad reminded himself, *the Professor had taken it further with more recent information.*

As Brad read the introduction he was struck by a word that came up. It was a portmanteau of 'religious delusion', and was used exclusively by atheists to describe someone who was ignorant of science and scientific methods and who thought Holy Scriptures were fact. The word was relusion. Brad typed it in as the Level Four password and a text file opened up.

The headline was something of a *non-sequitur*; *Level Four: Faith Works.*

Brad raised an eyebrow at the heading - the Professor had changed the order of the program. He also realised that by hunting for the password in Dawkins' book, he was effectively doing pre-reading for this level.

Religious faith is an almost universal phenomenon and for most of human history has provided an advantage to those who adhere to it. Religion has been responsible for improving social cohesion, been a source of moral values and yes, even knowledge and understanding. Religion has even been consciousness raising. It has been a phenomenon that unites people and helped people to feel more connected, supported and valued. In short it has been of immense benefit to humanity. What I am about to write may be something of a contradiction to these statements, however the aim of this Program is to be consciousness raising and a study of atheism is definitely consciousness raising. It is for this reason that this discussion is included (i.e.: the aim is not to turn people doing this program into atheists, it is to turn people into freethinkers such as those who are members of The Network of Freethinkers). Atheism and Atheist pride are just ideas to help make you aware of where our social and cultural norms come from and how they are shaped by language, ideology and evolution and are subject to change - just as all religious beliefs and all ideas are. You can be religious but still find the concept of atheism consciousness raising.

Brad gasped involuntarily. He congratulated himself on being ahead of the program and for finally proving a link between the strands of the investigation he was investigating. He spent a moment debating whether to read on, or call Detective Summers and Sergeant Pan over to share his discovery. He decided to read on.

And yes, this is an idea I have borrowed to an extent from others. Atheism is an important consciousness raiser since understanding it and the concept of atheist pride is eye opening. It incorporates our other levels too. Religion is a great example of an ideology and it is this understanding that religions are merely collections of ideas about how the world is or should be, that gives rise to the knowledge that religions are constructed. When you look at how interrelated many of the religions are, you can see how they have evolved. Look at Roman and Greek gods. Look at how Judaism, Islam and Christianity share a God and prophets, but how after their common origin they branched off and developed mostly independently – i.e. they evolved. The question then comes "what is the next step for religion?" and the answer is to commit apostasy. Apostasy means breaking from the word and involves renouncing your beliefs. We do similar acts all the time such as breaking up with a partner or quitting a job. When you do this your opinion of your partner or workplace changes from how you felt at the beginning of the relationship. So too with religion. This is not to undervalue or deny the benefit of religion, but simply an understanding that you can get your morals and values from elsewhere. In short you can outgrow religion. It is important to understand that this is not something to be ashamed of or to make excuses for; which leads to the concept of atheist pride.

Atheist pride is an application of the concept that is found in the concepts of Black pride and gay pride. It is the idea that it is ok to be an atheist, but also that the public's perception of atheism can or will also change just as it has for Black people and gay people. When you look at atheism through this lens, it can change your perspective. Importantly if you stop and think about it, it demonstrates that there are major shifts in the public's ideological opinion of many phenomena. When you contemplate the evolution of such changes and how the old point of view is considered, you begin to realise how transitory such notions are and how irrelevant they are to bigger questions of humanity. This is not to say that such issues are not important, but rather than focusing on black, gay or atheist pride, the real issue is why there are such divisions between groups of people in the first place.

I mean and why people can't just work together and get along? Imagine if they did! The things we could achieve. I mean look at what happens during war, when whole countries get behind a cause, the technological advances are huge. Now imagine that on a global scale, with free and liberal exchange of information, cooperation and interaction; we could wipe out hunger, explore space and planets and maybe even make contact with another species…"

Brad could imagine the dreamy look in the Professor's eye as he was writing the article. He smiled as he realised he was getting the same expression. The feeling of empowerment he felt with unlocking each level was addictive and Brad realised that the program was really changing his view of the world. Somehow, it was also making him happier and more confident.

###

Brad spent most of the night daydreaming rather than sleeping. His thoughts kept switching between Amy, the Program and the case. He could just 'see' how the course of his life had been shaped by the factors covered in the Professor's program and that understanding was making Brad re-evaluate his whole history. The thing was that this was a surprisingly positive experience.

I think I *am beginning to 'get' life!* Brad thought happily. *I can't wait to share this with Amy, she'll understand what is happening to me, and is probably the only one who could. Gee, I'm attracted to her, and yet I should be distancing myself…How can I know that so clearly and still want to see her?*

Brad felt restless again. *I always do the right thing so why I can't I just have this one wrong thing and have it be ok?*

###

Brad arrived early for his shift the next morning. He was surprised by the number of vehicles parked outside the station. Sally came over to him the moment he walked in and it was clear that something was going on.

"The brown stuff has hit the fan," she said simply.

"What, why?"

"You know the media release that was sent out last night?" Sally questioned.

"I knew one was being sent, but I haven't read it," replied Brad.

"It has created a bit of a stir. Unfortunately, it was phrased in a way that made it seem like the Professor had created a program that would make people more intelligent and that all you needed were a copy of the program and the powder to become smarter," said Sally.

"But that's true," Brad replied.

"Yes, but you don't go out and tell people that. I mean really. People will always focus on that big positive rather than the potentially lethal consequences, which is what we were really trying to communicate. We need people to dispose of or hand in their copy of the program and powder, not seek it out," Sally scoffed.

"Hmm," said Brad thoughtfully. *The powder. I can only imagine how much more I would be experiencing if I had it. Am I missing out by not having it?*

"Anyway the boss is holding a press conference to try to get things under control."

Brad did not respond. He was too lost in thought.

Sergeant Wendy Pan was having a tough time facing questions from the assembled journalists.

"Can you show us the program?" asked one.

"Where can we get the program?" asked another.

"How many deaths have there been?" asked a journalist named Verity Trouver.

"Six," Wendy said, picking the question she could answer. "There was another one overnight, which is why the report we released yesterday was so important. You are focusing on the wrong part of the press release. People are dying! ..." Sergeant Pan was emphatic, "... and you are trying to obtain the program that is implicated in their deaths?"

She shook her head in disbelief.

"The Federal Police have arrived this morning and after this press conference I will be briefing them on the case to date. We have established links between several of the deceased and ..."

"Are these people being targeted?" interrupted Verity.

"Why is it only smart people dying?" asked another journalist. Brad realised that he had not considered this aspect as a lead yet. It suddenly seemed very odd that only smart people were dying from the program. He made a mental note to follow it up later.

"No, it appears that they are not targeted, but all are members of a particular group," Sergeant Pan said.

"What group?" asked a journalist, almost shouting to be heard.

"We are not releasing the name at this stage," said Sergeant Pan, sounding exasperated.

"What is Leviathan Enterprises role in this?" asked Verity.

Gee, they certainly know a lot, Brad thought. *The Sergeant was right, they are conducting their own investigation and if I'm not careful they will figure it out before me.*

"Nothing as far as we know, other than one of the deceased was an employee of theirs. They have been very cooperative with us and have provided information that led to some of the leads we are following in the case," the Sergeant replied in a controlled voice, nevertheless her surprise at Verity asking about Leviathan flickered across her face.

"Are you sure Leviathan aren't involved?" Verity persisted.

Sergeant Pan glared at her and did not answer.

"What are the leads?" another journalist asked.

"We are not going to reveal that," Sergeant Pan said incredulously.

"What do you make of people selling the powder online?" asked a journalist who was near Brad.

Wendy was speechless. At the back of the room Brad tried not to laugh. The smile wiped from his face when he realised, *I should have known that.*

"What do you mean?" Sergeant Pan demanded.

"Well someone calling themselves E-pony-mouse is auctioning a tub. It started at ninety-nine cents but now over four hundred dollars," the journalist replied after looking at his phone for the latest bid.

Sergeant Pan hesitated. "We will be tracking that person and if it turns out that they are selling something dangerous, then they will be charged. Let me reiterate, the powder is most likely the cause of the deaths and should not be consumed. However, what is being sold is probably a fake since it appears that it was only a select group who were sold the program."

Brad knew the Sergeant couldn't possibly know that. He could see reasons why she would lie and, as he was contemplating them, he realised that this clarity was an improvement on how he would usually interpret such an event. Brad smiled as he realised that he was actually getting better at reasoning and considering more things at once. After the press conference ended, Brad could see that the Sergeant was in a bad mood. Although he had only known her for a short while, he could tell she hated giving evasive and unclear answers. He also guessed that since she had just taken a hit socially, she would want to re-establish her status and evolutionary fitness as leader, probably by taking it out on someone. Unfortunately for Brad, she called him straight into her office.

Interchapter

To: The Professor
From: Mathew Arnold
Subject: About your program

Hello Old Friend,
Your program is interesting, thank you for inviting me to be a part of it. I am hopeful that it will indeed help humanity progress. While I am happy to do as you request with RTI, surely there is more money and more purpose in sharing the program with a wider audience? We could then use the momentum to make some real social change and that is something that interests me greatly. Let me know how I can help make this happen.
Yours
Mathew
Arnold

Chapter Seven

"So Detective, do you have anything to say to me?" asked Sergeant Pan angrily as she slammed the door.

"What do you mean, Sergeant?" Brad tried to maintain his innocence.

"You laughed at me being uncomfortable in the press conference."

"Oh, you saw that?" Brad said, unable to hide his guilt.

"Yes," Sergeant Pan said tersely.

"It was only that I've never seen you being speechless before and it amused me."

Brad's honesty and lack of guile diffused some of the Sergeant's anger. She knew that she was more frustrated with herself for not controlling the press conference better than with Brad, but he was an easy target for her irritation.

"Let me be clear, Detective, when we are holding a press conference, we present a united front. You do not laugh unless I do. You do not smile unless I do," she dictated.

"Yes, Sarge," Brad responded automatically.

"That's Sergeant, Detective," she replied.

"Sorry, Sergeant."

"Fine. Now I am about to call in the Federal task force. There are three of them. Before they come in, let me say to you that I want this case settled as soon as possible. I don't like having them around and I don't like that they will take credit for our work and progress in the case. If they solve it I will be very upset. If the media solve it before either of us, I will be even more upset."

Brad nodded in affirmation.

"Now, in regards to what you briefed me on last night about the link you had proven between the Network and the Professor. Let's keep that to ourselves and see if we can investigate it further. Keep working on gaining membership since that seems to be the key to solving this once and for all," Sergeant Pan said.

"Ok."

"And get on the phone to the uni and let them know that the Feds are likely to be coming over. Better yet, accompany the Feds over there," the Sergeant ordered.

Brad tried not to smile at the thought of going to the university and being able to see Amy.

"Ok," he said as neutrally as possible.

"Alright then. You stay here, I'll go and get them and Detective Summers." Sergeant Pan said as she left the room. A few moments later Sally strolled in.

"Hey Brad. Did you get in much trouble?" she asked with amusement.

"No. Not too much, but I'd better not laugh during the

next press conference." They both smiled.

"So what are we going to do?" she queried.

"Let's see if the Feds can help us, which I now think they won't. Maybe they'll be able to provide a lead or something we can follow, but as I see it, all we need to do to is get through the Professor's program and join the Network. From there we can figure out the link between them and Leviathan and hopefully find something that will point to Dr Engels being behind the deaths." Brad surprised himself with how authoritative he felt.

"That sounds like a good plan. Well done, but is it that simple? What are we going to do about the people selling the fake powder and program?" Sally asked.

"Well first we have to prove it is fake powder... I suppose that if it isn't, that's a good thing since we then have another lead to follow. If they are a fake then at least we can finally make an arrest in this case."

Brad realised he was about to say "annoying case," but in fact that wasn't how he felt about it. He realised that he was enjoying the Professor's program and that it was also helping him professionally.

Sergeant Pan strode into the office with the Federal team strutting in behind her. It was clear that they felt like the rock stars of the police force and that they were here to be heroes. Brad suddenly understood why the Sergeant was so against them coming. It was unlikely that they would do more than go over what already had been uncovered, criticise the work that had been done, work inefficiently and then claim any credit if the case was solved, while the local police did all the legwork. Wendy was in the middle of the history of the case when Constable Paul Stavropolous knocked on the door and said that he needed Brad to come with him. Sergeant Pan scowled, "at least you are up to speed on the case."

He walked out next to Paul and they huddled conspiratorially as they walked through the office to the front desk.

"So what's up?" Brad whispered to Paul.

"I'm not quite sure what FONT is, but there's a member of it here who would like to talk to you." Paul replied softly.

"Do you mean the Network of Freethinkers?" asked Brad, his voice rising.

"Yeah, she said that, but added that not everyone reads left to right and that members refer to it as FONT," responded Paul.

"Hmm. That's interesting" said Brad, wondering how he might use this information.

"Yes, but that's not the interesting thing… she has a sample of the powder for us and…" Paul continued.

"What? She has a sample of the powder?" said Brad as he started walking faster.

"Yes, and she knows about the mark we discussed," Paul replied barely keeping up with Brad.

"Athena's?"

"Yes. She has a ring on her right index finger that has AΘE stamped in it," said Paul.

Brad was practically running now. He burst through the door to the reception desk and saw Jenny, the assistant from Leviathan Enterprises. She was formally attired and seemed as detached as the last time Brad had seen her.

"Hello again Officer," Jenny said coolly.

"It's Detective," Brad said. He had a sudden insight

into why Wendy kept correcting him when he called her "Sarge". When Amy called him 'officer' he just about melted but when Jenny did it, it provoked nothing but hostility in him. Same word, different interpretation, different semantic network triggered.

"Alright Detective, is there some place we can talk privately?" asked Jenny.

Brad guided Jenny to an interview room. Paul returned to the front desk and was almost immediately asked to sign a statutory declaration.

The interview room was bare, with only a desk, three chairs and the clichéd two way mirror that people in the adjoining room could look through. Jenny did not bat either of her delicately mascaraed eyes. She sat down like a model with her legs crossed, upright but with a slight lean forward and her hands delicately placed on her knees. Brad admired her appearance but found himself unattracted to her. Her absence of warmth meant that he felt like she would not make a great partner or mother and for some reason these seemed to matter. *Evolution in action again,* he thought.

"Detective, I have some of the powder you have been seeking," Jenny made no movement to hand it to him.

"Good. May I have it?" Brad asked.

"Yes, when we are done."

"Why else are you here?"

"There are some things you have to know," said Jenny neutrally.

"Like what?" Brad said with a confidence he wasn't sure he felt.

"First, I waive my right to an attorney and give you this information freely," said Jenny.

126

"Ok," Brad said, unsure whether he should go and get another member of the police force to join them.

"My former colleague Brentham, as you know, knew the Professor. Brentham was a wonderful man and one I admired greatly. He also knew the Dame," Jenny said.

Brad thought he detected some emotion from her but he wasn't sure. He nodded, indicating that he was aware of their connection.

"What you may not know, is that Brentham was the one who distributed the powder to the members of the Network of Freethinkers, who by the way are actually called FONT," said Jenny.

"You mentioned that to the Constable," Brad replied.

"Yes," Jenny said sharply, "however, he did that as a personal favour to the Professor and the Dame. Let me be crystal clear, Leviathan Enterprises was not involved in the distribution of the powder in any way," Jenny said assertively.

"Ok. I understand. What about the program itself?"

"Again, if there was an arrangement for that, it was a personal arrangement and nothing to do with the company," replied Jenny.

"Ok, I understand."

"Good. That is all I came to say." Jenny made a motion as if to stand up and leave.

"Well now that you have said that I have a question for you."

Brad felt a heightened awareness of the room and in particular of Jenny. He realised just how conscious he was of her features, posture, tone of voice and facial expression.

"You can ask, but I may not answer." Jenny said

coolly. Her facial expression did not change, nor did her posture, but a slightly larger intake of breath told Brad that she was working very hard to control what she said and did.

"You have a ring on your index finger that bears the mark of Athena. Why?"

Jenny's face displayed a flicker of surprise but it was gone in an instant.

"She's a symbol of wisdom and empowers me." Jenny's face barely registered a smile.

"What is her gift?" Brad demanded.

"Wisdom," Jenny asserted confidently, but once again, a large intake of breath before her response made Brad aware that he was surprising her. He decided not to pursue Jenny for more information as he knew that he was in a grey area in terms of legality and whether he could use the information he was given. Jenny noted his hesitation and took it as the termination of the interview. She reached for her bag, took out the tub of the powder and placed it on the desk. She said "the dose is one heaped teaspoon per level," and left without another word.

Brad took the powder with him and found a plastic evidence bag. He went to the kitchen and put two thirds of the powder into the plastic bag and then hid the bag in his desk. He put the tub in an evidence bag and went back to Sergeant Pan's office. The five Federal police turned to look at him as he entered the room. Brad sensed an air of hostility.

"Detective Thomas, I have just finished bringing these gentlemen and woman up to date on the case. What did Constable Stavropolous want?" Sergeant Pan asked.

128

"There was a member of the public who had brought in a tub of the powder," replied Brad, drawing out his response.

The Federal police members all jumped to attention.

"Where is it?" asked their senior member, Daniel Forrest.

"Here." Brad revealed the tub from behind his back.

"We'll take that," Daniel said enthusiastically, taking it from Brad. Sergeant Pan glared at Brad.

"It will go to our lab in the capital. We will have the results for you within two days. Thank you Officer Thomas," Daniel said with a smile.

"That's Detective," said Brad.

Wow, I'm actually irritated by them calling me that. Maybe it's because it makes it seem as though I am not as 'fit' as my rank's status says I am?

"Thanks, Detective," said Daniel without a trace of concern. He took the tub out of the bag to inspect it more closely.

"Hmm, this stamp is interesting," he said, pointing to a dark blue mark on the base. Brad's first thought was to recollect the stamp theft from his previous town. *Why can't I let that case go?* Brad took a closer look at the tub and instantly recognised the symbol from his research on the Dame. It was a laurel wreath around the symbol of the Grand Cross with the letters DCMG underneath.

"That middle bit is called the Grand Cross. It is the symbol of the order of St. Michael and St. George that the Dame was a Dame Commander in. Those letters underneath it are her post-nominals; so I would say that this is genuine" said Brad.

Hmm, I guess when that email referred to the Commander, they meant the Dame Commander. I get it now! Brad was pleased with himself for the way he was thinking.

Sergeant Pan looked suitably impressed. Daniel simply stated "we would have figured that out."

"So who brought it in?" asked Sergeant Pan.

Brad debated whether or not to tell the truth. Normally he wouldn't have thought about lying, but now he was more conscious of the impact of things he said. The Sergeant might be upset at him for saying it was Jenny in front of the Federal police and the Federal police would probably just go charging over to Leviathan without thinking about it. Brad knew that wouldn't work. In the end he knew that he would be held accountable by the Federal police and any omissions would probably come back to haunt him.

"It was the receptionist from Leviathan Enterprises," Brad said calmly.

Daniel looked ready to go storming off to their offices. Brad responded quickly; "But going over there would be a mistake. Everything is ultra-secured and they have a heap of government and military contracts, so I'm pretty sure that if you tried to gain access to anything, they would have a huge number of legal avenues to block you."

"So what do you suggest?" asked Daniel.

"Make an appointment to speak to Dr Engels or invite him to come and give a statement. Although I'm not sure what information you will be able to get from him. I get the impression that he's very self-disciplined and self-assured. He won't say anything he doesn't want to. Let

130

me put it another way, he will be the smartest guy in the room."

Brad was again surprised at his authoritative tone. The Feds looked at each other with a smirk. It was clear they were thinking *we'll see about that*. Brad knew they were making a mistake.

"Ok, then what?" Daniel asked.

"You guys have access to more records than us, so maybe you could research the Dame? We've already found a hidden account which she used to facilitate the distribution of the powder. Maybe you could find out who she sent it to? Also you will probably want to look over the evidence we have collected, in case there is something we have missed. You might see something by having a different perspective to us."

Once again Brad had the sensation that he was applying the lessons of the program to his life.

"That sounds like a plan," said Sergeant Pan crisply, indicating that she wanted the meeting to end. Then, quickly making eye contact with each of the Federal police agents, she continued "why don't you go and do that?"

As everyone got up to leave Brad looked at Sergeant Pan. "Sergeant?"

"Yes Detective?"

"May I have a moment?"

"Yes. Ok. Detective Summers, perhaps you can take these good people to the evidence room to look over the materials we have collected so far, so that they may give us the benefit of their collective wisdom?" the Sergeant commanded Sally with more than a hint of sarcasm aimed at the Federal police.

"Certainly Sergeant," Sally replied. "Follow me Federal police members," she continued good-naturedly.

When they had all left the room, Brad closed the door and turned to Wendy.

"I just thought I'd let you know that when Jenny brought in the powder I took a small sample so that we could do our own analysis through the Medical Examiner's office. Sam asked me to send her some when we got more and thinks she knows what it might be," Brad said with surprise at his lack of nervousness about revealing this information.

"Good thinking Detective and thank you for telling me. Send it over to Sam ASAP and let me know the outcome. In the meantime keep this as a need to know only item. We don't want the Feds to think we're undermining them," said Sergeant Pan.

She was impressed that Brad had taken the step to keep some of the powder for them, *at last he was showing signs of thinking*, she thought to herself.

"Sure thing Sergeant." Brad turned and left the room. He went to his desk, pulled out a second plastic evidence bag, put two teaspoonfuls of the supplement in it and then arranged a courier to take it over to the Medical Examiner's offices. He added a note to Sam to say that this was a secret sample and let her know the recommended dose that Jenny had told him.

Brad made an appointment for the Federal police to go to the university to see the Professor's office and spole to Jenny at Leviathan to arrange for Dr Engels to visit the police station. Brad went to tell the Federal officers that the university was not able to see them until the afternoon. The small room they were in was made smaller by having three people and several boxes worth of evidence crammed into it. They greeted Brad indifferently. He let them know the password for the Professor's computer and left them ruffling through the evidence to see what they could glean.

###

Now that he had some time, Brad decided to resume his attempts to make progress with the Program. He suspected that the password for the next file was related to the network of freethinkers and that Jenny had been giving him a hint by saying that not every culture reads from left to right, but when he tried 'font' as a password in both lower and uppercase form the file did not open, he also tried it as TNOF and tnof. He tried various other passwords such as atheism, godless and deity to no avail. Brad swivelled in his chair and thought about the passwords he had used to date, trying to find a common thread.

None of them would be found in a conventional dictionary he thought almost absently, but then realised that this was the clue he needed. *This must be to stop a brute force attack whereby a computer program could simply try one word after another from a dictionary to gain access.*

The next password he tried was FoNT and this time the file opened. Brad grinned. It was another video. He knew from Amy and the Level Zero file that the powder was meant to be taken just before commencing a level.

I need to know what this is like. I have to know what I am missing, Brad thought. He took out a teaspoon, carefully measured a dose from the two he had kept for himself and rested it under his tongue. He felt a slight tingle as the substance dissolved in his saliva and started being absorbed. Within a couple of minutes it was gone.

Brad placed headphones on his head and pressed play on the video. The Professor appeared on the screen. Once again he appeared to be in his home and was standing next to his television. He had that *I'm bemused and have never felt so alive* glint in his eye. Brad felt that the Professor must have been a warm and caring person. It seemed like he really wanted to help people through the program he had created. Brad did not feel like the powder was having any effect yet.

Level Five: Conflict

One of my favourite questions is how does conflict produce change? It is a seemingly innocent question until you try to answer it. Conflict is simply the state where one idea, action or group is not compatible with another, and it occurs in all knowledge domains as well as human relationships. Conflict is a fundamental phenomenon of the human experience and it is brilliant!

The Professor had a sly grin. Brad felt a slight tingling under the skin of his arms.

I mean think about it, the history of science is the history of conflict between theory and experiment, the history of humankind is the history of conflict in one form or another, things like matters of opinion or who owns the Crown or piece of land and so on. Conflict is vital as part of humankind's development both as a species and a people, but also as the mechanism through which humans have developed figuratively and literally. Obviously conflict is a driver of evolution...

Brad smiled again. He was seeing the subtleties of evolution everywhere he looked these days and it was already helping him read people more accurately. He noticed the tingling sensation was spreading up his arms.

…But conflict is a driver of a great many things and this is why I put it to you that it is only through conflict that change occurs.

The Professor paused as a series of slides flashed on the TV screen beside him. The slides were annotated pictures from history, economics, psychology, biology, chemistry, physics, sport, languages and human relationships. In each instance the slides contained pictures or graphs or a fundamental principle along with arrows labelled conflict and change. The slides were compelling evidence for the Professor's point of view.

The thing that I find interesting about this idea is that it is nothing more than a generalisation or rewording of Newton's first law of motion. Newton was one of the greatest geniuses who has ever lived, but he was also vindictive and nasty towards people who disagreed with him. His famous quote that he had 'seen further by standing on the shoulders of giants', was both a statement of a proud history of science and a put down of Robert Hooke who was short and had a stooped back, and with whom he was arguing. This conflict led to a significant change in how Hooke was perceived and he died a bitter man. But I digress, anyway, let us continue this theme concentrating on conflict and change.

You only need to imagine conflict to produce change, which means that change can be caused by virtual conflict, not only real conflict, which is quite a fascinating idea, but not the only one to consider. The other key thing, particularly with human conflict, is to learn to look for the source of the conflict and gauge some measurement of it.

For it is that gap between points of view, between contrasting understandings, that provides room for mutual growth, a fantastic form of change and … well, that is beautiful.

The screen dissolved to white. During the video Brad had felt his body temperature rise, and the tingling under his skin worsen. Now he felt breathless. He realised that the cause was the powder and understood why Amy had said it really made a difference. If it did as claimed and helped the brain develop new connections and improve its functioning, then combined with the program it could really change lives. Brad felt the urge to obtain more and regretted not taking more from the tub, but, as he told himself, he had only taken some to see what it was like and to get more of a sense of what was going on. Brad reminded himself that he also didn't know if the dosing schedule had changed or the potential side effects. Given how breathless he was, he guessed that he was probably taking the maximum dose.

Brad tried to imagine what completing a full course of the powder would mean for the structure of his brain and how he would feel. He knew he'd already made improvements to his thinking and reasoning simply by being more aware of his environment and human behaviour. He started daydreaming about what it would be like to be able to read every situation, to see more and make more links between what he saw and what he knew. What if he could really connect all his knowledge and draw on all of it at once? Brad took a moment to revel in the sensation of his view changing. Brad's breathlessness worsened and caused him to panic, *Oh no, what have I done? Am I about to die? How could I be so stupid and not think this might kill me? Help! I can't breathe.*

Just as Brad made the decision to try and get help, he felt the breathlessness and tingling start to decrease. A few minutes later his body returned to its normal state. *Wow, that really was a conflict for my body and it felt like it definitely caused some change. I could almost feel my brain being stimulated. Hmm, conflict really is necessary for change.*

Brad realised that the Dame must have reached a similar conclusion about the necessity for conflict and deliberately constructed a public image that conflicted with people's stereotypes of scientists to make them change their behaviour and take more of an interest in science. Brad wondered if the Professor had known this and if he did what might have tipped him off. His reverie was broken by the sound of his phone ringing.

"Hi Brad, it's Sam again," her bright tone lightened Brad's annoyance at his daydream being broken.

"Hi Sam," replied Brad enthusiastically.

"I've done the additional test I thought of and I know what is in the powder!" she said triumphantly.

"What? But I only sent it an hour ago," exclaimed Brad.

"We're not that far away you know," said Sam.

Brad reminded himself that he was meant to go over to her office and look at the tattoo in person.

"Oh. So what did you find out?" Brad asked.

"It's basically nothing more than a mix of GABA, fructofuranoside, a hint of green and a hint of brown food dye," said Sam.

"GABA?" Brad queried.

"It's a neurotransmitter called Gamma Amino Butyric Acid," said Sam as though they were words she used every day.

"So that's what makes the brain grow?" asked Brad.

"No that's the thing, ingested GABA does not cross the blood brain barrier, so there is no way it would affect the brain. If you wanted it to change the brain you would have to inject it into it. But even then, in adults it's role is inhibitory."

Brad imagined an injection into his skull and cringed.

"But I have a theory as to why it was added," Sam continued.

"What's that?"

"When taken orally, GABA has a side effect of making a person feel breathless and a tingling under the skin…" Brad felt a flash of guilt, "…so including it makes it feel like a dose is biologically active. But that's the thing – that is all it does, it does not stimulate the brain at all. The Dame certainly knew what she was doing."

"But the rest of the stuff?" he asked.

"That's what I mean – the rest of the stuff is nothing, fructofuranoside is another name for sucrose, which is table sugar. The GABA at the dose in the powder has no effect on the body other than to create the tingling sensation and moment of breathlessness."

It's more than a moment, Brad thought to himself.

"The whole thing is a placebo!" Sam said excitedly.

"So it's a fake?" Brad was incredulous, recalling how strongly he felt it was doing something to him.

"No, you're missing the point, the powder is designed to give a sensation when ingested. It must be to fool the person into thinking it's really making a difference to them. It must be used to enhance the effectiveness of the training in the program you told me about," Sam replied.

They both paused to consider the genius of the program. Brad understood why the program had taken years to evolve into its current form.

"Sorry, I'm still just marvelling at it all," Sam said quietly.

"Yeah I know, me too," said Brad.

"Did you know that the placebo effect doesn't only occur in humans?" Sam asked randomly.

"Huh?" Brad responded.

"Yeah, it occurs in animals too. You can give epileptic dogs medication for epilepsy or a placebo they will still show improvement," Sam said abstractly.

Brad had the delightful sensation of his mind being blown.

"What?" he asked with amazement.

"Yeah they've done lots of studies on it. The interesting bit is that when you give the placebo group the real drug they show even more improvement than when it is a placebo only. But you have to wonder what size component of the effect of drugs we take is due to the placebo effect," said Sam.

"Indeed," Brad replied.

"I also read a study the other day about hamsters having something similar to the placebo effect. When hamsters are made to believe it is winter time, their immune system slows down, regardless of whether it's winter or not. It all depends on an external cue. I found this interesting as it helps to explain why we can't simply will or think our way towards improvement, but need to take a pill. In essence, we need some form of external influence to initiate the placebo effect. After all placebo is Latin for *I will please*," Sam said.

"That must be why Brentham continued to take the powder. I mean he must have known it was a placebo, but took it anyway since it provided a fake conflict that made his brain change its structure," Brad said, mostly to himself.

"Now it's my turn to go huh?" Sam said with a smile in her voice.

"Don't worry, I think we've just made quite a bit of progress. But I still want to check, are you sure that the powder is a placebo is not just a hoax to throw us off? I mean it came from our main suspect so it could be…"

"No, I'm pretty sure that given what we know about the Dame, the Professor and Brentham that this is the genuine stuff. Leviathan probably gave it to us so that we would tell people that it's a placebo and you would stop investigating them. I mean from what I can gather they have a lot to hide," Sam responded.

"You're probably right. I mean if we tell the world the powder is a placebo it would really take the heat off them."

"So I guess that this leads to the question; should we tell the world?" Sam asked.

"I don't know, given that the Feds are here, we don't officially know this yet, so we'll have to hope that they reach the same understanding and announce it."

"I'm not sure if I should be hoping they do or not. But anyway thanks for the chat," said Sam.

"Not at all, thanks for the info," Brad said.

"My pleasure." Sam said as she hung up the phone.

Brad marvelled at the thought that the powder was a placebo. It occurred to him that the Professor's video contained all the information that was needed to work out that the powder was a placebo. The discussion of virtual conflict being all that is required to produce change was really the Professor's way of guiding the understanding of the power of placebos. Brad glanced up from his desk and saw the Federal officers approaching. He groaned as he realised it was time to take them to the university. Brad made a mental note to try placebo as a password for the next file.

On the way to the university Brad messaged Amy to let her know he would be coming over and that if she happened to be near the philosophy building at 3pm they could say a quick hello to each other. Brad drove on a bridge over the freeway but did not have time to admire the view of the city, which was wide but not deep due to a railway on one side and a river on the other. He drove alongside King's park that overlooked the city and as he reached the edge of the park the tall sandstone buildings of the university could be seen above the trees. The sight made Brad feel like he was getting closer to Amy.

Brad guided the Federal officers to the building without difficulty. Brad was amused when Daniel, the task force leader asked "why isn't building one next to building two?"

While the Federal officers looked around the Professor's office, Brad stood outside the room, hoping that Amy would show up. Unfortunately, she didn't and Brad was amused at the thought that the anticipation of seeing her was like a virtual conflict producing the change in his heart rate. Brad was pleasantly surprised when he realised that the absence of her reply did not make him feel like she was avoiding him. *I really am changing the way I'm thinking,* he thought.

In the car on the way back to the station, Daniel, the head of the Federal task force sat next to Brad as Brad drove. Brad had an unusual feeling of knowing vastly more than the people he was with. He was really enjoying the sensations the Professor's program was creating in him and this made him even more determined to keep going with it.

"So Detective, what do you make of the case?" Daniel asked thoughtfully. His focus on Brad indicated that he was evaluating him. It was clear that Daniel had waited for Brad to be driving to ask this so that his attention would be divided.

"It has me stumped. I mean we know there is a connection between the program, the powder and the deaths. We know the Professor created the program and probably co-created the powder with the Dame and that the two of them were in contact with Brentham at Leviathan Enterprises. Leviathan almost certainly knows more than they are letting on and their CEO Dr Engels and his assistant Jenny are just a little bit creepy and have had way too much control over what they have told us," said Brad.

"Is that why you wanted us to interview him?" Daniel asked.

"I guess so. We don't have enough grounds to arrest or subpoena evidence from them, so it would be great if you could get more out of them," Brad said.

Daniel paused as if he was trying to decide whether

Brad was on their side or whether he opposed their presence like his Sergeant.

"We had a look at the video of Brentham's death and ran it through a few filters we have and we managed to make out some words," Daniel said softly. Brad could only recall Brentham mumbling in the video.

"So what did he say?"

"Well it was a little unclear, but it sounds like he was saying 'departing the cave.' So it could be 'I'm departing the cave' or 'we need to be departing the cave' but I'm not sure. Does that mean anything to you?"

Brad focused on the meanings of the individual words and the images they produced in his mind.

"No," he replied slowly. "But if you were suddenly seeing connections between everything you had ever learnt, wouldn't it feel like you were departing a cave and moving into the light?" Brad said, before remembering that Amy had said that the Professor had mentioned something about needing caves.

"Yes I suppose it would," Daniel replied, clearly happy with Brad's response. "Our interview with Dr Engels will happen tomorrow. Dr Engels agreed on the condition that I alone interview him. I decided to accept the condition even though it is clearly a ploy on his behalf to control what is said. Is there any advice you would give me?" Daniel asked once again studying Brad closely.

Brad decided that solving the case was more important than politics. He realised that part of his motivation for this was selfish – it would free him to date Amy without guilt and enable him to pursue the higher levels of the program without interference from the Department.

"No … I mean other than not being rushed to give answers. He would probably be good at tricking you or blocking your line of questioning if you try to go head to head. Instead, if you give yourself time to consider your response you should avoid some of his traps," said Brad.

Daniel nodded, seeming to accept that Brad was on their side as he said to Brad, "thank you Detective. That is good advice."

###

That night at dinner Amy greeted Brad out the front of the restaurant. It was located on a street that was known for its cafes, restaurants and eclectic mix of specialty shops. The restaurant they had chosen proudly stated that it served a 'fusion' blend of Asian and European cuisines. Through the window Brad could see that it was dimly lit and intimate inside. As he approached Amy he felt a smile spread across his face and a surge of being in the moment.

"Hello Officer. I know it's only 6.55 but can we pretend it is 6.59?"

She put her arms around his neck and looked into his eyes. Brad barely managed to say "yes" before Amy gave him a long kiss. Afterwards she gave a contented sigh and said "that's better, I'm glad we got that out of the way. Let's have dinner."

Brad was shocked by her ability to keep him feeling an intoxicating mix of awe and affection.

"How did you manage to make that kiss seem like you have been thinking of nothing else all day?" he asked.

"Who said I haven't." Amy replied with a raised

eyebrow and wicked smile. As they walked into the restaurant, Brad felt conspicuous and was amused that he could feel his heart beating strongly. He felt as though walking arm in arm with Amy was a display of his evolutionary fitness and that everyone should be looking at him.

"So Brad, how is the case going?" Amy asked with interest after they had sat down and ordered some drinks. Brad hesitated. *How much should I tell her? She is still a potential witness.*

"Slowly. The Federal police arrived today and they are taking up a lot of time and resources," said Brad.

At least she could already know that from the paper, he thought.

"Yes, I got your text, I was out at training so I missed seeing you. Sorry I didn't reply until late, I had to have my phone off. And I did really miss seeing you and not only because I was suffering the unique torture that is butcher's paper and writing down a bunch of rubbish so it can be stuck on walls for everyone to look at. But I shouldn't complain since it gave me time to think about you." Amy said looking him in the eye.

"What about me?" asked Brad, his qualms about discussing the case with her disappearing as her allure enveloped him.

"That you are a great guy and I am a lucky girl to be dating you." Brad blushed. He was thrilled at the formalisation that they were dating.

"Why me?" Brad asked curiously. *I really want to know*, he thought.

"Well when I first saw you I could see that you were an honest guy."

Brad thought about his retaining some of the powder for himself – the first vaguely dishonest thing he had done for years and felt a twinge of guilt.

"And you looked a little lost, which was just adorable, and it was clear that you were a nice guy. Plus after the level on evolution I started seeing it everywhere…"

Me too, thought Brad, "… and I really wanted to see if putting on a display, and I mean that in a natural selection sense, would actually have an effect. It was the first time I have tried something like that and as it turns out it did work! Our lunch at the uni that day allowed me to see what an interesting guy you are and what potential you have as a person, and that made me want to see you again."

"So your flirting is a display of evolutionary fitness and a means to make me select you?" Brad thought back over their previous encounters and at the sense of fun he got from Amy. Now he understood why; she was actually having fun.

"I thought so. Didn't it work?" she asked with mock innocence and a slightly raised eyebrow.

"Well actually yes. I have really struggled to stop thinking about you long enough to focus on my investigation," Brad admitted with a wry grin.

"Awesome," laughed Amy, clearly pleased with herself. "So have you seen the Professor's powder online? I have and I am not sure whether I should try buying some or not."

"If I tell you something will you keep it to yourself?" Brad questioned. He knew he shouldn't be telling her what he was about to, but he wanted to be able to discuss it with someone away from the office. *Amy needs to know this,* he thought.

"A secret you mean?" Amy replied conspiratorially.

"Yes."

"Yes. I can keep a secret." They both leaned over the table so that they were close together.

"Ok, then. The powder is a placebo!" Brad whispered.

The shock in Amy's eyes was unmistakeable.

"No way," she said.

"Yes way. It has a substance in it that makes your skin tingle and you breathe more heavily for a moment, but that's all. The rest is just food dye and sugar."

"Wow." Amy was speechless.

"Why?" she asked eventually.

"I think understanding the placebo effect is one of the levels. It's all about using that idea that conflict produces change. When you really get into the placebo effect it is really fascinating. I mean did you know placebos even work on dogs?" Brad asked.

"No," said Amy, "that is interesting."

"Yes. Oh hey, while I think about it did you figure out what the Professor meant about people needing caves?" Brad asked, thinking that at least he could ask Amy something that might help the investigation. *Ugh, what am I doing? Is she a witness or suspect or not?* Brad thought.

Amy thought about his question. "Not specifically no, but maybe it's something to do with evolution. I mean humans have evolved from cave dwellers to where we are today. Why?" she asked.

"It was just something someone said, but we are not

sure how it fits yet," Brad replied.

"Speaking of evolutionary ideas, what did you think of the Professor's level on evolution? I mean you obviously have seen it and the one on change."

"Yes I have. They are interesting and you are right, once you start seeing things in terms of how they relate to surviving, reproduction and social relations, there is suddenly evidence for evolution everywhere you look," replied Brad enthusiastically.

"Did you like the bit about genetic memory?" Amy asked with interest.

"Yes that was really intriguing," Brad replied.

"It kind of reminded me of Lamarck. Did you study him in high school?"

"Only in passing, we really focused on Darwin."

"Yeah, us too, but you know his idea was that if a bodybuilder had kids they would be born with larger muscles or a giraffe straining its neck to reach higher leaves led to its offspring having longer necks? And how this mode of inheritance was dismissed by the theory of evolution, well I like how this idea of genetic memory is kind of a triumphant return of the theory," said Amy enthusiastically.

"Yes and conflict led to it being discarded and also to its return!" Brad responded with equal enthusiasm.

"Exactly." They both smiled at each other, the shared furthering of their thoughts was a bonding experience.

"So, I suppose I should tell you that the Professor put another level in between evolution and change..." Brad said. Amy leant forward again, her eyes alive. Brad loved the way her eyebrows came alive when she was excited. Her whole face was so expressive.

148

"It's on atheist pride. The Professor's basic premise was that in the future the treatment of atheists will be seen as similar to that which has been given to homosexuals, Black people and women," Brad said.

"Oh wow. Imagine the T-shirts!" Amy said with a grin. "Atheist and proud!"

She dissolved into laughter. Brad laughed too whilst also being struck by the beauty and naturalness of Amy's laughter. *She is so beautiful, have I fallen for her already? Am I really doing anything wrong by seeing her? I mean she probably would not even be needed in a court case… but I know the rules are really clear, she is involved in the case so I should either excuse myself from it or not see her. Besides she could be used to establish the Professor's intent and how that conflicted with Dr Engel's or whoever and to establish motive. But I see a future with her…*

Brad smiled at his last thought. He realised that he felt a connection to Amy that he did not want to break and knew that regardless of 'the rules' he would not stop seeing her.

At the end of the meal Brad walked Amy back to her car arm in arm and even though he didn't want to say goodbye let her go after they had made another date. Both drove to their respective homes with a broad grin on their face.

###

As Brad drove to work the next morning he felt like he was really earning his wage this last couple of weeks, notwithstanding the conflict over his relationship with Amy. He noted that he was only the third car of the regular day shift personnel to arrive. He brewed a fresh pot of coffee for the office, took one in to Sergeant Pan, who accepted it gladly and then made a beeline for his desk. He was eager to try to unlock the next level and quickly booted up his computer. His first password attempt was 'placebo' and it failed which Brad had suspected it would, but he was not out of ideas yet. He had woken up early that morning and, unable to go back to sleep his mind had drifted from Amy to the case and back. As he mused over passwords, levels and all the evidence he had collected he realised that the connections between the passwords and levels was more than just one being a clue to the other. The passwords were also about changing your perspective. He had learnt new words and ideas from what the passwords were, but what had really made him feel alert and literally sit up was the echo of something Jenny had said … "not every culture reads from left to right." Unlike some of his successful attempts at past passwords, Brad felt like he *knew* the password would be obecalp – placebo backwards. When Brad typed it in the computer pinged and opened the file. It was only two lines of text that read: Level Six: The powder is a placebo. Join FONT to access next level. They were followed by a picture of the Pansy tattoo including the Greek letters.

Interchapter

To: Dr Engels
From: The Professor
Subject: If you really want to change the world…

Greetings Doctor,
Thank you for your contribution to the program, I think that it really adds something useful, plus it gives us a mechanism to monitor the impact we are having. I like the idea of limiting Levels Nine and Ten to those who go through the initiation. As for Level Eleven and any others I develop, I think we should limit them to those who, through our monitoring program, we have determined are worthy of it. What do you think?
Cheers,
Michael

Act Two: Chapter One

Brad stopped. His mind was racing. He was sure that figuring out what was Athena's gift would be the final step to joining FONT.

Brad knew that the meaning of Athena's mark was related to the Greek for the word atheism. He jotted down the letters again; αθεος, alpha, theta, epsilon, omicron, sigma. He searched the internet for the uses of the symbols in mathematics and physics and learnt a lot about science but nothing that seemed helpful. He decided to give up for now and went and made himself a coffee. When he returned to his desk he took another look at the sheet of paper where he had been taking notes. He had scrawled that AΘE is Athena's mark with the AΘE underlined. He thought about Athena and that her mark was part of the word for atheism and that she was the goddess of wisdom and mused that this was a slightly ironic connection. He had tried atheism as being her gift but that had not worked. As he looked at the

152

complete word in Greek αθεος he recognised that if you took out Athena's mark you were left with ος or omicron and sigma. Brad typed these into an online translation service and discovered that omicron sigma meant "th" in English. He then tried each letter individually, mostly because he was a little frustrated and just wanted to do something, but what he discovered was surprising. "o" on its own meant "the." Brad felt his heart beat strongly, "Athena the" was a positive lead. When he typed "ς" in, it came back as "s." Intuition told him he was close to a breakthrough, he just needed the flash of inspiration to occur. He did not have to wait long.

It occurred to him that he should try applying his understanding of the Professor's levels to the problem, since this was meant to be another challenge to overcome to reach the next level. Brad considered that someone could have a different semantic network and ideological point of view as to how the symbol could be viewed. He considered going to see Paul again, but decided that the solution was unlikely to be as simple as reading Greek. He asked himself where the conflict was and decided that it was that ς on its own meant nothing, unlike the other Greek symbols. "So," he asked himself, "if that is where the conflict is, how can it produce change?" The answer hit him like a bolt of lightning. "ς" is an *evolution* of another symbol for sigma, one that in its capitalised form was $\sum$ and $\sum$ had a very particular meaning to people from a science background. Brad knew from helping his sister that it meant "sum." Brad felt like he was seeing with absolute clarity. Athena's gift was the sum. The plethora of interpretations of this made Brad certain he had solved the riddle. The sum could have meaning mathematically, biologically (sum of our genetics and environment), ideologically (the sum of ideals), semantically (sum of possible interpretations) and even the concept of Atheist pride involved the sum of a history of movements. The solution to *what is Athena's gift?* could even be seen as the sum of the levels to date.

Brad immediately called Eliza and progressed to the second passphrase entry.

"Congratulations you have been moved up the queue. For immediate access to the Network, please state the second passphrase in the form of a complete answer."

"The sum," Brad stated confidently.

"That is not the correct passphrase," came the reply. Brad was devastated. He was so sure he had the right answer. He wondered if this was another test.

"Please state the third password in the form of a complete answer," Eliza repeated.

Brad replied "Athena's gift is the sum," without really thinking.

"That is correct" Eliza replied, Brad realised that he had given too little information the first time. He was talking to a computer after all, and it was looking for an exact wording.

"Congratulations, you are now eligible for membership to FONT. To complete the process please call this number…"

Brad carefully wrote down the number which included its international area code. As he dialled the number he realised he was literally trembling with anticipation.

"Hello," a male voice said in a friendly tone. The

single word was enough to convey the authority of the man.

"Hi, I was told to call this number," Brad replied cautiously.

"By whom?" the voice responded.

"By a computer named Eliza…" Brad was about to say more when he was interrupted.

"That is excellent news. To whom do I have the pleasure of speaking?" asked the voice. Brad found that there was something about the voice that seemed familiar.

"Detective Thomas." Brad said without thinking. He mentally cursed himself for giving away that he was a police officer.

"Ah yes, hello Brad, we thought you might be getting close to giving us a call," the voice responded enthusiastically. Brad was shocked, they knew who he was!

"How do you know who I am?" he asked.

"We have ways…" the voice said mysteriously, "but when you asked Jenny about her ring it was pretty clear you were on track so to speak. She very nearly broke her composure and I can assure you that does not happen that often. I suppose I should let you know that I am Dr Engels."

Brad was floored and felt the way that he viewed Dr Engels and Leviathan Enterprises shift. He was also confused by Dr Engel's jovial tone, which was at odds with his previous interaction with him.

"You probably have a lot of questions, which is good, we like questions. But what you need to know is that in order to complete your membership to FONT you need to be interviewed by one of us, in this case me. Now obviously, this is an unusual situation since you are also investigating me for other reasons," Dr Engels stated matter-of-factly.

"Uh huh." Brad wished he could have been more eloquent, but his mind was still reeling.

"So what I propose is that you come over to the Towers to meet me at 11.23am and I will assess you for membership and answer some of your other questions about the melting brain deaths."

"Ok," Brad said, feeling like he could not refuse.

"Great, see you then. Arrive early so Jenny can make you a coffee. You'll need it," Dr Engels said jovially.

"Ok," Brad replied again. Dr Engels hung up the phone. Brad sat motionless for several minutes. Eventually he stood up and went to Sergeant Pan's office. He knocked on the door and opened it just as she called "come in."

"Hi Sergeant. I have some good news," Brad said with a grin.

"What's that? Did you get the Feds to leave?" Sergeant Pan asked sarcastically.

"No, but I've got an offer to join the Network of Freethinkers," Brad replied. He noticed the surprise on Sergeant Pan's face and felt like he was living up to her expectations for the first time.

"How?" she asked.

"I finished the Professor's program and solved the riddle of how to join them. It wasn't easy but I..." Brad began getting ready to launch into the story.

"What's the next step?" Sergeant Pan asked, cutting him off.

"I go and meet with them and they interview me. If I'm deemed worthy I get to join," Brad stated with more confidence than he was feeling.

"Any chance you could take Detective Summers with you?"

"No, this is strictly a 'me only' thing."

"Fine, so when is this taking place?" Sergeant Pan asked, the irritation returning to her voice.

"I have to leave now. I'll be back this afternoon," said Brad.

"Ok Detective. Go and join them, but remember that I can only afford for you to have one assignment for a few more days. Soon it will be back to regular workloads, so I guess what I'm saying is the clock is ticking. Oh and make sure you talk to Detective Summers about what you are doing and get her to drive you there, even if she can't go in with you."

"Yes Sergeant," Brad replied as he turned and left the room. He was relieved Sergeant Pan had not asked more questions about where he was going or who he was going to meet with. He was also pleased that this would give him an opportunity to have a quiet word with Sally about Amy.

Once they had left the station and were on the open road, Brad turned to Sally and said, "there is something I would like you opinion on …"

"Oh yeah, what's that?" she replied.

"You know our case involved the Professor and his university, well when I went over there the HR assistant and I got chatting and we wound up making a date."

Brad felt like he was in a confessional. Even though he was side on to her, Brad could see Sally raise an eyebrow.

"So are you telling me this to gloat?"

"No. It turns out that she was involved in an early trial of the Professor's program and potentially could be used to establish the significance of the program. Plus she knew about Dame Sagan creating the powder which could be important."

"So you finished your meal, shook her hand and thanked her for the information and left it at that?" Sally taunted Brad.

"Umm no," he admitted.

"So?"

"We've had a few dates and we're basically boyfriend and girlfriend."

"Hmm, so what do you want from me?"

"Well what do you think? How much trouble am I in?" Brad asked.

"Don't you think it's suspicious that she latched on to you? How do you know she's not more involved than you think?" Sally asked thoughtfully.

This wasn't the response Brad was expecting and he was about to retort with "because she isn't," when he realised that really he didn't know or have a compelling reason to think that Amy was not more involved. She had certainly managed to get information from him about his investigation and knew how it was progressing.

"Hmm. I don't know, but I don't think so. I was more concerned about the umm, propriety, of dating her."

"There was nothing wrong with the first date, but after that it is a little more grey, but and you've pretty much determined that she is not involved, so even if she were called to give evidence, what she'd be providing

158

would not be compromised. Well, unless you are also giving her more information about the case that might alter what she'd say. So basically don't talk to her about the case and you're fine."

Sally spoke openly and it was clear to Brad that she was trying to provide the best advice she could. Brad sighed in relief. *It could all be ok,* he thought just as they arrived at their destination.

Brad entered Ivory Tower and made the rapid ascent to Leviathan Enterprises, marvelling at the security and modernity of the system. The interior of the elevator was gloss white, much like the halls of Leviathan's offices. The doors opened silently. He was unsurprised that Jenny was there to meet him, but was surprised when she greeted him like an old friend.

"Welcome Brad. I'm so pleased you might be joining us. Let me get you a coffee. It was a macchiato wasn't it?" Jenny asked with a smile that Brad had not seen from her before.

Brad nodded mutely. Jenny left and returned a few minutes later. The coffee was as Brad had remembered it and in the same strange three layered cup. Brad savoured the flavour and feel of the coffee as much as he could, but it was still gone in three sips.

What am I getting myself into? Would it have been better if I had asked for a stronger drink? he thought.

Almost the moment he had finished the coffee, Jenny said that the Doctor would see him now. She led him to Dr Engels' office which was on the opposite corner to Brentham's. He rose as they entered the room and greeted Brad with a double handed handshake. The office was large and brightly lit.

"Brad, welcome," Dr Engels said warmly. "Clearly we need to have two conversations, one about you joining FONT and one about your investigation. Which conversation shall we have first?" Dr Engels asked rhetorically. "Let's let fate decide."

Before Brad could reply he pulled a coin from his pocket.

"This coin has Plato on one side and Ghandi on the other. Philosophy or action which is it to be?"

He tossed the coin and caught it neatly in his palm before slapping it onto the back of his other hand. When he lifted his hand it showed the Plato side of the coin, complete with the image of a cave and Plato's face.

"Philosophy it is then!" Dr Engels said with a hint of glee. He then opened a familiar looking tub and offered Brad a heaped teaspoon of the Dame's powder. Brad looked at the Doctor quizzically.

"Just because you know it's a placebo does not mean it won't have an effect, that is the beauty of placebos; they keep working even when you know they shouldn't. Which means that your brain will still undergo neurogenesis as a result of taking it."

Brad took the powder and placed it under his tongue. Once again it dissolved quickly. They both sat down in leather sling chairs that Brad immediately felt comfortable in. It was like they were designed to be sat in while enjoying a whisky and chat.

"Welcome to Level Eight. Imagine a room inhabited by people who have been imprisoned there since childhood," Dr Engels said without pausing, just as Brad felt the first tingles of the powder taking effect.

"They are constrained in such a way that their legs and

necks are fixed, forcing them to gaze at a wall in front of them, unable to move their heads. On the wall is a TV. Let me suggest that for the people, the two dimensional images on the TV would constitute *reality* and let us imagine that they are only able to watch CCTV footage from an office block. They would not realize that what they see are merely *representations* of reality from outside their room. Furthermore, the imprisoned people would 'assign credit and prestige' to whomever among them could remember which images they had seen, and make predictions about what was going to happen." Brad nodded to indicate he was following the line of thought.

The tingling under his skin was getting stronger. *That is a strange sensation, now that I know what to expect, it's kind of nice,* thought Brad.

"Now let us suppose that one of the people is freed. He is told that what he has formerly seen has no substance and is not real and that what he now sees – the actual office block – constitutes a greater reality. He is asked to identify some of the objects and people in the office. He is unable to, due to his confusion and that he still believes the two dimensional images on the TV to be more real. This freed person's discomfort is only intensified when he is shown the wider city and country. Over time though he is able to learn about the world and society and … cameras and TVs. He learns about literature, science, mathematics and physical laws. Wouldn't this change his perspective of the room he came from? Wouldn't he remember his first home, what passed for wisdom there, and his fellow prisoners, and consider them pitiable? And wouldn't he laugh at whatever honours or prizes were awarded there to the ones who were best at identifying which images followed which on the TV screen? Moreover, were he to return to the room, wouldn't he be rather bad at their game, given that he knows about the breadth of existence?

Now think about how the prisoners would view him. Wouldn't they say of him that he was freed but came back with his eyes corrupted, and that therefore it's not worth trying to get free? Wouldn't they reject his knowledge, his wisdom? The imprisoned people, ignorant of the wider world, the wider consciousness would see the freed man with his corrupted eyes and be afraid of him."

Dr Engels sat silently, while Brad digested what he had said. Brad suddenly understood that when Brentham had said something about 'departing the cave,' he was referring to a level of the program. He also understood that this level changed his perspective on those he had experienced before.

"Isn't that really the point of this program? To make people who complete it reject what they once knew and to seek out greater understanding? And to then understand that as their consciousness expands, their evaluation of their knowledge and what passes for true understanding changes," Brad said.

"Well done, that is largely the point of the entire program." Dr Engels replied with a smile.

"It's like the stories I've heard of people who have left cults... or joined them," Brad said amused at his boldness in stating the thought aloud.

"Yes, I guess that is true. I would like to say that we are not a cult, but such claims invariably make one more cult like, so suffice to say that while we have certain rituals and requirements, you are not bound to do anything or remain a part of us. Nor do we ask you to change who you associate with. We don't even ask that you associate with other members. However, before I tell you what we *would* like from you, we need to address the other reason why you are here."

Brad nodded in response.

"Yes, several of our members have died recently under very unusual circumstances. And I also have some unfortunate news. It seems that there are three other deaths that have not been reported in the papers yet, so you are probably not aware of them?"

"Can I get their names?" Brad asked.

"Hmmm." Dr Engels hesitated, "I guess that all depends. How are you going to use the information?"

"Well I would make sure that…" said Brad.

Dr Engels interrupted him, "How can I phrase this… I take it that you have not actually told anyone that you are meeting with me. Which means that you are at least partially doing this for you and because of what the program means to you. You are not recording our conversation, just so you know the lift scans occupants for such devices, nor have you indicated that you are here in relation to any particular case or crime, so I am wondering what this information will mean for *you*?"

Brad paused, partly due to the powder making him breathless.

"I guess that it would mean understanding more about who are members of FONT, plus it would make me look good in my department if I could 'discover' these other cases… more the first one than the second."

Dr Engels had watched Brad intently as he spoke. It seemed that his answer had satisfied whatever concern the doctor had.

"Ok then, the other members are Senator Jasmine Green, Mrs Isla Tomic and Dr Stanley Wiles. They were all inducted into our little group within the last five months," he replied.

"That seems odd," Brad said. The breathlessness was beginning to pass.

"Yes and no. It is possible that the entirety of the program when combined with the powder from the start causes the users brain to greatly increase its processing and connections," Dr Engels responded.

"Go on."

"There are twelve levels. What we have just been through, the analogy of the room – a modified form of Plato's cave – is Level Eight. Joining FONT is Level Seven and you know the other six levels. Level Nine we will talk about in a moment, but it seems that the problem is with Level Eleven and Twelve."

"So why are people dying?" Brad asked.

"Well it seems that Level Eleven to an extent, but especially Level Twelve, causes a chain reaction in the brain that makes every neuron fire at once and continue firing. All the excitatory neurotransmitters enter the synapses and for some reason are not broken down. This causes a catastrophic overload of the brain and after a short period of time complete degradation of the neurons. To put it crudely, the brain cooks itself or as those vile articles say – it melts. The Professor realised this and sent out a warning so we have stopped distributing Level Eleven and Twelve to our members. Unfortunately many of them already had them," Dr Engels replied.

"But you've seen them?" Brad responded with

curiosity.

"Actually no," Dr Engels admitted, "I was away doing a project for a government when Level Twelve came out so I've only seen Level Eleven. The project meant zero communication with the external world. When I was sent the Professor's warning I was able to choose not to open the file for Level Twelve – I had not even started trying to figure out its password. While I am still extraordinarily curious as to what was in it, I have quarantined the file so that I would not be tempted to open it," Dr Engels stated with the misgivings he had about the course of action evident in his voice.

"So do you know of anyone who would want to harm the people you mentioned or the program?" Brad was aware that his line of questioning was clichéd.

"There could be a few people and there is one in particular I am suspicious of, however I have no evidence that anyone is deliberately setting out to make people die," Dr Engels stated simply, giving the impression that he was speaking the truth.

"But the member you are suspicious of…?" Brad asked.

"Is a member named Mathew Arnold and I am arguing with him over the distribution of the program. He believes that it should be sold and distributed as widely as possible for maximum revenue stream and maximum social change. Mathew would like to use Leviathan's technology that enables us to create single access video files that cannot be copied or captured and charge for each level. He wants to sell the program online and make it so that when you solve the password for the next level there is a fee to then obtain the file" said Dr Engels.

"How would that work? Wouldn't someone just copy the file and then on-sell that?" Brad asked like he was a teenager telling their grandparent about technology.

"I won't bore you with all the details, but even if you had a video camera aimed at a screen when playing the videos you would only obtain an incomprehensible movie. We use a lot of frequency modulation, psychoacoustics and visual perception tricks like the McGurk effect to get the job done in addition to high grade encryption. But anyway the point is that I disagree with Mathew. The Professor did not design the program to make money and even wanted to give away the powder. But like most things the cost needed to be met somehow – so I suppose I should mention to you that normally participants would be asked to pay $2000 for levels one to six of the program," Dr Engels stated matter-of-factly.

The surprise showed on Brad's face.

"Before you go on about the exorbitant cost, we experimented with the price and that figure was where we found the greatest follow through to the benchmark of level six – finding out that the powder is a placebo. If we set the price too low people gave up too easily. If we set it much higher they just did not buy it," he continued.

"So this has been… sold?" Brad asked incredulously.

"And you are wondering why you have not heard of it?" Dr Engels said with a sly grin.

"Yes" asked Brad.

"Well the sale was restricted to members of Round Table Intelligencia." Brad was shocked, RTI was an international organisation for people with high IQs.

"That seems odd. Isn't the aim to make normal people think better not super smart people be even smarter?" Brad queried.

"Yes, but the Professor wanted to check that the program had relevance to all people and he had already used some normally intelligent guinea pigs at the university. Members of RTI are smart, that is true, but that does not mean that they either do not want to improve their thinking or do not need to. Plus we needed some seed money to fund the next stage and well, they are generally well off." Dr Engels eyes were bright, much like the Professor's in his videos.

"Next stage?" Brad asked.

"Yes, to distribute the program more widely and to have people monitoring its distribution. That really is the key. We need people to monitor how the program is being used and to control the way it is given out. If every single person was given access to it all at once, we could not predict the impact on society. This is what I am arguing about with Mathew. I mean could you imagine what would happen?"

Brad shook his head. It was mind boggling. "Is that why all the secrecy?" Brad asked.

"Well, we're basically attempting *social engineering*. People tend to have a negative view of that, even though it is what governments do through education, the media and historically, at least, religious organisations," Dr Engels said wistfully.

"ISAs." Brad said recognising the list of ideological state apparatus that Althusser had created. Dr Engels looked suitably impressed.

"Exactly. But you can't just go and tell people you

are going to change the way they think. They will see it as you trying to control them and that is something they rebel against. Plus it just sounds so fascist … or communist for that matter and we are neither. If anything we are humanists who just want people to continue to make progress and develop.”

“So how do you do it? Put it in a novel?” Brad asked with a sly grin.

“Pah,” said Dr Engels dismissively, “that would never work. Where’s the investment from the audience? Knowledge on its own does not transform thinking. The reason the program is the way it is, is so that the people who use it put in effort, perform thought exercises, try things, puzzle over concepts and really *process* the information. I mean this is not our first time at this you know?” He said with a mixture of pride and exuberance.

“What do you mean? What social engineering have you done before?” Brad asked.

“Well you know that project for a government I just mentioned? And how there was the change of government in Araspring?” Dr Engels questioned.

Brad nodded, “I read about it in the paper, but surely you are not laying claim to leading the civilian uprising that overthrew the government?” he asked incredulously.

“Not at all, but a while ago we went over there at the request of a government that shall remain nameless and put into place some very specific things,” said Dr Engels.

“Like what?” asked Brad.

“We taught key dissidents how to bypass government censorship and use social media to coordinate. We gave them a slogan that attracted people to their cause; ‘*the*

168

people want the regime to change' A simple statement, and it worked brilliantly. People were really attracted to it," he said.

"How was that attractive?" Brad questioned.

"Well it was not 'students against …' or 'parents against …' it was *we the people*," Dr Engels replied.

"That sounds familiar," Brad said with a grin.

"Exactly," Dr Engels said as they both smiled.

"We showed them where the weaknesses were in the old regime and on what grounds, literal and figurative, they could be beaten. Most importantly we broke down the steps into easily achievable tasks and effectively gave them a plan for how to achieve their goal. The wonderful thing about it was that the whole thing was led by the Araspring people themselves. It really was their victory. We just gave them a path," Dr Engels stated matter-of-factly. Brad was temporarily speechless.

"And you can see what happened when people tried to copy what we did in other countries, without really understanding how we did it. It was far less successful." Dr Engels shook his head with an angry sigh. "And also why we do not want journalists, police or people poking around or delving into our affairs," he continued.

"Yes…Ok then, so how do you intend to distribute the Professor's program?" Brad asked after a pause.

"We'll get to that in a moment. First there are a couple more things you need to know. I am the one who designed Eliza for the Professor. I did this because he was a friend of mine and I helped him manage the program but not develop it, or at least not most of it," Dr Engels said mournfully.

"So when you said 'that man is not a client of ours'

you were telling the truth." Brad reasoned.

"Yes, maybe not the complete truth, but the truth nonetheless. The fact that he was my friend meant that we did not have a confidentiality agreement like we have with clients, so I could forward his emails to you. Plus you needed them to help you understand the risks and potential of his program, especially at the higher levels," Dr Engels stated.

Brad tried to fathom what might be in Levels Nine, Ten, Eleven and Twelve. He guessed that there must be some additional 'key' to unlock or create more links between pieces of knowledge and that it would probably also involve some means of unifying understandings.

"Ok," Brad replied.

"The other thing you need to know, and probably have figured out already is that the membership of FONT is not really limited to ninety-one people. That is simply on the website as a clue. I have moved a file that has the indication of our real number to a server where the Feds should be able to find it. It is important that they know how many people are at risk and work harder to recover all the copies of Levels Eleven and Twelve that are out there. Too many lives are being lost," said Dr Engels.

"So how many members are there?" asked Brad.

"Of FONT, worldwide there are one hundred and four thousand, seven hundred and twenty nine, plus you if you are willing to join us?" Dr Engels said.

"Yes I am," said Brad after a long pause while he processed his shock over the number.

"Excellent. Of those members, only twenty-seven thousand and eleven have taken their membership to the next level, which is level nine but also involves a larger commitment," said Dr Engels.

Brad was still reeling from the numbers. The size of the potential consequences of the program had just gone from dangerous to catastrophic. What if nearly twenty seven thousand people were at risk of imminent death as a result of the program? What would this mean for the country or the world if such a group of intellectual people were removed from society? Brad was only half listening as Dr Engels continued.

"You can remain on this level with this awareness of how your consciousness has changed and still be considered to be member of our group. I should point out that we have many members who have taken this option, but to access the next level you need to pledge your support for our cause, which means helping others to realise their 'room' and to come out of their caves, be they literal or metaphorical, to help them see with greater consciousness." Dr Engels said.

Brad could see why people would stop at this point. Dr Engels was speaking like an evangelist and making FONT seem like a cult. However, Brad's curiosity was piqued and, as he reflected about where he was on his life's journey, he decided he was ready for something bigger. *At least I would be making a mark on the world,* he thought.

"What would I have to do?" Brad asked.

"This is the thing, we are not asking you to go out and recruit, at least not anymore. What we are asking is simply that you continue to live your life with the awareness, the consciousness you have gained from the program, to make well-reasoned decisions and to quietly and without forcefulness, help others to improve their consciousness. This does not mean telling them what is in each level, but simply helping them to become aware of the forces that are operating in their lives and the things that make them who they are."

Dr Engels was speaking quite quickly, like he wanted to get to the end of a script. He made the choice seem so reasonable, so noble and purposeful that it was hard to say no to his next question.

"So Brad, will you receive our mark – the Ultraviolet Pansy tattoo?" He asked with a raised eyebrow.

"Yes I will," Brad replied immediately and with conviction. Dr Engels smiled, Brad continued, "but I must ask why an ultraviolet tattoo?"

"So you can be marked without being marked," Dr Engels replied laconically. "But really it is a compliance technique, a hazing ritual that is a way of getting you to follow through on your commitment."

Brad thought about it for a moment. Hazing rituals were part of many organisations, fraternities and clubs. They made those who joined a more close-knit group and in some cases made joining the group more desirable through exclusivity. In this case the tattoo would make it harder for Brad to withdraw his support, to do so would not fit with his previous statements and actions. The Professor and, Brad guessed, Dr Engels, seemed to have thought of everything and had clearly designed the program to the *nth* degree. No wonder it had taken so long to develop, it was a masterstroke of manipulation.

"Excellent. Welcome aboard. You will need to go here…" Dr Engels handed him a card from his pocket, "at the time indicated. There they will give you the tattoo

172

and take you through Level Nine. We are in a bit of an unusual situation with you in terms of the other benefits of joining us. You did not follow the usual path of approval by the Professor. Normally he, or one of a very select panel, would accept a nomination and send an automated request to the professor's computer, which would then run the encryption program and distribute the files to the participants. The program would also tell the Dame and us to distribute the powder and update our lists. So as it stands you could well be the last member to join us," Dr Engels said contemplatively.

"But I am really pleased that you will be joining us. You will bring some diversity to our group and that is vital for the group's intelligence. This also means that – with your permission – I would like to keep an eye on you. Although that is not the only reason. You interest me – I am used to people with very different upbringings and professions being made members. You being a … less urban, and if you will forgive my assessment, not very successful person would make an interesting case study."

Brad nodded with a slight wince.

"This will also give me an opportunity to see if the program could really be used as the Professor intended – to upwardly legitimise the more general population, and that interests me."

"Ok. I could probably use the mentoring anyway." Brad said, as much to himself as to Dr Engels.

"So why are you so involved in this? I mean, I understand that there is a connection between you, the Professor and the Dame, but I'm not sure exactly how all the pieces fit together."

"Many years ago I wrote a thesis which was related to the evolution of neurons. Afterwards I wondered what the next evolution would be and created a neural chip that could be hardwired into the brain. I became really interested in the limitations of neural implants – what I created basically acted to stimulate the pineal gland and control some biological functions related to sleep cycles. The military wanted to use it and also adapt it to control the adrenal glands to make some super soldiers who could function across time zones or for extended periods of time. I tried to explain that the implant was specific to the pineal gland and could not be readily adapted, but they offered me a sum of money that was too large to refuse.

Anyway the implant could only control a really small part of the brain and did very little to improve thought and social functioning, which is what I had become interested in. So when the Professor came to me with his idea to create a program to improve thought, I provided him with a grant to fund his research. We became friends and I became more involved in what he created than I had intended or had time for, so I delegated some of the management to Brentham who was happy to do it even though it was off the books so to speak. I also knew the Dame and gave some updated contact information on her to the Professor. The Dame and I wrote a couple of papers together a long time ago, and she formulated the powder to the Professor's specifications and made sure that it would produce a physiological response without actually altering anything in the body.

"Ok," Brad responded, unsure of what to say.

"I also modified the program a little bit to suit some

of my own goals, but you'll learn more about that when you receive the tattoo and get access to Level Nine. In the meantime, please keep in touch and if you need any more information please ask." Brad nodded mutely.

"Until next time," Dr Engels said, as he showed Brad out of his office. Dr Engels used this phrase with members of FONT and people he considered to be friends. He liked it because it implied that he was looking forward to seeing them again, but also implied an obligation for them to meet again. In essence, it created an open ended invitation for them to meet and a tacit contract between them to do so. Since he had adopted the habit a few years previously he had found that his friends kept in better contact than before. He was amused that what seemed like such a minor change could have such a profound impact upon his social interactions, but this was the pleasure and benefit of having a strong understanding of how language is processed and stored. The phrase meant that when someone thought of the Doctor, they would also think "I must get in touch with him…" as they had a sense of unfinished business.

Interchapter

To: The Professor
From: Mathew Arnold
Subject: About your program

Hello Friend,
Are you sure you do not want to distribute your program to a wider audience more quickly? The current rate seems silly – if we keep going at the current pace, then it will take decades to produce noticeable change. Why not let everyone have access to the program so we can generate some change today? Let me know how I can help make this happen.
Yours
Mathew
Arnold

Chapter Two

As they drove back to the station Brad appreciated that Sally allowed him time to think.

"So how did it go?" she asked when they were nearly there.

"Good. I can prove a connection between the dead people, Dr Engels and Leviathan, but I'm not sure that anyone has done anything illegal. But the public are crying out for answers and I'm not sure that I can give them. The deaths are linked and caused by the program plus the powder, but it is unclear whether the program would work without it. The deaths are only affecting smart people because it was only distributed to people who were members of Round Table Intelligencia and only a proportion of the recipients joined FONT and accessed the levels that are dangerous. More deaths are unlikely, but if someone could get hold of the program they could start it up again and the deaths would resume. It's all just a bit nuts."

"Sounds like you have made a lot of progress, but do you have proof yet that no one has interfered with the program or the powder to make it fatal? I mean there are a lot of people who would like to teach RTI or FONT a lesson or target them because they think it would be terrifying if the intelligence base was wiped out."

"That's true. So I guess that despite having come so far, we're back where we began." Brad said mournfully. "I knew this case was never going to end."

"Don't worry. The Feds are here now and maybe they will take it off our hands."

Brad realised that he was at the point now where this would not affect his progress with the program and would actually be a relief to him. *But then, I am not one who gives in and like to see things through to the end. I mean, I sat my detective exam twice and applied for this station three times. Even as a kid I would play games with my sister to the end, even when it was clear I was going to lose,* he thought as they pulled into the station's car park.

"Hmm," said Brad still pondering what he really wanted. *Closure*, he thought, *I want the case closed and my relationship with Amy legitimised. So I guess I better step up and see this through. Maybe the Doctor will get the Feds off our back? I guess he is only a minute or so away from being here so I may know soon enough.*

They walked into the station and Sally went to inform Sergeant Pan of their progress. Brad was quickly bustled into the interview room where the Feds were preparing to meet Dr Engels. Two of the Feds were checking a video camera that they had set up in the adjoining observation room. As Brad walked into the interview

178

room, Daniel was moving a hidden microphone under the table.

"Hi Brad," Daniel said condescendingly.

"That's Detective," Brad replied assertively.

"Yes, ok Detective," Daniel said with a hint of mockery. "How did you go with joining FONT?"

Brad tried not to show his shock that the Feds knew about his morning's activity. He paused for a moment and realised that Sergeant Pan must have told Daniel about him joining FONT, probably in response to provocation from Daniel. Brad calmed down as he realised that Daniel didn't know the full extent of his knowledge.

"Is being one of the ninety-one good?" he asked with an air of playfulness.

"Um, yeah it is," Brad replied hesitantly.

"You know that there are actually more than that don't you? A *lot* more," Daniel said with a grin. It was clear he was trying to shock Brad. Brad continued to hesitate. He wasn't sure exactly how much the Feds knew or whether he was officially meant to know about the real size of the group.

"Really? How many are there?" he asked, managing to sound curious rather than sarcastic.

"There are…" Daniel paused deliberately for effect, "over a hundred thousand!" He announced triumphantly.

"How do you know that?" Brad responded even though he knew the answer perfectly well. Part of his brain pinged with the thought that his year nine drama teacher had done him a disservice by giving him a 'D'.

"Well, we managed to hack into their server and access their membership database." Daniel replied triumphantly. It was clear that he felt like this was a major achievement and that Brad's team would never have accomplished the feat. Brad kept his face blank but wasn't sure if his eyes were revealed him laughing inside. Fortunately, Daniel responded with "I can see you're surprised. You didn't think we would be of much help, did you?"

"No," Brad said, just managing to suppress a smile.

"And yet we've managed to find out something that you couldn't," Daniel said smugly.

"Did you also know that the powder is a placebo?" he continued, clearly thinking he was going to shock Brad even further.

Brad felt like he had found that out a lifetime ago, even though it was only recently.

"Really?" Once again, Brad was impressed by how he controlled the tone of his voice.

"Yes, the results came back from our lab. It is nothing but a mix of food colouring, sugar and an amino acid that has no effect when taken orally."

Brad remembered his breathlessness and the bizarre tingling under his skin and thought to himself *you try swallowing it and then tell me it has no effect.* Aloud all he said was "why?"

"That's the thing, it must be a scam to make money!" Daniel said triumphantly.

"So why are people dying?" Brad asked, amazed at how Daniel made such an illogical conclusion sound reasonable.

"We have a theory on that, it seems that all the people who have died are members of FONT and someone is targeting them. So all we have to do is find out who their enemies are and we will have our answer," said Daniel triumphantly, as though he had all but solved the case.

Brad finally succumbed to his emotions and shook his head in disbelief. Fortunately Daniel misinterpreted his body language.

"Now, now, there is no need to be afraid. Just because you have joined them doesn't mean you are going to die. It seems like it's only people that have been members for months who die, plus they all have the tattoo. You don't have the tattoo do you?" Daniel asked as though he didn't care about the answer. Despite knowing that he would receive it soon, Brad shook his head.

"We think that that's how they're killing them, by having a slow acting poison in the ink," Daniel said. Brad was surprised that he had not spent more time thinking about the ink as the source poison, but then Sam had said that she had tested it. He was confident that the ink was not why people were dying, but it still added to his apprehension about getting the tattoo in a month's time.

"Wow that's good thinking. So what sort of poison do you think it could be?"

"It must be something that is basically undetectable on a blood or tissue scan, so we're not exactly sure, probably something from a rare plant," Daniel replied.

"Interesting," said Brad.

"Isn't it just?" Daniel said.

Brad watched as Dr Engels arrived, flanked by one of the other Federal agents. He felt nervous as he realised he was unsure how to greet Dr Engels without giving their new relationship away. As he approached, Dr Engels stated a simple "Hello Officer" to Brad. Brad automatically replied, "It's Detective."

Brad mused that the Doctor must have known he would respond that way and that the naturalness of his immediate response would conceal their more recent connection. Brad left the interview room and went to the observation room next door. He watched through the two way mirror.

###

Dr Engels sat down silently and waited for Daniel to speak. Daniel placed a box on the table and let it sit there. They waited for seventeen seconds until Daniel asked, "So Doctor, I was told that inviting you here would be better for us than if we stormed into your office."

Dr Engels nodded in response.

"And I can see that you are not in a talkative mood…" Dr Engels shrugged his shoulders, "which I thought might be the case. So let us make a deal."

"What kind of deal?" Dr Engels replied cautiously, his rich voice far more authoritative than Daniel's.

"Let us play a game, if I win you talk freely with us and if I lose you may leave," Daniel said slyly.

"What is the game?" asked Dr Engels.

"Chess," Daniel said with a smirk. He opened the box and produced a chessboard which he set up on the table while Dr Engels watched silently. He placed the white team on Dr Engel's side of the table.

"I'll even let you start," said Daniel smugly.

From the adjoining room Brad could see the Doctor's eyes light up. What he could also see were the other two Federal police opening a computer chess program and setting the difficulty to maximum. They were going to

182

put the Doctor's moves into the program and relay the computer's response to Daniel. So this was their plan, they were going to cheat their way into getting the Doctor to talk. Brad felt like running in and warning the Doctor, but knew that this wasn't possible. He was simultaneously aware of the irony of this urge, given that just this morning he'd wanted to arrest the Doctor. The conflict between his duty and his emotion was one that Brad realised he was having to deal with more often since beginning the program and he took it as a sign that he was maturing as a person.

"You've already lost," Dr Engels said confidently. Daniel could not hide his delight at the Doctor's self-assurance.

"So do we have a deal?" Daniel replied.

"No you misunderstand me. Look at the board, you have already lost," Dr Engels said, raising his hands from underneath the table and gesturing towards the chessboard.

Confusion flickered across Daniel's face "So do we have a deal?" he repeated.

"I can't make a deal when the result is already known. Let me explain, you have set up the chess board as two sides opposing each other." Daniel nodded and his body language said "well duh."

"And what is the next step. One of us makes a move – probably moves a pawn forward and the other responds. We go back and forth until one of our Kings are captured and the game ends. One team has achieved a victory and the other has lost a battle."

More nodding from Daniel.

"And then what, we play another game? Go for best

two out of three? Do you not understand that by forcing one side to lose, you both wind up losing? By setting up the 'us and them' dichotomy, you make a truly free exchange of information impossible. I mean look at the board, there is a clear divide between the two sides, just like there is between us."

Dr Engels once again swept a hand over the top of the pieces to indicate what he was talking about. Brad noted the gap of four rows between the different coloured sets.

"No one can truly win from this starting state. What you need is to bridge the gap between the groups."

Dr Engels quickly moved the black and white pieces closer together so that there were no rows between them. "But this is still a losing state. What you should be aiming for is for there to be only one group, without internal discrimination like what is currently represented here." Dr Engels quickly moved around all the pieces until they alternated black and white.

"This is the true victory. When you have achieved this state, no one loses because there is no conflict. In fact everyone wins." Dr Engels continued to keep his voice calm and spoke softly but urgently.

Brad could see the beauty of this point of view and how relevant it was to the Professor's program. If conflict was the cause of change then if you changed the conditions so that conflict was removed, then harmony could occur. It was clear that Daniel did not know how to respond. He had gone in with a plan that he thought was ingenious and would trap Dr Engels and it had backfired spectacularly.

Brad wondered if Daniel realised that Dr Engels was in fact giving him the key to getting information out of him. It was simple. Come to him as a friend and he would help you. Come to him as an enemy and he wouldn't. Brad realised that by joining FONT he had effectively become the Doctor's friend, which is why he had been so open with him. He also realised how skilfully he had been turned from an enemy into the Doctor's friend, even to the point where he now felt protective of him. Dr Engels had shown him the greatest victory was not conquering yourself, which Brad acknowledged the program was helping him achieve, but in turning your enemy into your friend. This realisation made Brad feel more protective towards the Doctor and he wanted to put an end to the interview. However, it was clear that the Doctor was more than capable of fighting this battle. Daniel turned to look at the two way mirror. It was clear he was lost.

Bam, you lose. Turning to us for support just means you no longer know what you are doing, Brad thought. The Federal officers beside him practically slapped their heads in disdain.

"So Dr Engels, what do you propose?" Daniel asked eventually.

"Simply this; ask what you want of me, but don't expect me to explain myself, infringe on the privacy of FONT or its members or betray any of Leviathan's contracts or contacts."

"Fair enough," Daniel said as though he was giving permission for the conditions for the interview. It was clear to Brad and the two Feds beside him who were groaning and mumbling, that from the moment Dr Engels had arrived, everything was happening on the Doctor's terms.

"What is Leviathan Enterprises involvement in the deaths of …" Daniel listed the names of the deceased.

"Leviathan Enterprises has no involvement other than being the location of one of those deaths," Dr Engels said passively.

"Do you know the Professor?"

"Which one?" Dr Engels replied laconically. Brad laughed to himself. Dr Engels probably knew dozens of professors.

"Michael Episteme," replied Daniel, just managing not to rise to the bait.

"Yes, he was a personal friend of mine. The world lost a great mind when he passed and I miss his company immensely."

Brad could hear the honesty of the emotion in the Doctor's voice.

"Who might want to see you harmed?" Daniel asked, quickly pouncing on Dr Engels momentary dropping of his guard.

"Did you not understand what I was trying to teach you through the analogy of the chessboard? I aim to turn people who are against me into friends. So I don't think anyone would want to see me harmed," Dr Engels replied after a pause.

"What about people who would like to see Leviathan Enterprises or FONT harmed?" Daniel continued, his voice rising slightly.

"Now that is a different question. Leviathan has had a number of people protest against it over the years, due to some of our contracts and the fact that we have to be secretive. I will email you a list. As for FONT, there are a few, but the main one is a man named Mathew Arnold.

186

He is trying to obtain copies of the Program that he can sell for himself."

"Well doesn't he have them already?"

"The videos he had played only once and the text files ran more like a video, line by line, again only playing once, effectively he no longer has a copy of the program. Besides, he joined at a point where it was not really necessary for him to work through the lower levels," said Dr Engels.

A chill ran up Brad's spine. He realised that by getting the files from the Professor's computer he had circumvented the security features that controlled how the files were distributed and how they played. He gasped as he suddenly understood the value of what he had and the overwhelming urge to make it more secure. The Professor's laptop was in evidence storage so the only copies were on his USB and work computer. He made a mental plan of action for the moment the interview was over.

"Couldn't he have simply recorded them?" Daniel said like he was stating the obvious.

"No," said Dr Engels firmly.

"Why not?"

"We have made it so he can't," Dr Engels replied.

"How?"

"We understand visual perception. You only perceive about fifty percent of what is actually in front of you, you know. We exploit that," stated Dr Engels.

"No, I see it all," Daniel replied defensively.

"No you don't. In your eye there is a blind spot where the optic nerve leaves the eye. The image that is projected onto your retina is upside down and two dimensional. Your eyes focus on a point and reduce the resolution of everything else. Your perception is a mental *process* not a direct experience of reality. Your brain fills in the gaps between what is seen and unseen. It is the conflict between your sensory experience and your expectations that causes your brain to change how it interprets the sensory information and give you the perception of a complete image. We take advantage of this and some technological creations of ours in order to make filming the video fail," Dr Engels said like he was talking to a child.

Hmm that could almost be another level of the program, Brad thought, I mean if you don't experience reality directly and your perception of it is an illusion created by your brain then we need to really rethink how we know anything or at least acknowledge the limitations of our perception as a way of knowing. Brad stopped to congratulate himself on such a deep thought. He had the 'spotlight on me' feeling again and enjoyed it immensely.

Poor Daniel, he is so ignorant of the significance of what the Doctor is saying... A month or so ago that would have been me. The program really is helping me see further.

"Whatever. What do you want us to do?" Daniel asked in exasperation. Next to Brad the Federal police just about went into apoplexy. Their leader was offering their services to their suspect! They both swore under their breath.

"It would be nice if you could control the hysteria around the Program. Ever since the media reports about the Dame and Leviathan Enterprises, we have been inundated. Plus the people selling fake powders and programs should be prosecuted, they are putting lives at risk."

"We are already working on those things." Daniel replied.

"Well, work harder," Dr Engels said unintentionally sounding rude. "Actually scratch that, think more. I mean your strategy here today was woeful. Thinking you would trick me into playing chess against you, when you have people in the next room feeding you moves..." Daniel looked guilty, like a dog caught stealing from a plate of food, "...and stop trying to work against me. I actually want to see you succeed. I want this shut down so that control over the Program reverts to Leviathan and people stop pounding at our doors trying to buy some magic powder."

Brad realised Dr Engels was stating the truth and was acting in his self-interest, which struck Brad as being in line with evolutionary mechanics. The more he thought about it the more he realised that everyone in this case was acting in their own interest. *I must remember that as an investigative strategy – identify who benefits from the crime.* Brad had an epiphany about the last case he had in Northam. *So in those thefts, the conflict is that stamps were stolen as well. So maybe the people who committed the break-ins made it look like teenagers had done it to conceal their real motive... So who benefits from stealing the stamps? Someone who knew their value. Who knew their value? Stephen, who they were stolen from and Chris from the collectibles shop who had valued them three months before they were stolen. Chris must have done it!* Brad wanted to run out of the room to go and test his theory.

"You are capable of more…" Dr Engels prodded Daniel gently.

"What do you mean?" Daniel asked in a state of exasperation.

"The rate at which someone can consciously *think* is about four hundred words per minute, which is about triple the rate humans speak at, double what they read at and ten times the rate at which they hand write. You have the capacity for greater consciousness and greater thought," replied Dr Engels sincerely.

The Doctor had allowed warmth into his voice for the first time in the interview. Brad felt the compassion in what he was trying to do for Daniel. Unfortunately, Daniel did not understand and terminated the interview. Dr Engels left without another word.

The Federal police rushed into Daniel and started berating him over such a poor interview. Daniel protested that they had agreed on the strategy together and suggested listening back to the recording. When they played the recording back the first voice was Daniel's and it was clear. When Dr Engels spoke it was very hard to understand what he was saying. As they listened to the whole recording, the only time it was clear what the Doctor was saying was when he showed some emotion.

"He must have had a jamming device," Daniel said angrily.

"Or simply understood how the recording worked. I mean he must have been able to guess where you had hidden the microphones," Brad countered.

In fact he probably had his hand over it. I mean didn't you notice his hands were under the desk? No wonder he made the sweeping gestures, it obscured the fact that the rest of the time his hands were under the table, Brad thought with amusement.

"No, I think he had some form of jammer. Next time let's make sure we pat him down or scan him," Daniel replied stubbornly.

"It's late. How about we all go get some food and rest, and regroup tomorrow?" one of the Federal officers suggested quietly. It was clear she felt that the interview had been a waste of time and no one was in the right frame of mind to achieve more that night. Daniel agreed and they left for the day.

Brad took the opportunity to phone his old police station. He was soon speaking to his old Sergeant.

"Hi Sargeant."

"You know to call me Sarge, Brad." Came the reply.

"Yes Sarge," Brad replied with a wry smile. "So the reason I'm calling is about those break-ins that occurred just before I left."

"Yes."

"Well I think I know who committed them."

"Good, because we never did arrest anyone. So who do you think it was?"

Brad explained why he thought Chris from the Collectibles shop was behind the thefts.

"You might be right you know, he did tell everyone he inherited a decent sum of money. That could easily be a cover for the proceeds of the thefts."

"So will you arrest him? Maybe I could come up and interrogate him tomorrow?"

"No can do."

"Why not?"

"He's left the country and moved overseas. Best I can do is put a flag on his name with immigration so that if he returns, we can grab him."

Brad cursed his inability to solve the crimes earlier.

"How's life in the big city?"

"I still don't feel like I fit in yet, but I've made some progress in the last month or so."

"Good. I hope it all works out for you."

"Thanks Sarge, speak again soon," Brad said as he hung up the phone.

Should I feel elated that I solved the case or upset that they got away? But since there is nothing more I can do about it, maybe I should just let it go. Brad let out a long sigh and had the strange sensation of a weight being lifted from his shoulders. Before leaving the building Brad did a virtual 'shredding' of the Professor's files on his computer. The safety of the files wasn't what kept nagging at his consciousness though, it was the thought that the tattoo might in some way be involved in causing the deaths and that he was due to get his soon.

Interchapter

To: Michael
From: Dr Engels
Subject: Contribution

My Dear Professor,
I received this from Mathew yesterday and thought I'd forward it to you for your information.
Dr Engels

Hello Doctor,
The Prof and I disagree about distribution of the program. I feel that we'd be better served by sharing it with a wider audience, but he won't help me, can you? I know you have ways of making people do what you want, so could you please convince him to share the latest version of the program more widely? It will help make the social change we want, happen more quickly.
Yours,
Mathew
Arnold

Chapter Three

The next week saw a shift in the public attention that was being given to the case. Only one more death was reported and the Federal officers charged a few people for fraudulent behaviour and then claimed what a magnificent job they were doing. Brad knew that it would be unlikely that the people would spend any time in jail, but at least the arrests had stopped people selling fake copies of the program and powder online. A natural disaster overseas at the end of the week meant that the story had stopped being reported all together. However, people were still interested in the whole Melting Brain Affair and the story maintained a life on the internet. People wrote a number of conspiracy theories as to why it was no longer being reported, the main one being that the program was being suppressed by the government. *It is more likely that Dr Engels is the one suppressing it,* Brad thought after reading one such theory.

During the week, Amy and Brad had shared three

more dates and Amy had asked him to meet her parents. Brad had offered that she meet his the night after hers. They'd both grinned when making the dates since it was a clear elevation of their relationship. Amy had teased him that she would probably have to spend the night with him afterwards just to maintain the pace of their progress as a couple. Brad had laughed. *I wish I could fast forward time*, he'd thought.

Brad had begun spending a lot of time in Amy's apartment and each night he made what felt like a long drive home to his own home. Amy's apartment was on the top floor in a block of twelve and the three flights of stairs needed to reach her front door felt like nothing to Brad on the way up, but were never ending on the way down. The apartment itself had two bedrooms, and a modern kitchen. One of the bedrooms was used as a study. On their latest date, Brad had used Amy's kitchen to make them his signature dish – a herb crusted lamb rack and a treacle tart for dessert.

"The treacle tart was my Grandmother's recipe, but the lamb rack is my own," he said to Amy after they had enjoyed their meal.

"The tart was amazing. I don't think I've ever had one before, but I really liked it," Amy said.

Now they were sitting on opposite ends of Amy's couch with their feet entwined and cups of peppermint tea by their sides. Brad told Amy about some of his progress in the case and shared his understanding up to level seven. Amy was still shocked about the powder being a placebo, but over the last week her initial anger had given way to forgiveness as she realised how brilliantly conceived the Program was.

"Man, they really went overboard designing the program didn't they? … So how did you solve the riddle of what Athena's gift is?" Amy asked curiously.

"I pieced it together by analysing the letters in the tattoo. I guess I was lucky that I had the image to begin with, whereas normally people in the program would not get it until they solved level six. But once I found out about the mark of Athena, well actually it still took a lot of thinking and applying of the lessons of the program, so I don't know. I guess that I was just so determined to see this whole thing through to the end. I am gaining so much from it that I just didn't want to stop my advancement. I need to see this through for me."

"That is certainly a good insight, just like how you solved Athena's gift. Kudos."

Brad beamed like he always did when Amy complimented him. She had a knack for boosting his self-esteem and he felt like the extra confidence she gave him was making him a better person. As they continued to discuss the levels, Amy stopped him suddenly when the topic of evolution came up.

"You know how you asked 'why me?' a couple of weeks ago?" she asked quietly.

"Yes" replied Brad.

"Well I didn't give you the complete answer." Amy continued ashamedly.

"Ok" he replied cautiously, suddenly afraid of what she might say.

"You know how from my office you can see a lot of the uni?" asked Amy quietly.

Brad nodded.

"When you were wandering around I saw you interact

196

with a couple of young children as you were asking for directions. If you remember it was quite late in the day and the day care had just closed."

"So?" questioned Brad.

"Well, it sounds silly now, but you were a natural. At least that's how it looked from the window. I remember thinking that you would make a great father and that excited me, it was like a display of your evolutionary fitness. When we met, I saw how humble you were and you were just so cute, looking all lost and out of place. So, since I had started to think about you as a father, I also started to think about you as a partner and after talking to you, albeit briefly, I was sure that we were compatible, so yeah, I um… put on a bit of a display." Amy had curled up slightly while talking and seemed shy. Brad had never seen this side of her before and he found it alluring. As he admired this new side of her he realised that there was more to her shyness than having to admit she had not been completely open with him.

"Are you now trying to get me to talk about whether I want kids or not?" Brad asked, his eyebrows rising.

"Actually, yes. That is very insightful of you," Amy replied with a sly smile.

"Yeah, I seem to be getting better at that these days. But to answer your unasked question, yes I do want kids but maybe not for a year or two, ok?" Brad paused for a beat before his eyes widened in realisation of the implications of what he had just said.

"Wait don't answer that," he cried.

"Ok," Amy said with a broad smile.

"Ok I won't answer, or Ok is your answer?" Brad questioned.

"Both!" Amy said with a wicked grin.

Brad resisted the urge to playfully hit her with a cushion. He laughed. "I've been thinking it for a while now and I know we've only been dating for a few weeks, but since you have just agreed to have kids with me, in principle at least, I want you to know that, Amy, I am in love with you."

"I love you too" she replied immediately and then dived on top of him for a kiss.

###

Brad had to wait nearly a month to receive the tattoo. In the final week leading up to it he had thought about nothing else. *I don't think the tattoo is responsible for the deaths as those whose brain melted had a very mixed timeframe between receiving it and dying, but still I don't really know what I am getting myself into. I wish I could just let it go, but I have to know more. None of the ideas in the levels to date are worth dying for so what is the big secret with the rest that made people put their lives at risk, even after the Professor sent out his warning and the publicity around the affair? Would I be prepared to die just so I could know everything? I don't know if I have an answer for that*, Brad thought.

He had found the location on the card from Dr Engel's easily and had been surprised to see it was further around the river from the university and on the edge of the city. Brad had imagined that such a site would be clandestine and in some dingy and obscure building. Instead he was looking at Mount Hospital and the medical suites next door. The only unusual thing was that he was visiting out of normal hours and looking for a dentist's office. Brad arrived on time and knocked on the door at precisely 9.07pm. As he had approached the building he had not seen any signs of life from inside, yet the sliding doors opened instantly. Despite the normality of the doors closing, when they did so it seemed ominous. Brad found room 102 on the ground floor and knocked on the door of the darkened room.

"Welcome. Come in." A voice with a slightly French accent beckoned as the door opened. The woman to whom the voice belonged was slender and clad head to toe in black. The exception was a bright red streak in her hair. Despite her clothing and sense of style she was tanned and had a healthy glow about her and not a single visible tattoo. She introduced herself as Emily Rousseau. Brad entered the offices and was led to the dentist's room and made to sit in the chair. He looked around in mild surprise.

"Before you ask, we need the ultraviolet light and magnifying lens to see what we're doing, plus it's a clean room," she said warmly.

"Well that explains the dentist office then," Brad said.

The dentist's suite was white and looked sterile. As Brad sat in the dentist's chair he could see a flat screen TV on the ceiling. He could easily imagine patients watching something while their mouths were worked on. However, it was currently turned off.

"So I am authorised to give you the tattoo in your left or right ear and introduce you to Level Nine, but I must warn you that once you know what it involves it will change how you view the other levels. The tattoo is also not one that can be undone. The ink we use is not like other inks. The only advantage is that it won't show. We also don't use anaesthetics. Part of the ritual is the pain.

So, having said that do you still want to go through with this?"

"Yes" said Brad with conviction, "but are you sure the ink is safe?"

"Absolutely," Emily said with a confidence that was inspiring. Brad nodded his agreement for her to continue.

"Ok then. We will need to strap you down to the chair for reasons that will become obvious as we go through. Your hands will remain free and it is only your head that we strap down. We will even give you a quick release button that will undo the strapping, but just make sure that you warn us as much as possible first if you are going to leap out of the chair. I mean you don't want a punctured eardrum or eyeball," said Emily with a small grin.

"Who is we? There is only you here," Brad asked quizzically.

"Yes but I am representing the organisation of FONT and acting on their behalf. Therefore I am we," Emily said with a hint of a smile.

"Ok. Let's get started," Brad said, trying to sound confident.

Emily strapped Brad's head to the dentist chair.

Gee that's tight, Brad thought as his pulse increased. When it was clear that he could not move his head Emily put on some magnifying glasses and got started. She attached the inkwell to the needle and started the machine going. The whir and sight of the needle made Brad cringe.

Emily saw him shudder. "Don't worry this is not a dentist's drill, we swap it out for a tattooing needle," she said with a smile.

As the needle approached his ear, Brad felt a chill run up his spine. He shivered involuntarily and hoped he would not do it again when the needle was making contact. The sound as it got closer and closer to his ear was torturous and Brad was sure Emily was prolonging the experience as much as possible.

As Emily pressed the needle into Brad's left tragus for the first time, he was filled with a sense of impending doom. The sting of the needle and the intense sound, made it feel as though the needle was inside his ear. Brad was suddenly grateful his head was strapped to the backrest of the chair as he fought the overwhelming urge to leap away.

The pain was intense. There were a large amount of nerve endings, particularly at the base of the tragus leading into the ear canal, right where the tattoo was going. Brad had the surreal sensation of the strong pain triggering an almost pleasurable sensation, particularly when he focused on why he was experiencing it. The process lasted nearly an hour. The difficulty was in getting the Greek letters done correctly, Emily explained to Brad when she was done and had put some antibacterial ointment on and a bandage over the wound.

"So you can take the bandage off and shower in the morning, but keep it lukewarm and try not to let water get into your ear. Also it may itch and flake as it heals, but don't scratch, don't pick and don't moisturise as it will interfere with the healing." Emily wagged her finger as she spoke.

"Ok…That was weird…" Brad began.

Emily interrupted him, "Let me guess, you found it

somehow pleasurable?"

"Yes," said Brad curiously.

"That happens. The endorphin rush and sense of purpose to what you are doing changes your perception of the pain. It's weird isn't it? The brain is so amazing."

"Yes."

"It's also part of the operant conditioning you have already been through." Emily said with a smile.

"What do you mean?" asked Brad.

"Well think about the rush you experienced when you figured out each level," suggested Emily.

"Yes, it was great."

"And what happened next?" Emily prompted.

"I was given the information about the next level," Brad replied.

"Exactly, so you paired the idea of reward with new ways of thinking. We were training you to find new ways or new lenses for looking at the world as a positive experience," said Emily.

Brad stopped to consider what Emily had said. He admitted to himself that he had found the thrill of solving the puzzle of each level and shift in his perspectives to be addictive.

"Anyway come sit with me in the next room, so I can take you through Level Nine."

Brad followed her and she led him into a staff room. Emily poured Brad a glass of water and sat opposite him.

"Here is a scoop of the powder. It may be a placebo, but it is all part of the ritual."

Brad smiled and put the powder under his tongue. They sat in silence as it dissolved and was absorbed. Emily seemed to know exactly how long to wait as she spoke at almost the same moment Brad felt the first tingling under his skin.

"Level Nine is actually quite straightforward and follows on from Level Eight. But saying that it's the next logical step is not quite accurate. Anyway the first thing you need to do is read this quote."

Emily took a card from her pocket and handed it to Brad. It read:

"Until philosophers rule as kings or those who are now called kings and leading men genuinely and adequately become philosophers, that is, until political power and philosophy entirely coincide… cities will have no rest from evils… there can be no happiness… in any other city than one in which Philosopher Kings rule." (Plato, the Republic)

Brad placed the card on the table and looked at it for a while in silence.

Emily continued; "The view that people have of philosophers is that they have no understanding of day to day life and do nothing but hang out in cafes and mutter about the meaning of life. They never live a truly adult life as they are too busy trying to think deep thoughts. If this perception were true, philosophers are the last people who we should or would want to rule. However, in his book *The Republic*, Plato corrects this misunderstanding and argues that the fact that philosophers are the last people who would want to rule is precisely why they should. He argues that only those who do not wish for political power can be trusted with it. FONT agrees with this point of view and takes it to the next level by asking that you continue the training you have experienced to date, in whatever field you are in, and work towards becoming a

Philosopher King. That is, we ask you to get into positions of power, not for power's sake but to make decisions based on reason and for the greater good. We are aiming to change the world, by changing how it is run. We are not interested in you going out and changing individuals *per se*, what we are saying is that philosophers are people who can be trusted to rule well. They are both morally and intellectually suited to rule. They won't be corrupted by people attempting to sway them away from what is right for the greater good. The members of FONT are asked to support each other in this goal, in accordance with local laws."

Emily stopped and sat silently, while Brad gathered his thoughts over what she had said. His first thought was that this level basically turned the program and FONT into an initiation for a cult and this disappointed him immensely. But it also occurred to him that they were not asking him to do anything specifically. They were asking him to make his own interpretation of their request and to simply have some ambition in his chosen vocation and to use thought when making decisions and make decisions based on their merit and not for political or personal gain. They were simple ideals but would be quite complicated to put into practice.

"So how will I know who to help? Do I get a list of members?" Brad asked with some surprise. Emily smiled a wry grin and her eyes shined.

"That my friend, is the thing…You won't. We don't have meetings or anything and don't be disappointed, but there is no secret handshake either," Emily said with a smile.

"So what is the point of having a Network of

Freethinkers if you can't use it?" Brad asked, feeling a faint, but rising anger.

"Relax Brad, the point of not knowing who to support is that you will support decisions on their own merits and help other members by helping create a social *milieu* in which the right decisions can be made and *enacted*. And before you get worked up again, you do have access to the Network, it's just that the contact comes in the form of a mailing list. We have over a hundred thousand members all around the world, so we have chosen an anonymous mailing list that is for distribution of philosophical ideas and research. In short, it is continuing education without being defined as a level," Emily said proudly.

"So if everyone who has completed level eight is a member of the list what is the point of Level Nine? And why was I made to go through to Level Nine before I found out about it?" Brad queried.

"Yes, normally you would be given access to the list the moment you achieved Level Eight, but given the extraordinary circumstances around you joining us, Dr Engels decided that you should have to wait until now to get it. Incidentally, not everyone is offered access to Level Nine you know. Your interview is an assessment of who you are and whether you are worthy of access to this level. The extra commitment you have now made means you will also be given access to a second email list. This list is exclusive to members who have achieved Level Nine and above." Emily said.

"Above?" Brad questioned, despite knowing of the higher levels he knew nothing about them.

"Yes, there are another three levels that the Professor

completed before he died. My understanding, is that they provide a logical framework for unifying knowledge. Level Twelve is meant to be mind-blowing, but unfortunately a little too literally. But then I have only gleaned this in passing as I have not progressed beyond Level Ten. As you know the Professor wanted the last two levels destroyed as they were implicated as the cause of death in several of our members. And as far as possible that has been done. But you are right, Level Nine is a bit different to the other levels and that is probably because it is the only level that was not created by the Professor. Dr Engels created the social engineering side of the program which is Level Nine. The Professor did the rest – for him it was an intellectual challenge to create the program. Dr Engels saw the potential to link to a broader social movement and added in Level Nine, with the Professor's full consent."

Emily was giving Brad her full attention and he found himself totally focused on what she was saying.

"Well that explains a lot," Brad replied thoughtfully.

"But back to the second list. This list is more interactive, you can pose questions or queries to it and contribute responses. Think about how powerful that is. You have access to over twenty thousand of the most aware and visionary minds on the planet. It is also a means for tracking the progress and spread of the program as you could also use it to provide details of people you would like to receive the program," said Emily.

Brad paused to consider how significant and how powerful that network would be. He could ask them about any key decision or problem he had and the anonymity of the group meant he could do so with boldness and freedom.

"So you monitor us?" Brad asked.

"Yes."

"Big brother is watching you…" Brad said absently. Emily laughed softly.

"Yes that is true, it is like you are being watched, but think about it, if the program were suddenly given to everyone and millions of people became more conscious of the factors that were holding them back, more aware of their oppression through ideological institutions, and more conscious that they can reject those institutions and still be proud, happy and productive…" Emily trailed off.

"There would be anarchy or civil war!" Brad said, alarmed.

"Yes people would not be governed. Which is why we need Philosopher Kings in place to elevate society in a controlled manner," said Emily.

"I think I get it now," Brad said, once again recognising the danger in what could be.

"Which is why this level is important and only for selected members and why we control things to the extent we do. And that is why only those select people, the ones who have the tattoo, such as yourself are the only ones who can nominate people to be given the program… or at least could." Emily said.

"Ok," Brad replied, automatically wondering who he would give it too, even though he knew the answer was that he couldn't give it to anyone. His first thought was about Amy, but he wasn't sure what effect it would have given her previous exposure and their discussions about it to date.

"But unfortunately, our usual processes and checks and balances have quite literally died a tragic death. Which means that in fact we are no longer accepting new members and you are our last new member. Dr Engels will continue to coordinate the program and monitor its success and now that Brentham has passed he will also do any necessary administration, but that is all. We are in a holding pattern for the foreseeable future. Which is probably not a bad thing, we were growing very quickly," said Emily.

Brad nodded. He was upset that he would not be able to give the program to others, but he consoled himself that this was not the most important thing for a member of the program to do.

"The next thing is minor, but we need to know. Obviously you obtained the files from the Professor's computer, what has happened to them?" Emily asked.

"I deleted them from my computer last week," replied Brad.

"What about the computer itself?" Emily asked without pausing.

"It's in police storage."

"Good, are there any other copies?" Emily asked quickly.

"No," said Brad without thinking. Emily had watched him very closely as he responded. Apparently satisfied with his response she continued, "Ok then. So now that we have covered that. Let me ask you a question."

"Ok."

"How are you thinking these days?" Emily said.

"What do you mean?"

"Well, I have seen your transfer file and report to your current police department. Your work ethic and honesty were praised, but your last Sergeant thought that you would only ever be a good Detective and never a great one because of a lack of insight," said Emily.

Brad was surprised at how unconcerned he was at the invasion of his privacy.

"And yet, you managed to complete seven levels of the Professor's program before joining us, which must have been somewhat life changing."

Brad nodded in affirmation. He mused to himself that all of the information that was in the Professor's levels was nothing new, but the context in which he had covered the information and the way he had felt compelled to put it into practice meant it had a value greater than the sum of its parts.

"In effect you have gotten out of your own way. So I ask you again, how are you thinking these days? This is your chance to put those thoughts about thinking that have been circulating into a cohesive statement so take your time with your answer."

They sat in silence for thirty-seven seconds while Brad gathered his thoughts.

"Clearly," Brad said, surprised at the certainty of his response. "It's like I was colour blind and now I'm not. There is an extra level of detail in what I see and it's beautiful. I feel like I am seeing what is really in front of me. I am open to multiple interpretations of situations and the possibilities they bring."

Brad realised that the first part of his description could equally apply to his relationship with Amy as she had brought a new level of colour into his life.

"And how does that feel?" Emily leant towards Brad as she asked the question softly.

"Incredible," Brad said as the realisation flowed through him. He felt more invigorated than ever before.

"I think you're ready to change the world. Have fun."

Emily quietly slipped out of the offices. Brad sat in a thoughtful silence for twenty three minutes. As he gingerly touched his ear, he realised that today, instead of leaving a mark on the world, it had left one on him, both literally and figuratively. Brad stood up and quietly left the building, making sure to lock the door behind him.

Interchapter

To: Doctor Engels
From: The Professor
Subject: A Caution

Greetings Doc,
Thanks for the message about Mathew. He worries me. I fear he may act rashly and choose his own course of action. I believe our method to implement and monitor the program is the right one. A rapid upheaval in social values has a tendency to be short-lived as people to fear or avoid change, especially social. What we need is a gradual raising of awareness, one that is organic and through many agents rather than a one man crusade that Mathew wants to rage. Do you think we can change his mind? In the meantime, I will not send him any new levels I create.
Cheers,
Michael

Chapter Four

"Detective, can you join me in my office?" Sergeant Pan asked Detective Summers early the next morning.

"Sure," Sally replied confidently.

They silently walked to Sergeant Pan's office. Sergeant Pan shut the door when they had walked in.

"I have a case for you," Sergeant Pan said. Sally tried not to look upset, she had several active investigations and another one would not make solving them any easier.

"I know you're busy at the moment, but this is the sort of case you want to get. The good news is that it's a contained case, almost a locked room mystery. A Japanese man was killed this morning in what appears to be an improvised attack – he was stabbed in the neck with a pen."

"Wow," Sally responded involuntarily. While she knew pretty much anything could be used as a weapon this was the first case she'd had where a pen had been the murder weapon.

"And there are five witnesses. And we are confident that one of them did it, since the Japanese man's screams attracted people to the scene. We think they got there so quickly that the killer pretended to be offering assistance," Sergeant Pan said.

Sally could see why it would be an interesting case.

"But don't most people ignore cries for help?" she asked.

"Yes but this is the unusual bit about the case. The murder occurred in dense bushland, meaning that they could not see each other, or, unfortunately, the murder taking place. So they each thought that they were the only ones who could respond and they did," replied the Sergeant.

"Interesting," said Sally.

"I told you, you would like this one. Plus all five witnesses are waiting to give statements. The Constables who brought them in are just requesting a detective to join them for the interviews. So off you go," Sergeant Pan said.

"Ok," Sally replied positively.

Half an hour later, Sally went back to her Sergeant. She knocked on her office door and walked in hesitantly.

"You know the straightforward, easy case you gave me this morning, well I'm stumped," she admitted.

"What?" Sergeant Pan said in surprise. "What's the problem?"

"Well, they all say that they found the man bleeding out and dying. He was barely conscious when they found him and the only word they could make out from what he said was 'Subaru.' I have checked and none of them drive a Subaru vehicle, so I am really not sure who to suspect. They all said that they heard the cries and ran to the scene. They all arrived at roughly the same time. Three of them clearly heard the word Subaru, but as I said that seems to be a dead end," stated Sally quietly.

"Ok then. How about I give you some assistance on this?" Sergeant Pan asked.

Sally nodded, pleased that the Sergeant was willing to personally help her with the case.

"Detective Thomas is back on normal duties, so I will assign him to help you," continued Sergeant Pan. Sally tried not to show her disappointment that she had misunderstood Wendy's statement or that Brad would be the one helping her.

"Give him a chance. He is getting better," Sergeant Pan said, as she motioned for Sally to go.

###

That morning Brad was ten minutes late for work rather than the half hour early he had been for the last few weeks. His ear was stinging but not bandaged when he walked into the station. He wanted nothing more than to get a coffee and sit quietly at his desk for a few minutes. Instead, he was summoned straight to Sergeant Pan's office.

"Starting late this morning are we?" the Sergeant asked. Brad struggled to tell if she was being sarcastic.

"It's ok," she continued good-naturedly, "I know how hard you have been working lately."

Brad breathed a sigh of relief.

"I didn't call you in here about that, though. There's been a murder that I would like you to help solve."

Sergeant Pan efficiently outlined the circumstances of

the murder and the investigation to date, including that Sally had not made much progress.

"Since you're on normal duties, you are to help out Detective Summers and see if you can make more progress together than she has alone," Sergeant Pan stated.

"Ok," Brad replied as the Sergeant directed him out of the office. Sally met him at the interview rooms and briefed him on what they knew. The five witnesses were a mixed group. There were two teenage students who had been cutting through the parkland to get to school. They were the ones who'd insisted that everyone stay until the police arrived. There was also a short but muscular Australian who reminded Brad of the English 'Chav' and the American 'Redneck.' He was what the Australian's call a 'Bogan' and was wearing shorts, thongs and a sleeveless t-shirt that revealed a Southern Cross tattoo on his right arm. The other two witnesses were a housewife who had been out walking her dog and a French tourist.

Brad thought through the facts as they were known and tried to identify where the conflict was. He was getting used to doing this even though it was not quite what the Professor had discussed. He found that seeking the conflict in a problem was the path to its solution. In the case at hand he could see the conflict was coming from the interpretation of Subaru as referring to a vehicle. He thought about how his interpretation of Greek letters and the Greek word for atheism had changed, shifted and been completely rebuilt, and decided to change how Subaru was being interpreted. Instead of referring to a car, he thought about the symbol that was the company's logo and that the car manufacturer was named after a constellation of stars. Brad put himself in the dying man's shoes and realised that the last thing he saw was stars and so he related it to what he knew, the northern hemisphere constellation of Subaru. But that could also be a misinterpretation of the Southern Cross particularly if your vision was a bit blurry as you were losing consciousness. Brad felt giddy as he realised that the Australian was the killer.

Brad wondered if this was how other detectives felt. *If only I was like this when the stamps were stolen. I would have solved that case easily. The stamps were the only things of value that were taken. It should've been obvious.*

Brad then noticed that the Australian also had some Japanese characters tattooed on his left pectoral muscle, which only became visible when the Australian was leaning forward and Brad could see down his t-shirt. Brad guessed that the characters primed the victim to think of a Japanese phenomenon. The three characters reminded Brad of a martial art tattoo his self-defence instructor had, had when he was at the police academy. If the Australian was a martial artist that would mean he would also know exactly where to strike. Given the location of the stab wound there was a good chance Brad was right.

"I know who did it," Brad said as casually as he could.

"Yeah right," Sally replied.

"No, really," Brad responded.

"Ok then smarty pants, who?" questioned Sally.

"The Australian," Brad said with a grin. He explained

his reasoning. Sally was impressed and felt like she'd underestimated him.

"So what strategy do you think we should use?" Sally asked. "I mean we pretty much have only circumstantial evidence."

Sally was curious to see if Brad would actually come up with a strategy. Brad considered what it would take to get the Australian to confess if he were the murderer. He concluded that the officer should come in as a friend as the killer probably would have an oppositional stance to police officers. The officer should act as though they had proof it was him, for example eyewitness statements, since this could be possible given the circumstances. The officer should make it seem like they want to help him. This would have the effect of causing conflict and confusion in him, thereby changing how he intended to respond to the police officer. The solution to his confusion should then be presented casually, something along the lines of "so it would make things a lot simpler and reduce your punishment if you confess. This would also give you the opportunity to explain yourself and relieve yourself of the burden of the crime."

The officer should play up that the police understood it was a crime of anger and not premeditated and that they could reduce the degree of the charge, but only if he told them his side of the events. Brad relayed his thoughts to Sally. She listened attentively to his strategy and asked Brad if he would go in and do the questioning, since he knew what was required.

"No. I think you should do it. He looks like he would have a hard time confessing his sins to a man. I hate to play the gender card, but I think it needs to be a woman for the strategy to work, so you will have to do it," Brad said.

"Ok," said Sally reluctantly. She took a few deep breaths, replayed the strategy in her mind and told herself that it would work. She breezed into the room and greeted the Australian like an old friend.

Five minutes later she had the Australian in tears and the confession she was after. Sally excused herself from the interview room saying "that she would just get the statement typed up" for the Australian to sign. She only just managed to conceal her grin as she exited the room. When she saw Brad she was compelled to hug him.

"Thank you! That worked beautifully," Sally enthused.

"That's ok," Brad replied as nonchalantly as possible. Inside he was mentally jumping up and down with excitement. He thought about how he had just created conflict in order to produce change and realised how useful that would be for him as a strategy in the future.

Sally knocked on Sergeant Pan's door. The Sergeant opened the door in one swift motion.

"Sergeant, I…" Sally began.

"How have you gone on the case?" Sergeant Pan interrupted.

"That's the thing, we've solved it and even got a confession!" Sally replied triumphantly.

"Well done, see I knew you could do it," Sergeant Pan replied.

"That's the thing, Sergeant. I didn't," Sally admitted.

"What do you mean?" Sergeant Pan said.

Sally explained how Brad had solved the case and

worked out how to get a confession from their suspect.

"That's really good thinking," Sergeant Pan responded, "he really is coming along well."

To herself she thought *maybe we will make a great detective out of him after all*. She was thinking about applying for a Senior Sergeant position that was coming up in a nearby station and that she would have an opportunity to nominate her preferred successor as Sergeant if she was successful. Suddenly it felt like there might be a new contender…

Interchapter

To: The Professor
From: Dr Engels
Subject: I have spoken to Mathew

My Dear Professor,
Unfortunately, my conversation with Mathew did not go well, he is determined to find a way to spread the program. We argued extensively and there was no way of changing his mind. I told him that I would find a way to stop him, equally he told me he would find a way to succeed. So we shall have to wait and see who triumphs. I will be out of contact for the next month as my next commission must be absolutely untraceable. It will be quite a change to be 'radio silent' for a while.
In the interim, keep working on the next level and the activities to stimulate neural growth. I will be in touch as soon as I get back.
Warm Regards,
Dr Engels

Act Three: Chapter One

The next few months were a whirlwind for Brad. His success rate at solving cases improved and was developing a reputation as being a good person to ask for advice. Detective Taupo had even started saying 'not bad for a country boy' and smiling at him. Constable Paul had attended a few crime scenes with Brad and started to look to him as a mentor and Brad felt more confident than he ever had in his life. His relationship with Amy helped cement the feeling that he was truly living up to his father's motto and making a mark on each day. Both his and Amy's parents had seen the happiness each brought to the other's life and had given their blessing to the relationship. No one objected when Amy and Brad moved in together.

The Federal police had left and declared that they'd solved what the media had dubbed "the Melting Brain Affair." Their announcement that "it was a natural reaction of brain chemicals that occurred in a few select individuals due to their consumption of a placebo that tricked their brains into a state of hyper-stimulation," had riled Brad. Daniel had nodded sagely while holding the press conference and implied that this understanding was purely a result of the Federal officers' work. He did not mention how Dr Engels had run rings around him or how the agents had not discovered anything that wasn't already known to the local Police department. The "Melting Brain Affair" was declared closed and given a token paragraph in the papers. The journalists conducting their own inquiry had not uncovered anything to alarm the public or supersede the official investigation. The public had mostly moved on, especially after the deaths stopped occurring and it didn't seem like something that could be caught. There was still a small online following that promoted conspiracy theories and existed through blogs and tweets, but for the most part the story had died.

Brad was attending a crime scene one morning when he received a call from Dr Engels. Brad recognised the voice immediately, despite having only a small amount of contact with him since he had reached level nine.

"Good morning Detective. How are you?" Dr Engels asked.

"Fine," Brad replied automatically, then realising that Dr Engels deserved more than a rote response continued "actually, I'm better than fine. My life is great at the moment."

He looked around at the horrific crime scene in front of him, but his assessment did not change.

"I'm very pleased to hear it," Dr Engels said warmly.

"What can I do for you today?" Brad asked.

"Well, I just want to confirm a couple of things since I am having some trouble with one of our members," said Dr Engels.

"Ok, fire away."

"First, just wanting to confirm that you deleted any files you copied from the Professor's computer and that his computer is safely in your police department's storage facility?"

"That is correct," Brad responded.

"Excellent," replied Dr Engels. "Secondly, you did not make any other copies that you still have?"

"No, I had made a copy onto my home computer, but deleted them a while ago." Brad responded.

"Thank you. You have been most helpful." Dr Engels replied and then hung up. Brad was confused. He would have expected more conversation from him but he did not have time to dwell on it as he was required to deal with a distraught father who had just attacked and more than likely killed a neighbour who had indecently assaulted his daughter.

A week later Brad received a call early in the morning when he was on his way to the station and told not to bother coming in. Instead he was to go straight to a crime scene at a nearby residence. Sergeant Pan sounded distracted as she gave him the assignment, but Brad had heard rumours she had applied for a promotion, so he wondered if she had been successful. As he arrived at the crime scene his phone rang again.

"Good morning Detective. How are you?" Brad recognised the same friendly tone of Dr Engels that he'd spoken to the previous week.

"Still great, just like last week," Brad replied warmly.

"I'm very pleased to hear it," Dr Engels said pleasantly, "But that is an odd turn of phrase, how would I know what you were like last week?"

"Well, we spoke last week, when you phoned me," Brad replied with amusement.

"I'm sorry, I did what?" Dr Engels said sounding alarmed.

"You phoned me last week," Brad replied, sounding less sure than before.

"I can assure you that I did not… Wait, what did we talk about?"

"Uh, the Professor's files and what happened to them," Brad replied.

"What specifically did you say to me?" Dr Engel's asked sounding concerned.

"That I had deleted them and that the Professor's computer was in our storage centre."

"Ok. Please let me finish what I have to say before responding," Dr Engels said.

"Ok," replied Brad.

"I was calling to say that I had heard a report that your home was broken into last night. I wanted first of all to check that you were alright and then to check that nothing related to the Program or especially copies of the program were stolen. I did not phone you last week and our last contact was a month ago when you called in for a coffee. This concerns me greatly. You may talk now," Dr Engels said.

"Someone broke into my apartment?" Brad asked incredulously.

"Yes," replied Dr Engels.

"Do you know who?" Brad asked.

"Maybe. I would guess that it was an associate of Mathew Arnold who was looking for your computer to get the Professor's files," said Dr Engels.

"He was the one you were arguing with about the Program."

Brad was good with names, something that he had developed through occupational necessity.

"Yes. A couple of weeks ago we had quite a heated argument about it. If we weren't such gentlemen, we would have come to blows. He wanted me to give him a complete version of the program that could be duplicated. I refused and told him I would never give him one and that even if I wanted to the Professor had the only set that was not copy protected. The Professor's computer authorised each new enrolment and sent them the files when it was online. This was a necessary check and balance for the Program, we had to control it as Emily and I have explained to you. My, our, point of view is that the Program should continue to be supported as it is and you are the last member we will admit. Anyway, as a result of our conflict Mathew resigned from FONT, I'll forward you the email. He also shouted that I could not control him, nor stop him from doing what he wanted with the Program and that he would find a way of obtaining one," Dr Engels said matter-of-factly.

"But I only have or had the first six levels. What's the point in only having those?"

"He needs them so that even without the Professor's computer he could make a start with his plans to distribute the program more widely. If he could get both, that would be even better, plus level twelve might be recoverable from the Professor's email program. The rest he could readily replicate on his own."

"Well why doesn't he just make new videos?" Brad asked.

"Good question, the short answer is that he basically started at level seven so he does not know exactly what is in them. Besides he would want to be able to sell them as the authentic program."

"But surely he could get that from other members or the mailing list?"

"It would create suspicion for him to ask for them, plus if they are on the list then their copies have played their one time. But then there is also the long answer: Mathew and the Professor were friends for decades and neighbours until the Professor's wife passed and he downsized his home. Their families were very close and he would think that distributing the program as the Professor created it, would be a way of honouring his friend and creating a shared legacy. It's similar to my motivation for continuing the administration of the program – it's my way of honouring the Professor. He was a great friend to both of us. However, I encouraged the Professor to not allow Mathew access to any more levels after Level Eleven and Mathew has been a bit upset with me since then. So I imagine that his ultimate goal is to get Level Twelve for himself."

"And so Mathew thought he could get levels one to six from me?" Brad asked.

"Yes, and maybe a clue about Level Twelve." replied Dr Engels.

"Why?"

"Well what did you tell him? He probably had a voice

analyser verifying what you said."

"I said that I had deleted the files from my home and work computer and that the Professor's computer was in storage. Which is true," Brad replied.

"Ah that must be it, he must have been looking for your computer," said Dr Engels.

"But I deleted the files," Brad protested.

"Surely you know that pressing delete does not actually remove the file from your computer? Mathew must have thought he could get your computer, restore the files and then copy them," Dr Engels responded.

"I do know that, which is why I used a shredding program that completely removed any trace of the files and copied over the space thirty-one times," Brad said with a hint of smugness.

"Oh, that was good thinking," Dr Engels said, sounding impressed, "so it was a waste of his energy and effort."

He chuckled in amusement. "Serves him right," he said under his breath.

"How could someone phone me and sound exactly like you?" asked Brad.

"Remember Eliza?" queried Dr Engels.

"Yes, of course," replied Brad.

"The technology that I used to create her, was not created in isolation. Meaning that I had help and the person who helped me was Mathew. My skill was in designing the chip that she is housed on and some of the software. Mathew designed the speech analyser."

"Oh," Brad said quietly.

"Did anything strike you as odd about the conversation?" asked Dr Engels.

"Actually yes, it was very abrupt, since I joined FONT I'm used to you being more talkative."

"That was probably due to him not having the variety of language on file to sustain a conversation without you becoming suspicious. I mean think about when you spoke to Eliza, it was only after you had spoken to her for a while that something in her speech jarred with your expectation and you figured out she was a machine," Dr Engels said confidently.

"How did you know that is how it happened?" Brad said, amazed at Dr Engels.

"That's how it happens for everyone. Well, except for the smarty pants who understand why she is called Eliza. We want people who would persist when faced with a challenge. It's important for the next step," he said.

"Huh?" Brad replied.

"I'm guessing you solved the riddle of Athena's gift from the tattoo you saw on the *melting brain bodies*," Dr Engels said the phrase with derision, "… and not the level six file and that you never realised that if you played around with the colour and contrast settings of your monitor when you were at FONT's homepage, you would find a hidden copy of the pansy image? Dr Engels continued.

"Huh," Brad said again, as he realised how other people were able to join FONT.

"Don't worry, we are getting distracted. Mathew is becoming dangerous, given that he is resorting to breaking and entering in order to obtain the files. How secure is your storage department?" asked Dr Engels.

"Very. It's guarded, alarmed and offsite. I mean once a case has gone cold or been closed the evidence is moved to an offsite location. He wouldn't know where that is." Brad replied.

"Actually the site is listed on the police department's website, along with a warning that it is not where you should report crimes," said Dr Engels.

"Really?" Brad responded.

"Yes. You might want to give them a heads up that they may be about to be robbed." Dr Engels suggested.

"You really think he would break in there?" Brad asked incredulously.

"No. I think he would be much smarter about it," said Dr Engels.

"What do you mean?" Brad asked.

"Let me put it this way, if I was going to rob it, I would verify the procedures and requirements to gain access and then gain access."

"Yeah but we wouldn't just tell you that," Brad replied.

"No, *you* wouldn't, but did you know the Police department has a media liaison officer who reviews scripts and provides feedback on accuracy of procedures. They even loan out genuine uniforms, squad cars and will even block off streets for you if you ask nicely and pay a small to exorbitant fee," Dr Engels said.

Brad shook his head in disbelief. "There's no way."

"I'll give you a moment, look it up." Dr Engels challenged Brad.

Brad moved his phone from his ear to in front of him and put it on speakerphone. A few clicks took him to the police department's website. Sure enough there was a "media liaison" link detailing all the services Dr Engels had just described.

"Wow," he said after a moment.

"So what I would do is get them to make sure I knew exactly what to do. I would get an associate I could reasonably distance myself from to undertake the actual task and get him or her to get the evidence for me," Dr Engels said, as though he had given the idea much thought.

"But…" Brad was about to protest when he thought about how the person at the desk at the storage centre would not know who was a real or fake police officer and if they had the correct uniform, badge and car the thief would be able to walk straight in and back out without anyone feeling even a modicum of suspicion. There was a strong possibility that no one would ever know a crime had been committed. It was a genius plan.

"Sure it would cost a bit to set up, but really it would be quite effective. The only difficulty would be knowing which evidence boxes to ask for. But that could be solved with either hacking the Police's internal database or stealing your computer which would probably have the information on it," Dr Engels continued.

"But my computer wasn't at home, in fact I don't even live there anymore, I moved out two weeks ago and sublet it to someone else," said Brad.

"Why?" asked Dr Engels.

"To move in with my girlfriend," Brad replied with a smile.

"Congratulations," Dr Engels said with sincerity, "that is a big step for a relationship… I know Mathew well and he would triple check things, so I take it you have moved in with her rather than signing a lease on a new place?"

"Yes," Brad replied, "But we are also looking at getting a bigger place together."

"You might want to call the storage facility and ask them to put a hold on giving access to the particular boxes of evidence. Knowing Mathew, he would want all the original copies of the program that existed, otherwise he would not have a monopoly on them. So he probably would have planned for all the copies to be stolen as close together as possible. And knowing him he has probably been planning this for a month or two; his phone call to you was just to confirm that there were no more copies available…"

"Ok, I'll have to do it when I get to the office, I don't have access to my desktop with the box numbers now," said Brad.

"Please be as quick as possible," Dr Engels implored.

"I will. I'll see if I can get someone else to cover this case and get back to the station ASAP," said Brad.

"Excellent. Thank you, Brad. I do appreciate it, until next time." Dr Engels said warmly.

"Bye," Brad replied.

Brad hung up the phone and looked at the scene in front of him. Despite his urge to get to the station, he felt compelled to at least give the scene a quick look over. He was pleased to see that Constable Paul had been allowed to go on a call out. Detective Taupo was with him. Brad realised he had been sent here to delay him from discovering the news about the break in to his home.

Brad greeted them both warmly and then joked to Paul, "It's good to see you out from behind the desk."

"Yeah I think I've mastered the arts of signing stat

decs and certifying photocopies. It was time for a bigger challenge," Paul replied with a laugh.

Brad looked around. In the doorway of a brand new home there was a gunshot victim who was wearing nothing but shorts. The house employed all the latest building technologies. It had solar panels, double glazed windows and a fake lawn to save water. There was a tattoo of a gun on the torso of the victim that showed clearly against his white skin. It seemed to Brad that in a heated moment the tattoo would look like a real gun and could be used to threaten an attacker or scare them off. In this instance though it seemed as though it must have provoked someone to shoot him, maybe in self-defence. The person who had done the shooting was in handcuffs and could be heard saying that he was sure the victim had drawn a gun on him and that he'd shot him to protect himself. *It was a reasonable argument*, Brad thought.

Brad asked Detective Taupo for an overview of what had happened. It seemed that the victim, Tony, was a drug dealer and informant to Detective Taupo. Despite his vocation, the Detective Taupo liked Tony due to the leads and information he provided. The suspect was named John and he had only one prior record for possession. When he'd been arrested for that charge he had become violent with the officer in question and it was only through a plea bargain that saw him plead guilty to the possession charge that the assault was dropped.

Brad went over to speak to John.

"Hi my name is Detective Thomas. You were involved in some unfortunate circumstances today. Are

232

you able to give me your version of events?" Brad said calmly, working hard to build rapport with the man.

"Yes, I knew Tony," John said indicating the body, "he sold me dope from time to time. Anyway I came over to get some from him and heard a lot of shouting and yelling as I approached the house."

John seemed keen to tell his story.

"When I got closer it had gone quiet. I came around to the front from over there."

John indicated he had walked beside the side fence of the house to approach.

"As I say it had gone quiet, so I thought it would still be ok to ring the doorbell. When I did I heard Tony scream 'you have some nerve coming back here, I'll kill you, you know.' He flung open the door and it looked like he was reaching for a gun so I drew mine and shot him."

Brad thought about the story. It was plausible, but seemed a little too neat. John had even confessed to buying drugs, which was the opposite of what he'd expect a suspect to say. It was almost as though he was trying to convince Brad he was telling the truth and probably figured that a misdemeanour charge would be infinitely preferable to murder. It was like he'd worked out his own plea bargain already. Brad thought about how he could get more information out of him, without tipping him off to his suspicions.

"So who was Tony arguing with?" He asked warmly, giving the impression that he was just trying to get the facts. The friendliness and lack of hostility made it seem as though he believed John and did not doubt the story.

"I don't know," John replied.

"Male, female?" Brad questioned.

"Female," John said after a pause. Something about John's eyes looking up and to his right, made Brad sure he was lying.

"And what were they arguing about?" Brad asked gently.

"Apparently he had sold her some bad drugs and she was upset about it, she was yelling that she would tell the world about his snitching. He did that you know," John replied.

Brad got the impression he was projecting his own story onto what Brad guessed was a fictional woman.

"So you could hear them clearly?" Brad continued.

"Yes, they were yelling really loudly," John said emphatically.

"Did you recognise the voice or hear a name?" asked Brad.

"No, she must have left as I came up and gone that way." There was a path that lead in the opposite direction to where John had approached from, which made this plausible.

Brad called over Detective Taupo and Paul and asked Tony to repeat his story. He listened carefully as John repeated that he had heard arguing and had approached the house anyway and that he had mistakenly shot Tony in self-defence.

"So you approached the house even though you could hear an argument?" Brad asked, maintaining the warmth in his voice.

"Yes, I really wanted to buy some drugs," John said, without hesitation.

"Ok, so you are willing to accept that we have to

charge you for that?" Brad said sounding reluctant.

"Yes. I guess so," John, said with a hint of enthusiasm.

"Constable Paul would you kindly write up a misdemeanour charge for this man for attempting to purchase an illegal substance," Brad said as though he was sorry for having to say it.

"Ok." Paul quickly read him his rights.

John almost looked pleased at the charge. Brad looked him in the eye and continued, "And also charge him with the premeditated murder of Tony."

John, Paul and Detective Taupo looked shocked.

"Why?" they all asked in unison. Brad knew he had his man. An innocent person would have said that they "didn't do it," but guilty people wanted to know what gave them away. Brad continued to look at John.

"John, take a look at the house. Every window is shut and according to your story so was the front door when you approached. This house is built to the latest energy efficiency standards, which means double glazed windows, in wall and in ceiling insulation and brick outer walls. These features are great at keeping heat in or the sun out of a house and also do the same for noise. In other words, there is no way you could have heard an argument that occurred inside the house. I put it to you that it was you he sold the bad drugs to and that you wanted revenge," Brad said matter-of-factly.

The guilty look in John's eyes told the policemen that Brad's version of events was correct.

"Ok, I did it but it he deserved it. He should not be able to get away with selling rubbish." John cursed Tony loudly. He launched into a tirade about why Tony deserved what he got for being a snitch and how he had done the world a favour. Once John was safely in the squad car, Brad quietly pulled Detective Taupo aside and asked if he would mind finishing up the processing. Detective Taupo agreed and said, "I think I'm going to have to start calling you city boy. That was good."

Brad was not quite sure how to take the compliment, so he smiled, said 'thank you' and quickly walked back to his car.

I can't believe that worked. Who knew philosophy could have practical applications? Brad thought to himself while grinning wryly.

Since his initiation to Level Nine, Brad had started formal study of philosophy through a night course at the University. He'd convinced Amy to do it with him and it gave them their first 'couple' activity. It also meant that on the days when they had their evening classes, Amy caught the bus in to the University and Brad drove them home together. Brad had been particularly taken by one of the concepts covered in the class - the idea of fallacies. Since reading about them he'd started trying to use them to make better decisions in his life and work. In particular he had enjoyed the concept of the straw man fallacy, which he recognised as being frequently used by opinion piece writers. In effect, Brad had just used this technique to make John confess. The straw man involves a pattern of argument where Person A has a particular belief about something. Person B presents a superficially similar belief - belief Y. This belief is a distorted version of the original argument and can be more readily attacked, leading to the conclusion that the original belief is flawed. The fault in logic is that the original

236

belief has never actually been attacked.

Brad had just made it seem as though the core of John's argument was hearing a fight when it was really that he felt threatened. Brad had made a single aspect represent John's whole story, which he successfully countered, making it seem as though this meant that his entire version of events was false. If John had been smarter he would have seen that finding a flaw with one aspect of his story did not alter the idea that he'd felt threatened and was defending himself. Brad laughed. This was the first time he could remember feeling intellectually superior to someone. The sobering reminder was that the straw man argument was also the main one used by politicians to discredit their opponents or justify reasons for changing an opinion.

Once he was seated in his car, Brad took out his phone and called the station. He asked to speak to Sergeant Pan.

"Ah Detective. How are you going?" she said as though she was waiting to hear from him.

"It turned out that it was murder not self-defence. I managed to get the perpetrator to confess. Detective Taupo is bringing him in now," Brad said absently.

"Good work. How did you get the confession?" Sergeant Pan asked curiously. This wasn't what she was expecting him to say.

Brad quickly explained his reasoning and tactics omitting the information about the straw man and followed up with "but that is not why I am calling."

"I guess you have heard about what else happened this morning?" Sergeant Pan said, sounding unsurprised that he wanted to discuss something else.

"Yes, someone broke into my apartment. Or at least the apartment I used to live in," Brad stated simply.

"What do you mean?" Sergeant Pan asked.

"I moved in with my girlfriend a couple of weeks ago. Someone else lives there now," replied Brad.

"Oh," Sergeant Pan responded, sounding a little surprised, "so how did you hear about it?"

"A neighbour," Brad said vaguely, "what did they take?"

"Your, I mean their computer and portable hard drives, two TVs and a coffee machine," Sergeant Pan replied. Brad thought back to what Dr Engels had said they might be after.

"Hmmm," Brad mumbled aloud to himself.

"Obviously you cannot investigate this, since you have a connection to the case, but do you have any thoughts as to who might have done it? I mean it could be random, but we can't discount it being targeted simply because it's your old apartment. I'm sorry I couldn't tell you about it earlier and had to stop you coming into the office, but as you know there are procedures to follow," Sergeant Pan stated.

"Actually I do have an idea as to what they were after. You remember the Professor, Leviathan and that whole saga?" Brad asked.

"You mean the melting brain affair, of course I remember it," Sergeant Pan replied distastefully.

"One of the things that came up in that case was that someone was trying to locate the original files of the Professor's program and that they were prepared to go to great lengths to get it. Nothing came of it during the investigation, but perhaps they finally thought of a way

238

to get it, namely stealing my computer in case I had a copy on there," said Brad.

"And did you?" Sergeant Pan asked abruptly.

"No. But then it wasn't my computer anyway," Brad said with a smile.

"So do you know who this person is?"

"I can't confirm who they are yet, but let's take this as a working hypothesis and ask what they would do now that they had failed to get a copy from me. I think they may even be desperate enough to break into our storage facility to get the Professor's computer from the boxes of evidence," Brad said.

Sergeant Pan made a noise to indicate she was following his reasoning.

"In which case, we need to alert the facility to not let anyone check out or view the evidence from that case. In fact I was about to head in to get the box numbers from my computer, in order to do that. I can't access them from here. Can you do that for me and give them a call?" Brad asked, realising he was talking to Sergeant Pan as though she were an equal. He was not used to feeling like he was on par with people at his own level, let alone a superior officer and he enjoyed the sensation of feeling respected.

"Ok," Sergeant Pan said, amused that Brad was giving her orders, "I'll get right onto it. How far away are you?"

"Probably seventeen minutes," Brad said.

"I'll see you then," the Sergeant replied. As she hung up on Brad, she realised that he was demonstrating the characteristics of a leader.

Sergeant Pan was not the sort of person who would wait by the door for someone, nevertheless, she was doing a good impression of it when Brad arrived at the station. He was escorted straight to her office and asked to sit down. For a change the Sergeant sat in the chair next to Brad rather than on the other side of the desk.

"Detective Thomas, let's put aside the break in at your old home for the moment."

Brad nodded in agreement.

"When I phoned the storage facility to ask them not to allow anyone to access the boxes and to alert me if they tried, everything started well. Unfortunately, they then said for me to hang on a moment as those numbers were familiar," Sergeant Pan said. Brad nodded again, indicating he wanted her to continue.

"Then they said that the boxes had been examined yesterday morning," Sergeant Pan stated quietly. Despite suspecting that this might be the case, Brad was still a little surprised by the revelation.

"I have asked for the footage from the evidence room to be sent over."

They looked over at the Sergeant's computer as if they were expecting it to ping on cue.

"When I asked them about who had requested the box, they scanned and emailed me the login sheet and claimed that they had checked the person's ID and that they had arrived in a squad car and standard uniform," Sergeant Pan said.

The computer suddenly pinged.

"Hmm, thirty seconds too late," Sergeant Pan said. They both gave each other a cautious smile.

A moment later they watched the video file that was

streaming to the computer. It showed a man in police uniform walking from the evidence warehouse to the viewing room. He was trailed by another officer who was wheeling a trolley with four large boxes on it, who put the trolley in the room and then left. Inside the viewing room, the man in police uniform took out his laptop and placed it on the desk. He opened the first box and almost immediately opened the second. It was clear he was searching for something in particular. The Professor's computer was in the second box, the man pulled it out and placed it on the desk. He then moved around the desk, temporarily blocking the line of sight of the camera to the computer. He sat down on the other side of the desk and opened the computer. He appeared to look at it for a while, then put it away closed the box and called for the duty officer to return the boxes.

"Did you see that he switched the computers? You can tell that was the purpose of the visit since that model is not Police issue. Plus what could he possibly be looking at? I mean the computer has been in storage for months. There is no way there is any charge left in its batteries," Brad said, mostly to himself.

"I think I did." Sergeant Pan rewound the video and they watched carefully. The two computers were the same model and the switch carried out expertly. It was clear that the person knew exactly where the camera was in the room. They watched several more times. Thankfully the resolution on the camera was high and in colour.

"But how can we prove it?" asked Sergeant Pan.

They watched the video again.

"Take a look at the SD card slot," Brad said quietly

but urgently. They watched the video again. As the man moved from one side of the desk to the other a memory card disappeared from the computer on the left side of the desk.

"At least we have proof that he swapped them or took something from the evidence box," Brad said quietly.

"Yes, but who is he? And which police station does he work for," Sergeant Pan asked.

Brad thought about where he could have come from.

"I would guess that he's an actor," said Brad.

"Huh?" Sergeant Pan said in surprise.

"Well let me put it this way, we don't recognise him. Only four stations store their evidence at that location. Why not run his picture through our database. I would bet that there is no match for any officer in any of them, despite him being naggingly familiar," Brad said.

Sergeant Pan extracted the image of the man's face and inserted it into their facial recognition program. This gave her a moment to think. She realised the flaw in Brad's idea. *And he was so close to making it sound plausible* she thought to herself.

"Let's say you're right. Aren't you forgetting something?" Sergeant Pan asked.

"What?" He asked.

"Well, he arrived in a genuine squad car, was wearing a real uniform and had a real ID badge," Sergeant Pan said trying not to gloat.

"True, but we probably gave them to him," Brad said, just managing not to smile.

"What do you mean?" she asked.

Brad outlined the theory about the theft being planned by someone and then set-up via a media liaison officer.

"And if I'm right it also provides us with a lead. I mean all we would have to do is talk to the media person and see what services they have been providing recently. I would bet that there is a script they have been helping with for a cold case type show," Brad said.

"Ok then," said Sergeant Pan, admiring the scientific approach Brad was taking. He had put forward an idea based on circumstantial evidence, but then proposed a testable hypothesis that would provide support or opposition to the idea.

The database pinged. No match was found.

"It looks like the first hurdle for your theory has been passed. Why don't you get in touch with the liaison officer and see what you can find out. In the meantime, let's keep this quiet. If you're right then the less suspicions we can arouse the better," Sergeant Pan said.

"Agreed," Brad took the hint and left quickly.

Sergeant Pan was impressed at the creativity that Brad had displayed in order to generate the lead about who had robbed the storage facility. He was really developing exponentially at the moment and was displaying the reasoning that would make him an excellent Sergeant. Her promotion to Senior Sergeant would take another seven weeks to process, during which she had been asked to nominate up to three candidates to sit their Sergeant's examinations. For the first month after Brad had transferred, she was sure he would never move beyond being Detective. He was now at the top of her list for promotion. *I'll have to talk to him later*, she thought.

Chapter Two

Mathew Arnold surveyed his surroundings. His apartment and offices were the equivalent of Ivory Tower, except on the other side of the street. His building's official name was Franklin Plaza but it was more commonly called Ebony Tower due to its proximity to Ivory Tower and black exterior. Mathew took off his shoes and scrunched the plush carpet with his feet. It was an old habit that he used to ground himself before big events. And he was about to experience the biggest event of his life. Not only did he now have the Professor's computer and more importantly the program's files, but he would also have access to Level Twelve, which he had been denied until this point. He was pleased that his two pronged attack to locate the files had worked and that the months of planning had been worthwhile. He'd doubted that he would be able to get the files from Detective Thomas, so he'd decided to go after the source as well. It was a bold strategy that had worked perfectly. His agent had performed brilliantly and swapped the computers without a hitch. Mathew was excited by the perfection of the plan; no one knew anything had been taken.

He plugged in the computer and turned it on. Mathew was unsurprised to find that it was password protected. In fact he was prepared for it. He had hacked the University's IT department and discovered the Professor's password. It had taken him nearly half an hour, which indicated that the University had good security.

It took Mathew next to no time to find the folder with the files in it. Mathew had effectively started at level seven when he joined FONT, so he had to work through the program like a novice, albeit with the advantage of some understanding of what was in each level. He was able to open the first couple of files without difficulty, but was briefly stuck with the password for level three. When Mathew viewed the first three levels, he was surprised by their lack of significance and insight and realised how it was the program as a whole and the connections that the users of the program had to make that was genius. Just enough had been left out to make people work for their understanding and that made all the difference to the success of the program. As Mathew watched and read each file he could see the steady progression of thought in each. It was a refreshing reminder for him of the thought journey he had been on throughout his life. The journey had set him on the path he now found himself, ready to change the world and become extraordinarily wealthy at the same time.

The next two levels took him another half an hour to

unlock. He found himself stuck on level six, which frustrated him since he needed to check them all. After two hours he gave up and decided to work on his marketing strategy for the program. He knew the existing two thousand dollar price tag was too much for most people and although making money was the main goal of his acquisition of the program, he also wanted it to be distributed widely. He decided to set the price at four hundred and ninety-nine dollars. He kept having the nagging thought that even though this would make the program accessible to people, it would not change the world.

###

Brad tried phoning the media liaison officer but was told that the officer was out on set today and would be out of contact until tomorrow. He sent the officer an email saying that he needed to speak with him as soon as possible.

As Brad was driving home he thought about an email that Dr Engels had forwarded him. It was from Mathew to Dr Engels and had simply read:

Dear Carl,

I am afraid that I cannot agree with you on the position you have taken over The Program. I believe the Professor would want it to continue to expand and that us making a reasonable but not outrageous profit from it is also perfectly ethical and rational. Since you will not support me to achieve this, with regret, I must renounce my membership of FONT. I hope we can remain friends.
Yours,
Mathew
Arnold.

Brad was disproportionately excited to discover Dr Engels first name. As he was smiling to himself and picturing the email, it struck him that how Mathew had signed off was odd. Brad could not get the phrase 'Yours Mathew Arnold' out of his mind. As he pictured it he realised that it was the capital letters that bugged him. They spelt Amy backwards. Brad pulled over the car. *Amy. Could Amy be Mathew Arnold?* The idea seemed ridiculous. *Mathew Arnold was a man, wasn't he?* But Amy knew about the program and had become close to him when he was investigating the case and she even admitted to putting on a display to attract him. Brad acknowledged it had worked brilliantly, he was smitten by her. Amy also had the drive and the ambition to seek higher levels of authority and influence, which was a Level Eight or Nine quality.

Maybe she knew more than she was letting on? Brad tried to dismiss the thought that she was Mathew but couldn't. He reasoned that even if she wasn't, when he looked at their history from this perspective it seemed highly suspicious.

And besides, isn't this how I wished I had thought in the stamp case? Plus, Sally also thought it was suspicious that Amy had become involved with me. Brad told himself again that he was being silly, but in the end he decided that he'd have to investigate the thought and that would mean making a detour to the pet shop on the way home.

Brad arrived home before Amy and started making dinner. She breezed in a short while later and gave him a long welcome-me-home kiss. Brad soon served the salsa stuffed chicken with peas and roasted carrot, capsicum and potato that he'd made. They sat at the kitchen bench as they ate. During dinner Brad told Amy that he'd been called into Sergeant Pan's office just before leaving.

"What did she want this time? Did she give you another case?" Amy asked curiously.

"No she didn't. She said that she'd been told that she was going to be promoted to Senior Sergeant and that her position as Sergeant would be available soon," Brad said, stopping short of the full story.

"Why would she call you into her office to tell you that?" Amy asked, while looking him in the eye and touching his hand.

"So that she could also say that she would like me to sit my Sergeant exams so that I could go for her job," Brad said with a smile.

"What did you say to that?" Amy asked, her eyes widening.

"That I was flattered that she felt me worthy of the role and that I would be delighted to attempt the exams. I perhaps should've given it more thought because the next sitting is in two weeks, right around the time our assignment for Uni is due," Brad said, realising how busy he was going to be for the next fortnight.

"Don't be silly, you'll do fine at both. So, do you have the revision materials for the Sergeant's exam?" Amy asked confidently.

"Yes," Brad said, pointing to two large folders on their dining table.

"Well then. How about I clear up the dishes and you do an hour or so of study?"

Brad nodded in agreement. Their interaction felt so natural that Brad found it hard to believe she could be deceiving him.

"And don't worry, I'll do all the cooking until then, I don't mind eating a little bit later, if it means that you are able to do some extra study. Just make sure you use the time for study, ok?" Amy said.

Brad nodded again. He was grateful that Amy was so supportive of him, but now that his suspicions of her had been aroused, he could not help but see this as a means for him to become more endeared to her. Brad dutifully went and sat at their desk with the intent of starting to study. He found himself distracted by Amy clearing the table. The way her hips moved as she held a plate in each hand and walked from the dining area to the kitchen was hypnotic.

An hour later they went to bed. Brad lay awake for an hour until he was sure Amy was asleep and then reached for the torch he had bought at the pet shop on the way home. The torch was a black light that was normally used to detect cat urine, but could also be used to check for ultraviolet ink. He picked it up and turned over to Amy. She was asleep on her side. He turned the torch on and shone it on her ear. From his point of view he could clearly see that nothing was glowing in her ear. She did not have the tattoo on her left side. As he was thinking about a way to get her to turn over she spoke unexpectedly.

"You could just ask me you know?" Amy said as Brad recoiled.

"Ask you what?" he asked, trying to sound innocent.

"If I am a member of FONT or not," she replied sleepily.

"What do you mean?" Brad countered.

"Oh please, when I'm woken by a purple light shining in my eye, it is not really reaching to say that you were trying to check me for one of those tattoos you've spoken so much about," Amy said.

Amy rolled onto her back and shuffled up the bed until she was sitting upright and turned on the bedside light. She paused briefly as if debating whether to talk more or simply let Brad check her other ear. After a moment she used her fingers to brush her hair away from her ear and lay her head on his stomach to let him check her right ear. She made the movement seem trusting and somewhat sensual, which made Brad feel like a fool even before he saw that she didn't have the tattoo. As he turned off the torch Amy pressed her hands against his torso to prop herself up, looked him in the eye and said gently "by the way don't think that I'm not upset that you didn't feel like you could just ask me the question and get an honest answer. Can you tell me, are you checking me because you don't trust me or because you don't think I would be with you unless I had an ulterior motive?"

Brad thought about how to respond. He felt an immediate connection to the second option.

"Yes there is a part of me that says you are too good for me and that our relationship is too good to be true," he replied.

"Good, don't lose that," Amy interrupted with a sleepy smile, as she rested her head on his chest again. Brad involuntarily kissed the top of her head.

"But I also had a silly thought today that your ambition, focus and logic are all consistent with levels of the program that you were not exposed to and then there was a silly thing that your name appeared in reverse order in someone's email sign off and it just got me thinking the wrong way," Brad said.

"Some things are just coincidence you know. I mean if I had not seen you out of the window before you came up to the office, who knows if I would have felt the same about you. And I was only looking out because Mr Horace asked me to see if I could see anyone who looked like they were trying to find our office as he wanted to go home. I'm ambitious, in part because of the fact that the bit of the program I was exposed to, helped me see and determine a pathway, but I was ambitious long before that. I mean you don't do ballet for as long as I did without being a certain type of person," Amy said, looking up at him. Brad nodded. He realised that Amy had never lied to him and felt stupid for the first time in months.

"You will have to make up your betrayal to me in some way that I will determine later," Amy continued light heartedly, "…maybe take me away for a weekend somewhere, I'm not sure. But for now I'm going back to sleep."

Amy rolled off him, turned off the light and curled back up to go to sleep. Brad noted that she dropped almost straight back to sleep, a sure sign she was unfazed by his suspicion. For Brad, sleep took another forty-seven minutes to achieve.

Chapter Three

Brad was pleased to be able to get into work the next morning. His case load was light and he hoped to have time to sneak in more study for his Sergeant's exam. He was in early enough to brew a fresh pot of coffee for everyone. Five minutes before his shift was due to start, his phone rang. Brad sighed, reminded himself to send a message to Amy that he was sorry for his brain fade the previous day and answered the phone. It was Peter, the media liaison officer returning his call.

"Hi Peter, thank you for returning my call so promptly. I was just wondering if you were helping anyone with a TV show at the moment and what things you have been working on recently?" Brad asked.

"Sure, I'm currently an advisor on four TV shows, reviewing two books for accuracy in police procedures and have about three scripts for movies I'm checking," Peter said proudly. Brad got the impression that Peter thought he was more important than he really was.

252

"Tell me about the TV shows," Brad asked.

Peter mentioned two that were well known and had been on TV for a few years. Brad discounted them. Then there were two new shows. One was set in a futuristic society where police officers had a robot companion that could process crime scene evidence, meaning all the forensics were done on the spot and the other was a cold case show that saw old cases get re-examined by a new police officer to try and solve them.

"That last one sounds interesting," Brad began, "can you tell me more about it and who is behind it?"

"It's some new guy. It's called *Thaw*. The guy has bags of money and is adamant about getting all the details right. I mean who really cares if a cop draws his gun the wrong way or does part of the investigation on his own rather than with a partner as long as the story is good?" Peter said as though he should be in charge of it.

"Uh huh," Brad replied.

"I told him there were too many of that type of show on TV already. But he didn't listen to me and said that his show would be different. It would feature a principal cast of six actors who change roles each week, so one of them would be the good guy one week and the bad guy the next. One would be the Sergeant one week, then Detective the next and so on. I told him that's not how TV works but he didn't listen. He even wanted the first two or three episodes in the series to be the *same script* with the actors rotating roles. I mean really! It's an easy sell for the actors, but the public? Come on…"

As Peter was talking Brad realised that the rotational roles were a key feature to enable the robbery of the storage centre to occur. Peter could be coaching one actor in uniform while another, still in uniform could go off and commit the robbery. Given how movie sets operate it wouldn't be hard for an alibi to be created for the person who committed the theft.

"So who's in it?" Brad asked.

Peter named the actors involved, three were well known TV actors, one was a genuine movie star and the other two were unknowns.

"Who's the guy with the money?" Brad questioned.

"The producer, Nicholas Machiavelli," Peter said.

Brad stifled a laugh. The name was an obvious pseudonym. Even Brad knew Niccolo Machiavelli had written a book that argued that it was ok for people in power to seek to maintain that power using immoral actions, or more colloquially that *the end justifies the means*. Brad and Amy had discussed the notion in one of their classes.

Brad debated what to do next. He decided that he needed to go to the set and speak with everyone involved.

"Is Nicholas there today?" Brad queried.

"I think so," Peter said.

"Great, I'd like to talk to him and the cast, if I may?" Brad asked.

"Sure, I'll let them know you are coming," replied Peter.

"No, please don't do that, I'd like it to be a surprise," Brad said.

"Fine." Peter hung up without saying goodbye.

###

Brad drove to the set as quickly as possible. He quickly found the right location since he'd been given directions when signing in upon entering the studio. When Brad reached the set he had to walk past the catering table and was surprised at how much food they had available, but then he reasoned that there were actors, producers, directors, lighting technicians, writers and many more people on set during the shoot. The amount of people walking around still surprised him as he was expecting just a few actors and a director. He soon spotted Peter standing behind the catering table eating a donut. Brad reminded himself that stereotypes are often formed from a grain of truth. Peter saw him and came over, greeting him like a long lost friend.

"Oh Brad, I'm so glad you could make it!" he gushed. "Did you find us ok?"

"Yes," Brad said trying not to smile.

"Let me show you around," Peter continued as though he owned the place. "So, I'm in charge of checking scripts and procedures and keeping an eye on the car, uniforms and badges we have loaned the production."

You could've kept a closer eye on them, Brad thought.

"Here we have…" Peter proudly rambled on.

"I'm sorry to cut this short, but I would really like to speak to the producer Nicholas, if I could?" Peter looked crestfallen.

"Oh I'm sorry he left a few minutes ago for an important meeting with the writer," Peter replied sorrowfully.

"Did you tell him I was coming?" Brad asked.

"Oh no. I mean I may have mentioned that a colleague was coming to visit me and that your name would need to be added to the approved list," Peter said guiltily.

"Did you tell him my name?" Brad questioned. Given that Mathew had organised a break in to his former home, it was obvious he would know Brad's name.

"Of course, how else would he add you to the list?" Peter said with a childlike smile.

Brad swore under his breath.

"But don't worry, I didn't tell anyone else you were coming," Peter said conspiratorially.

Brad sighed and decided to interview the cast and crew even though his primary target was not there.

He started with the cast. Interviewing them was a lengthy affair as they were constantly being called on to go to make up, costuming, read throughs, rehearsals and actual filming. Brad suddenly understood why only eleven minutes of actual content was produced each day.

The first two actors were the movie star and an unknown. Their interviews were quite similar. Both were trying something new to expand their repertoires. Both hoped that the TV show would bring them some critical acclaim and introduce them to a new audience. Each liked the idea of swapping roles each week so they could show the diversity of their acting ability. Both hoped that the show would progress beyond the first six commissioned episodes as they were hoping for more regular work. Neither knew about the police storage site as they were not involved in those scenes.

Brad then interviewed one of the regular TV actors, named Brandy. She was a petite blond who had appeared on several soaps and was hoping to get onto a more serious TV show so that she could be seen as more than just a soapie star. As Brad was interviewing her he could not help but think that she was being a little naïve as she was too attractive and too bubbly to be on anything else. Unless she went through a physical transformation and toned down her personality, it would be unlikely that she'd achieve this goal. Brad asked her where she was the previous morning.

"Here. We were rehearsing the evidence scene. It's this great scene where the Detective goes to the evidence store," Brad cringed at the term; that wasn't what the police called it, she made it sound as though you could just go there and buy evidence; *On sale now, three positive DNA tests for the price of two*! Brad smiled wryly to himself.

"The scene is where the detective gets the box of evidence from the store after a heartfelt request from a new friend. As they go through it they discover that the original investigators had missed a big clue and that they have a new lead to follow."

Brad was pleased that he now had solid evidence linking the production to the theft.

"By any chance did the scene involve you stealing a computer from the box?" Brad asked slowly.

"Yes!" Brandy replied sounding surprised. "How could you know that?"

"Just a hunch," Brad replied nonchalantly.

"We rehearsed it extensively, I'm pretty good at it, watch." Brandy grabbed two donuts from the catering table and placed one on the table in front of Brad. She walked round in front of him, facing the donut and temporarily blocked it from his view. Her swapping of the donuts was obvious and clunky. She moved aside and proudly said "ta da! I have swapped the donuts."

"Wow," Brad said managing to sound sincere rather

than sarcastic.

"I know, you couldn't tell right?" Brandy asked.

"No," Brad replied, just managing to keep the sarcasm out of his voice. Brandy beamed.

"I know. They said I wasn't that good at it, at least not as good as Simon but I think they're wrong," she said quickly.

"Definitely," Brad said encouragingly, suddenly keen to talk to Simon. He quickly finished up with Brandy and wished her well with her career. He had to wait for Simon to finish shooting a scene and when he came over to Brad he was in a police uniform. Brad's heart thumped and he felt a little bit numb as he recognised Simon from the storage theft video. Brad decided to arrest him.

"I'm sorry to have to do this to you, but you are under arrest for the theft of evidence relating to a criminal investigation."

This is the first time I've ever felt guilty about arresting someone, he thought.

Simon looked shocked at the charge.

"This is a joke, right?"

Brad advised him not to talk until they were back at the station and his lawyer was present.

"I have no idea what you're talking about, so I don't know what I could say that would get me into trouble, but ok, I'll stay quiet until I can speak to a lawyer."

Simon was true to his word and did not say anything further until they were at the station.

###

Back at the station, Brad immediately put Simon in an interview room and had him call his lawyer. He then called Sergeant Pan to meet him in the adjoining observation room. Sergeant Pan appeared in the doorway within two minutes. Brad quickly explained what he had uncovered and that he now had evidence to support his theory that the storage facility was robbed by someone pretending to be a police officer and that they'd used the media liaison officer to obtain the proper uniform, car, badge and procedures. Sergeant Pan was impressed; something had really clicked for him since he started at this station.

Together Sergeant Pan and Brad interviewed Simon. His lawyer was unusually quiet during the interview and only conferred with his client a few times. It was clear that Simon had committed the theft and he readily admitted as much, but had laughed at them when he was told that he had done so from a real police storage facility and not a TV show set.

"It was a set! They had converted an old warehouse and hidden the cameras because of the reflective surfaces. We rehearsed back at the production lot and moved to the set. It was great too we got it in one take," Simon said proudly.

Sergeant Pan and Brad were incredulous. It was clear that Simon was bewildered by their interest in the TV show and its production. Sergeant Pan and Brad got Simon to give a sworn statement while being assessed for lie detection. They used the standard polygraph as well as the newer technologies of voice risk analysis and the Silent Talker Lie Detector. Unfortunately for them, it was clear that Simon was either an exceptional actor or telling the truth about his version of the theft. He really was innocent of committing a crime, in as much as he did not knowingly commit an offence and had been duped into doing it. Sergeant Pan and Brad consulted. They had a number of misgivings about charging Simon for the theft – even though they could probably get a conviction since it was clear that Simon had committed the theft. The extenuating circumstances would mean that he would most likely get a good behaviour bond.

They decided that they would not charge him if he helped them get to Mathew. They struck a deal with Simon and his lawyer, and Simon soon told them everything he knew about his mysterious producer Nicholas Machiavelli. It turned out that he didn't know a lot other than he had been unusually involved in the computer swap scene rehearsals and it had been his call as to which of the actors would get the role for the 'on location' shoot. Nicholas had told Simon that the people he would meet were also actors.

"So why wouldn't you rehearse with them first?" Brad asked, thinking that there was a hole in the story.

"It was not unusual for us to rehearse with different people to those we filmed with. That was the nature of the set, we would swap roles all the time," Simon said earnestly.

It was clear to Brad and Sergeant Pan that Mathew had made it so the actors would not be suspicious. After they had concluded the interview and allowed Simon to go back to the set, Brad was back at his desk pondering the latest developments. As he thought, the idea that Mathew Arnold was a figment kept intruding into his consciousness. The way he had used an alias on the set made it seem likely. Brad knew he had made a mistake about thinking Amy could be Mathew, but what if the

260

proposition that Mathew could be an alias for someone else was right, but the conclusion that it was Amy was wrong. In that case the logical person would be Dr Engels. He had known the strategy that was used to rob the storage facility and was the only source Brad had that Mathew Arnold existed. And even that was just a few emails and statements from the Doctor. The more he thought about it the more logical it seemed that Mathew was really Dr Engels. What better way to distance yourself from an action than by creating a figment who you could use as a scapegoat. Brad felt angry and as though he had been used and lied to. He grabbed his keys and drove to Ivory Tower. When he arrived the guard did not admit him to Leviathan Enterprises until Brad had flashed his badge and a call to Jenny.

Jenny showed him straight through to Dr Engels' office.

"Hello Brad how are you?" Dr Engels asked warmly. He motioned for Brad to take a seat.

"I've been better," Brad said, sitting down.

"Oh why's that?" Dr Engels asked.

"You were right," Brad replied through gritted teeth.

"What about?" Dr Engels asked curiously.

"The way Mathew robbed the storage facility," Brad said.

"Really? I'm a little surprised by that." Brad quickly outlined the scale of the production and what he had uncovered. When he finished explaining the way the theft had occurred, Jenny reappeared with two macchiato coffees.

"We can't have you miss out on one of these," she said in a friendly tone, offering Brad his choice of the two. He and Dr Engels each took one. Jenny left the room and shut the door behind her.

"The thing that gets me is that this is the exact way you said it would be done. And that bothers me," Brad struggling not to sound hostile.

"What are you getting at?" Dr Engels asked, maintaining his friendly tone.

"That you are behind the theft, there is no Mathew Arnold or if there is then he is you," Brad said icily.

Dr Engels smiled.

"So are you here to arrest me?" he laughed.

"Do you admit it?" Brad asked quickly.

"No," Dr Engels said.

They both paused.

"Your reasoning is sound you know, but there is another conclusion you could have reached," Dr Engels said warmly.

"What's that?" Brad asked.

"That Mathew is a real person and needs to be stopped," Dr Engels stated.

"But how would that explain that he used your idea. It at least indicates you were working together," said Brad.

"Not at all," replied Dr Engels.

"Of course it does," Brad retorted.

"I agree with your proposition and your conclusion is valid once again, but there is another alternative conclusion that I am amused to have to tell you in this context, because it is Level Ten of the Professor's Program." Dr Engels said with a broad smile.

Brad reeled at the mention of the Program and the next level. He had assumed he would never get to know about it.

"The reason Level Ten is not on the Professor's computer is that it is only four words long and would normally be emailed or told to a FONT member when they had displayed a certain level of reasoning and had nominated a few appropriate members. They would then have to process its meaning to really understand the level. It is quite a common expression actually. It's just that when you put it in this context it becomes so much more meaningful," Dr Engels said with a smile.

Brad knew Dr Engels was just dragging out the revelation of the level to see if he would glean it intuitively from what he was saying. Brad thought through his reasoning in reaching his conclusions and tried to think of it as a logic problem like the ones he had been studying. He realised that another conclusion could be that Mathew had thought of the same idea independently. Brad thought back through the Program and the section about Newton. Brad had researched Newton afterwards and found that several of his ideas had been discovered independently by his contemporaries. In other words *great minds think alike.* Brad stopped.

"Great minds think alike," he said aloud. Dr Engels beamed.

"Exactly. Congratulations on divining Level Ten. Intuition is a perfectly valid form of knowledge you know. To me, it is the unconscious connection of information that makes its way into working memory via the speech centres in the brain. This is why it is almost as you say it, that you are aware of the thought," Dr Engels said.

Brad wasn't listening. He was lost in thought about

Level Nine and the idea of philosopher kings. If the assumption that great minds think alike was true, then it opened up new understanding of how the members of FONT, particularly those at Level Nine, would operate. It was inspiring.

"I think you understand now why Mathew might have come up with the same idea," Dr Engels said gently.

"And I can assure you he is a real person. I can't give you his address or personal details as that would be a breach of our privacy agreement," Brad remembered signing the agreement when he had joined FONT at Level Eight. It was a straightforward privacy policy. He had not given much thought to the fact that there was nothing in there about protecting the names of members, but plenty about their contact details other than an email address.

"So without breeching our policy there is not much more I can do to help you, although I have every confidence in your detection abilities and that you will catch him soon. What I can do is give you a photo of him since it is a personal photo and copyright lies with the person who took the photo, not who is in it." Dr Engels said.

Dr Engels stood up and went to what looked like a blank wall and waved his hand in front of a section of it. "My ring has a near field communicator device in it" he said as the wall seemed to recede slightly before moving to the side with a slight swoosh. Brad had a flashback to his first visit to Leviathan and Dr Engels swiping a card to open doors.

The card was fake! It was a ruse so that if people stole it for access to the facility they would take something useless...wow it's like a placebo, Brad thought.

As the door moved away it revealed what looked like a large bookshelf. It was stocked full of photo frames filled with pictures.

"These are all photos of my friends. Most of them also happen to be members of FONT as well. This is Mathew," Dr Engels took a photo off a shelf as Brad walked over and handed it to him. The image was of Dr Engels and another man. Both wore suits and were pictured with their arms around each other's shoulders. Mathew was a little bit taller than Dr Engels and had more grey hair. His eyes were brown and there was something about his grooming that said he was a wealthy man. Despite his grey hair he appeared youthful.

"That was taken two years ago. He has gained a kilo or two since then but is still pretty much the same person," Dr Engels said softly. He called Jenny back to the office and asked her to make a colour copy of the image. She returned a minute later and gave Brad the copy and Dr Engels the original photo.

Brad took the photo and carefully folded it so that it would fit in his shirt pocket without putting a crease through Mathew. Dr Engels and he sat back down. Brad finally drank his coffee. Even though it was lukewarm it was still better than what he was used to at the station.

"So, hmmm," Brad said, not quite sure of what to say.

"Let me put a thought into your head. What are the consequences of great minds thinking alike?" Dr Engels asked.

Brad allowed himself time to consider the question. The coffee made him feel more alert, even though he knew that the peak caffeine level in his bloodstream would not occur for another hour. Another benefit of the placebo effect.

Several consequences occurred to him. If great minds did think alike then given similar pieces of information they would reach the same or similar conclusions. This would mean that they would act similarly in a given situation. If they were all Philosopher Kings and in positions of influence then there would be a definite movement that could be observed. It would also mean that there was a standard of thinking that could be defined as 'great' and that a test could be designed to check if one did indeed display great thinking. Brad mused that IQ tests had been trying to do this for many decades and still could not definitively achieve such a measure. Maybe the test couldn't be standardised but replaced with something like an interview by other people who were great thinkers and that would be the test. Brad realised that effectively, this was what the Program did. Brad relayed these thoughts to Dr Engels. He listened attentively and smiled encouragingly throughout.

"Congratulations you have achieved what I like to call level 10 step one. Don't let me saying it that way make you think that it is not an achievement, because it most definitely is, and you are really close to step two. Step two is to acknowledge that patterns in thinking lead to patterns in knowledge. Which is like taking level one, the links between pieces of knowledge and semantic networks and ramping it up several orders of magnitude, which really is the journey the Program puts you on. This is the key understanding that drives the next two levels. I say that with confidence even though I have not seen Level Twelve, because it is a major step to understanding how to unify knowledge." Dr Engels stopped to let his words sink in.

Brad thought about taking the idea of linking bits of information and taking it further to seeking patterns in bits of information and then relating this to patterns in thought. It was heady stuff that he knew would keep him awake at night, particularly as he sought out patterns in his and others' thoughts.

"Hmm." Brad did not know what to say. He hoped that his grunt conveyed his message that he was really processing the idea and had understood it, rather than a lack of interest.

"Yes, it is not something you can just respond to. But that's ok," Dr Engels said good-naturedly. "But there are other things I was doing before you arrived, so I am sorry, but I am afraid that I will have to cut this a little short."

"Plotting world domination?" Brad asked with a grin.

"Not today. Just a way to make a merger that will create job losses seem like a win for all involved. It will need some thought and planning. The merger creates synergies for the companies that are beneficial and mean that they can make the most of a technology I created for them, so I do take some responsibility. This is also why I really want to make it a win for all, and why it will need some thought."

Brad took the hint, thanked Dr Engels for seeing him and left quickly.

Brad drove home slowly and distractedly. He was honked at more than one set of lights for missing the change to green. By the time he got home he was quite a bit later than usual. Amy greeted him as he walked in the door saying that his dinner was nearly ready and that he should get his books out to study.

Amy gestured towards a bottle of liquor on the kitchen bench, "If you study hard, I will reward you later. If you don't, I'll just reward myself. Ok?" Amy said with an air of playfulness, apparently forgiving him for the previous night. Brad knew that he would try to study hard, but that he would be distracted by his thoughts.

Chapter Four

The next morning Brad left a message at the station that he was going straight to the set of the TV show in the hope of catching Nicholas/Mathew. When he arrived, he had trouble getting through the security gate as he wasn't on the list. It was only after the guard had phoned the station and Sergeant Pan had confirmed that Brad was there on official business that he was let through. The guard apologised to Brad for the precautions and said, "You would be amazed at what people do to try to get in here and see their favourite stars."

Brad realised why Peter had put his name down the previous day. It had unfortunate consequences, but it was understandable behaviour.

The studio was already a hive of activity. The actors were getting their make-up done and the lighting people, set dressers, camera operators, microphone operators and director were scurrying around setting up the scene for shooting. The scene for the day was a police officer played by Simon, telling 'Paula,' who was played by Brandy, that he'd caught the person who had murdered her parents eleven years ago. Brad laughed to himself at the idea of the effervescent Brandy acting like she'd had a traumatic life and shedding tears of relief at the news.

Brad made his way to the dressing room. Brandy and Simon greeted him and were promptly told off for moving by their respective make-up artists. Neither of them had seen Nicholas since the previous morning and were not sure when or if he would be back. Production would keep going without him as there were other producers and besides, all he really did was interfere with what the director wanted to achieve.

Brad showed Brandy the photo of Dr Engels and Mathew Arnold.

"Is Nicholas in this photo?" Brad asked.

"Yes," she replied.

"Can you point to him?" Brad said, having the sudden thought, *if I don't prompt you, who will you identify?*

"Sure," Brandy said as bubbly as ever.

Brandy waved her finger around dramatically before letting it rest on Dr Engels. Brad felt his heart rate skyrocket. He'd been tricked, *Dr Engels really was Mathew Arnold and responsible for the break in!* Brad's mind was flooded with thoughts about how skilfully Dr Engels had manipulated his thinking about him. Just as he was catching on that he was really Mathew he simply showed Brad an alternative point of view and let him do the work to change his mind. And now Brad had given him time to flee.

It's like the stamp case all over again, I am an idiot. Brad groaned at his foolishness.

"Just kidding, this is Nick," Brandy said and pointed to the other person in the photograph. "I have no idea who that is," she continued, pointing to Dr Engels.

Brad did not know what to say, he took a few breaths and tried to slow his heartbeat.

Oh man that was evil, but I should have trusted my gut. What was it the Doctor said 'intuition is a valid form of knowledge?"

Simon took a look at the photo out of the corner of his eye and grunted "Nick is the guy on the right." He managed not to move his head or lips. His make-up artist smiled in amusement at the feat.

Brad was relieved that they had both indicated the same person. The make-up artists also nodded their agreement. Dr Engels had told him the truth. Brad breathed another sigh of relief. Simon grunted again and somehow communicated that he wanted to talk to Brad. The make-up artist indicated that she'd be finished soon, so Brad said he'd wait for Simon to come out to the set.

Simon appeared a few minutes later and handed Brad a thick envelope. "It's a copy of the script for the scene you were interested in. Nicholas had scribbled some notes on it," he explained. Simon indicated that after the 'on site' shooting a couple of days ago he had been told that scene would now be shot in the studio. Brad could see that unless Simon specifically brought up the extra shooting of the scene no one would ever know it had taken place. And why would he? Actors were used to scenes being changed or dropped, shot multiple times or being altered. They were used to not being told reasons for things. All Mathew needed for his plan to work was for people to behave normally…

Back at the station a short while later, Brad sat at his desk. There were two neat piles of folders on it, one on either side of his computer. Brad opened the envelope Simon had given him. As he looked at the script he tried to process it through his senses. Brad listened to the sound of the paper, felt its weight and looked at what it was telling him. He could smell the remnants of the catering table on it. The handwriting from Nicholas was a few annotations about where the camera would be relative to the entrance to the room and the table. Brad realised he now had a tangible link to the theft from the storage facility. He looked at the paper again and picked up one of the sheets to see if there was a watermark or some other useful clue. He was disappointed that there was no watermark and closed the script. He looked closely at the crumpled cover and realised that the crumpling was due to the page being 'eaten' by a photocopy machine. Someone had straightened out the page and fed it back into the machine. As a result it had the partial imprint of a company logo in the corner. Brad imagined a secretary or some person doing the copying, having the machine jam a few times and giving up and then next person along being Mathew with the script. Brad recognised the partial image. The logo was of a prism separating light into its colours and the colours forming an anchor. The company's motto was 'solutions anchored in science' and they were called Sci-Co. They were a highly regarded firm that took a scientific and inventive approach to problem solving for other organisations - if the other organisations could afford them. Sci-Co were known for being expensive to hire, but they did guarantee results.

Brad went to find Sergeant Pan to tell her what he'd uncovered. He found her in the kitchen, silently sitting sipping a coffee. Brad had never seen her spend time like that before. Clearly she was in a contemplative mood.

"Hi Sergeant," Brad began.

"You can call me Wendy if you like," she replied. Brad was floored. Her insistence on being addressed by her title had been unrelenting. He wasn't sure what threshold he had crossed to earn such privilege, but he felt a connection to her that had not been available previously.

"I think I have found the person responsible for the break in to the storage facility," said Brad gently.

Wendy smiled slowly and deliberately, Brad had pretty much become her 'go to' guy.

"Well done. So who, how, where, when?" She asked.

"Mathew Arnold, by finding a logo for Sci-Co on a script, at Sci-Co's HQ, as soon as I confirm he is there," Brad replied.

"So what do you need from me?" Wendy questioned, making it clear that she was ready to mobilise whatever resources he would need.

"Permission to get a warrant to access Sci-Co's personnel records to locate Mathew, then if I am able to confirm that he does indeed work there, to help me get an arrest warrant and give me someone to help go and arrest him," Brad replied confidently even though he was thinking on his feet.

"Done, take Detective Summers," Wendy replied.

"How do you know I'll be able to confirm that he is there?" Brad asked.

"You have not been wrong about things like this for a while now and if I must say it, you are becoming an excellent detective." Wendy paused. "I hope you are studying hard for your exam next week?"

"I am," replied Brad, thinking about how well his study was going. His high level of motivation had made the learning fun.

"Good. Now bring me whatever forms you need signed and get going. It'd be great if you could finally make an arrest in regards to that whole melting brain affair. Really great," Wendy said with a smile and detachment that Brad had not seen before.

Brad raced out of the kitchen. It was as though he had drunk the pot of coffee that Wendy had got her cup from. A short while later he'd confirmed that Mathew worked at Sci-Co and was in fact a partner in the organisation. Sally and Brad chatted about their exams and Wendy's impending promotion while they waited for the arrest warrant to be emailed through by the judge.

"You know you'll get it don't you?" Sally asked. Brad was unsure about how she felt about her opinion.

"No, I don't think so," Brad replied.

"Oh please, you are her shining star," Sally said with a hint of bitterness. Brad was shocked. He had never been anyone's favourite and while he knew that he'd experienced a high level of success recently, his focus had been on the personal satisfaction he felt not on how others might view him as a result. Brad was enjoying not finding work such an effort. It was like he'd spent his professional life in second gear and had just discovered the third and fourth.

"I don't think so. I mean it took me seven years to get

this job, I bet it took you only the minimum of four. Plus you have been a detective for longer than me and are more experienced," Brad countered.

"We'll see," said Sally neutrally. She liked Brad as a friend and found it hard to be upset that he was achieving things, still her own ambition and desire for the Sergeant's job gnawed away at her. If one of them did get the role it would be interesting to see how they each coped with the other's change in status.

The computer pinged and Brad quickly printed the arrest warrant that had come through.

"Let's go," he commanded Sally as he grabbed the paper from the printer and raced towards the door.

When Brad parked the police car in the loading bay out the front of Franklin Plaza, he was amused that he could see Ivory Tower in the distance. From the street the building certainly lived up to its 'ebony tower' nickname by looking like a large black piano key sticking out of the ground. Brad and Sally made their way to the reception desk and got directions to Sci-Co's floor in the building. A swift elevator ride later, they found themselves at another reception desk asking to be taken to Mathew's office.

The receptionist dutifully led them to a corner of the building, knocked on the door and asked if Mathew would mind talking to some police officers who were here to see him. Mathew agreed and ushered the woman he was talking to out of his office. Sally gasped as she recognised Diane Singh, a famous mathematician and entrepreneur who had revolutionised the use of algorithms in the grocery industry. Sally whispered to

Brad "what could she possibly need Sci-Co for?"

"I don't know," Brad replied as Mathew walked over and greeted them warmly. Both Sally and Brad recognised Mathew from Dr Engels' photo. Brad thought that Mathew was putting on a good show of not presenting a guilty conscience or being caught out. He also noticed that he was not wearing shoes.

"So, Officers, what can I do for you?" Mathew asked genially.

"That's Detective," Sally and Brad said in unison.

"So, Detectives, what can I do for you?" Mathew replied without missing a beat. He returned to his desk and sat down before beckoning Sally and Mathew to take the two seats in front of it. Brad could just see Mathew's feet clenching and unclenching under the desk as they approached. Sally noticed as well and it reminded her that she'd not seen Brad spin in his chair for months.

"We are here to arrest you," Sally said gently.

Mathew laughed. "What on earth for?" he asked curiously.

"For orchestrating a break in of a police storage facility and the theft of a computer from an evidence box," Brad replied firmly.

"I have not heard of any such break in on the news. When did this occur?" Mathew asked with an air of innocence.

"A few days ago," Brad replied.

"So why do you think I did it?" Mathew said.

"First let me read you your rights," Brad said more as a statement than request.

"Ok," said Mathew without any concern.

Sally and Brad alternated sentences of the rights Mathew had as a suspect in a criminal investigation. When they finished Mathew smiled "that was beautiful. Really stereo, I like it. I acknowledge that I am aware of my rights." He finished while maintaining an amused tone. "I think you will find that I was out of the country when the break in occurred, so I'm sorry you have had to go to the effort of coming here."

Sally looked at Brad with confusion. Brad gave her a reassuring glance and turned to Mathew.

"Actually we have witnesses who say you weren't, and even if you show us plane tickets and receipts, we know you were in fact here…Nicholas." Brad replied.

Mathew's face rippled with surprise. In an instant it was gone.

"Nicholas?" he queried.

"Besides, even if you were away, we're not accusing you of committing the actual break in," Brad said, ignoring Mathew's question.

"So why are *you* arresting me for it then?" Mathew directed his response to Brad and then looked at Sally and Brad as though they were school children.

"You are the one who masterminded the break in and had someone commit it for you," Brad asserted.

"Masterminded? Who masterminds crime anymore?" Mathew asked wistfully.

"You," said Brad pointedly.

"I think you'll have a hard time proving that," Mathew replied, anger creeping into his voice.

"Well I, I mean we, don't," Brad replied bluntly.

"You haven't said much," Mathew said to Sally, "I take it that Detective Thomas here has driven this investigation?" Sally nodded.

Brad realised that he had not told Mathew his surname when introducing himself and that Mathew therefore knew more about who he was than he let on. Turning to Sally, Mathew said "Would you mind if I made a full confession? It will be on the record and I will allow him to record it if you want, but I will only do so if Detective Thomas and I are alone."

Sally looked to Brad for confirmation. He nodded and Sally walked out, shut the door and waited. She was disappointed that she could not hear their conversation as the thick carpet and well adorned walls of the office captured their voices.

"Good. Before we leave, may we talk freely and *off* the record? We can then have a separate chat on the record for the sake of your partner," Mathew asked with a twinkle in his eye.

"Ok," Brad accepted, leaving the voice recorder he had placed on the desk turned off.

"Do you know how I keep tabs on the Doctor?" Mathew said, the geniality of his earlier conversation had returned.

"No," Brad said.

"I have a video camera pointed at the entrance of his building. It's the best I can do given the strength of his security. Which is how I know that you have visited him several times – certainly more than if you were just being a police officer. So I take it you are a member?" Mathew queried.

"Of what?" Brad replied innocently.

"Let's not play games. Are you a member of FONT or not?" Mathew said firmly.

"Yes," Brad admitted.

"What level are you on?" Mathew asked.

"Ten," Brad said with some pride.

"Congratulations," Mathew said genuinely, "would you like to know what Level Eleven is?"

Brad's heart skipped a beat and his ears pricked up like a German Shepard's. Mathew could see the temptation in his eyes.

"All you have to do is give me a ten minute head start," Mathew said clearly understanding how tempting this offer would be.

Brad thought about how easy it would be to give Mathew an opportunity to get away. He could easily give an ambiguous command to Sally and leave Mathew alone for a moment and then blame his disappearance on poor communication. Given his recent success and vested interest in solving the case, no one would think that he had deliberately let Mathew get away. Brad had received offers of bribes before, but this was the first time he had been tempted to take one.

"I can assure you that Level Eleven will change your life. It makes the connections so clear," Mathew said dreamily.

Brad thought back to the ideal of the Philosopher King. Such people were meant to be so seeking of truth that they were incorruptible. Brad wondered how Philosopher Kings would react to bribes of wisdom. After quite a few moments, Brad made up his mind. Brad realised he could do it.

"No. I'm sorry but I *won't* do it," he said firmly to Mathew, making it clear that he was exercising his free will.

"I can respect that. You understand that I had to try?" Mathew asked.

"Yes," said Brad.

"I'm guessing that the Doctor helped you to pick up my scent so to speak?" Mathew said.

Brad was unsure of how to reply.

"I take it from your pause and lack of denial that he did. This is ok. I am not angry at you and I will keep that bit of information between us. But I am angry at the Doctor. Let me tell you … that, that man, your Dr Engels, is a placebo," Mathew said with bitterness. "He gives you a suggestion and you turn it into the action he wants."

Brad recognised the truth in the statement.

"He says such simple things, like would you mind taking a personal interest in social phenomenon X, but due to great minds thinking alike, your response to that suggestion is reasonably predictable, so you wind up doing the action he wants without him having to ask you for anything specifically. He is insidious. You do what he wants without even knowing it. I mean look at you. He told me that he would find a way to stop me from making the program commercial and now here you are, doing his bidding," Mathew paused. The last statements were as much to himself as Brad.

"Do you know how he keeps tabs on FONT?" Mathew asked after a moment.

"No," Brad replied.

"Within the senior members there are a select group of one hundred and eighty one people who are what the Doctor calls 'centurions.' I should know since I was one until I resigned. They monitor their hundred or so

280

designated 'collaborators' and report up the food chain to Dr Engels or the Professor, at least until he passed away."

Mathew displayed some emotion at his mention of the Professor. It was clear that he had great admiration of him and mourned his passing. To Brad this seemed at odds with his actions.

"And so they monitor you all to see who is doing what, what effect the program is having and perhaps more importantly who they deem worthy of the next levels," Mathew continued softly.

"So are there a lot of people who have seen Level Ten?" Brad asked.

"Yes," Mathew said, "and Level Eleven and Twelve. Not that the Doctor will let me see Level Twelve. Which raises the question…"

"Why weren't there more deaths?" Brad interrupted.

"Exactly and the answer may shock you…there were," Mathew said, looking Brad in the eye.

"Yes I know about the other three deaths that weren't reported," Brad replied.

"No Detective, there were a total of one thousand, six hundred and sixty-seven deaths around the world including the ones you know about," Mathew countered.

The shock was visible on Brad's face.

"Dr Engels used his influence and favours to suppress the reports and by assuring people that no further deaths would occur. He even closed the powder plant. That's why it went away so quickly and why the Feds disappeared without making any arrests," Mathew gave Brad time to process the information.

"And now there really won't be any more deaths

because you, as an instrument of the Doctor, have stopped me spreading the program," Mathew said mournfully, "and since I don't think that you would be here unless you were certain of a conviction, I think we should now go on the record?"

Brad nodded affirmatively and pressed record.

"I Mathew Arnold have been arrested on suspicion of having responsibility for a break in and theft from a police storage facility. I have been read my rights and I waive my right to an attorney. I confess to this crime freely and of my own volition," Mathew began.

He proceeded to give a full description of how he had planned and orchestrated the crime and concluded with several references to the strength of Brad's detective work. Brad realised that he was probably confessing to reduce his sentence and would use his cooperation as an excuse to be placed in a minimum security prison, but he didn't mind since he had stopped the distribution of the program and achieved a major arrest. Brad did have a nagging thought that perhaps he was been set up for a fall.

###

During the car ride to the police station, Mathew had time to think about the change that had just been imposed upon his life and plans. Ever since he had been exposed to Level Eleven a few months previously, his view of the world had changed dramatically – as had his plans for what he wanted to do with the program. He acknowledged that a small part of him was pleased he had been arrested, but his overriding thought was that now he would never know what was in Level Twelve. He'd found a folder in a cloud storage program that appeared to contain a copy of the level. He would never have known about it or been able to access it without the Professor's computer. The security was first rate and Mathew was frustrated that he could not simply hack his way in. His desire to open the file had even made him bring in Diane Singh to see if there was a mathematical way of cracking it. Since Level Eleven Mathew's understanding of humanity, society, physics, space and time were reaching new heights. Previously his awareness had been in chemistry and physics, but now he was becoming aware in biology, geology and psychology and he was able to link these subjects in thought and ideas. He was beginning to unify. He could see how all physical events might be linked and dependent on one another. Time, awareness and thought were no longer the separate things they appeared to be.

And yet there was the last level – the key to making that final connection that would link all of his knowledge completely. He was desperate to hear it. His desire was insatiable. He was aware that the information, the final piece in the file could cause his brain to disintegrate or melt. The chemicals in his mind would react too much when assimilating and accommodating the knowledge of that level. Yet he had to know. How his late friend had been able to live at such high levels of awareness and knowledge for so long was something Mathew could only guess at. It seemed to Mathew that his friend must have had some means of controlling the 'level' of thought at which he was operating. This alone could explain how he had been able to survive for long enough to record the information for Level Twelve and begin distribution of it. Mathew decided that he had only one

course of action available to him to get Level Twelve
and it was one he hoped he would not have to make.

Chapter Five

A week later Brad and Sally sat their Sergeant's examination. They decided that if one of them got the Sergeant's role they would not be bitter towards the other person. They resolved that if they did start to harbour some resentment that they would discuss it, and that they would work with the other person not against them. Sally knew that Brad had the inside running for the position as long as he did well on the exam and scored close to her and was unsurprised when he was offered and accepted the promotion another week later. What did surprise her was that he almost aced the exam and was easily the top performer, outscoring both herself and Detective Taupo.

"So how did you do it?" Sally asked curiously.

"I think I just studied differently. I mean, I used to just try and memorise facts and try to remember who, when and what. This time I did it differently. I linked what I had to learn to other pieces of information and really tried to create scenarios where I could use the information I was reading. I guess the deeper level of processing made the information stick a lot better and easier to recall."

Brad smiled to himself at his insight into what had changed.

"Plus I was significantly motivated for it by Amy."

He had meant this innocently enough, but Sally had covered her ears in mock horror and walked away saying "ewww." Brad was grateful for the humour and knew that they would actually work well together with him as her boss. He decided that he would let her and no one else refer to him as 'Boss' to keep less of a barrier between them.

That night Amy had been thrilled with his news and the next day her parents came round and gave Brad a card. Amy's mother apologised for Amy's father signing the card as being from "the Leorates" rather than their first names, as he had signed it thoughtlessly. Brad also had emails from his parents and sister. His father had said that he knew Brad tried to live up to his personal motto and that it was pleasing to see him doing it over the last year. He added "it's easy to dwell on the absurdity of our existence, but leave that for the existentialists, well done on finding someone who gives your life meaning."

Brad kept his sister's email from Amy because in it she had written the line that now he would have "enough money to buy all sorts of things, maybe even a ring." He did feel an affinity for his family's assertion that Amy made him a better person. Dr Engels also called and offered his congratulations and thanked him for embodying the spirit of the eighth and ninth levels. Brad smiled and felt like a pawn in Dr Engels scheme, but one who was very happy to play the role.

The trial of Mathew Arnold went quickly. It was high profile, due to the extraordinary setup of the theft and boldness of the plan, as well as the fact that an already wealthy and intelligent businessman would go to such lengths to obtain an intelligence raising Program. The trial did reinvigorate people's interest in the Program and one particular speech that Mathew gave in his defence became a viral video:

"We are born with three fears: the fear of loud noises, falling and the unknown. We can overcome the first two fears relatively easily, but overcoming the unknown can only come through understanding. Understanding removes the 'unknowing' and frees us from our last fear. As a result we can be truly free and truly happy. That is all I wanted to bring to the world. That is all I wanted to share. I know there are copies of the program out there and I hope this mission will be fulfilled by someone."

Mathew made himself sound so noble and virtuous that the public began to rally behind him. "After all," they cried, "no one had been harmed, he'd returned the computer and cooperated fully with the police."

Despite the pleas, the judge sentenced Mathew to two years in a minimum security prison and reminded the public that he had been responsible for breaking into a secure and restricted government facility and the theft of evidence.

###

Early one afternoon, a month after the trial, Dr Engels' intercom buzzed. "I have a call for you, it's from

Panopticon Prison," Jenny said cheerily through the intercom. Dr Engels frowned. He only knew one inmate from that prison and he had helped put him there. He picked up the phone and was asked by a guard if he would accept a call from prisoner Eight-One-Nine, also known as Mathew Arnold. Dr Engels sighed and agreed.

"Greetings Mathew," he said.

"Hello Old Friend, how are you?" Mathew asked in a friendly tone.

"Fine, how are you?" Dr Engels replied.

"Oh you know, so full of energy I feel like I'm in a cell," Mathew said with a laugh.

"So, to what do I owe this pleasure?"

"Cutting to the chase so soon?" Mathew asked in mock disappointment.

"Well what else should I say? You know I'm sorry that our disagreement led to you being where you are, but you also knew that I would take action to stop you and that I really had no choice," Dr Engels stated.

"While I'm not sure that you didn't have a choice, I have thought of a way you can make it up to me," Mathew said.

"Oh yes. How's that?" Dr Engels asked curiously.

"Bring me Level Twelve," demanded Mathew.

Dr Engels felt like he had been punched in the stomach, "I can't" he gasped.

"You can. I know you have a copy," asserted Mathew.

"It's quarantined. Even if I could, what about the consequences?" Dr Engels asked with concern.

"Let me deal with the consequences. Plus, if the same thing happened to me that happened to the others, then you will never have to deal with me again," Mathew said.

"But the ethics," Dr Engels said with urgency.

"You and your ethics. All the great studies of human nature from Zimbardo to Milgram to Harlow, are the ones that have violated ethical boundaries the most strongly, so don't talk to me about ethics. Plus, this from the man who has changed governments, incited wars and caused how many deaths? Just for the pleasure of seeing if he could do it," Mathew said, suddenly sounding angry.

"There have been far fewer deaths from my intervention than if others had used more conventional means. Not that I admit to having done any of those things," Dr Engels replied defensively.

"True, but if you are arguing about the ethics of your personal involvement you would find yourself on the wrong side of the right and wrong dichotomy."

"Fair enough. But past behaviour is no justification for future behaviour," Dr Engels said philosophically.

"I have missed our chats you know," Mathew said, suddenly sounding wistful.

"Me too," Dr Engels replied.

"Let me put it another way. I am in a medium security prison, because the minimum security ones were full and it is hell. Do you know what it is like to be the only intelligent person in a crowd? I see so much and they, they are all so ignorant. They don't even know why they are in here," Mathew said exasperatedly.

"I'm pretty sure they know what they were convicted of," Dr Engels said with a laugh.

"That's not what I mean. They are so unaware. They

don't know why they were driven to behave the way they did and it's driving me insane. I would feel less alone if they put me in solitary," Mathew said sounding frustrated.

"I understand," Dr Engels said empathetically. He really meant it, if he was in that situation he would be unhappy too.

"Maybe you could teach them?" he asked Mathew.

"No, that's not for me; that was the Professor's job. I wouldn't know where to begin," Mathew said.

"But you know the Program, maybe you could modify it or something?" Dr Engels suggested.

"No. I am not a teacher. There is no way I could handle their inane questions… At least if I had Level Twelve, I could complete the unification and live in that knowledge. It's like I am on a cliff with a parachute and down below is paradise and I can only reach it with a push. That push is Level Twelve. I need it," Mathew said, aware that he sounded like a junkie.

"But if it causes you to die?" Dr Engels questioned.

"Then I'll live with it," Mathew said laughing again, mostly to himself.

"I'll have to think about it some more. I'll let you know soon," Dr Engels hung up his phone.

Dr Engels spent the rest of the day thinking about the morality of the decision he was facing. He put aside his own interest in Level Twelve and decided that if he found that it was morally acceptable for him to give the file to Mathew then, while he would regret not having access to the information himself, he could live with that regret. Dr Engels wished the security that was on the file allowed for it to be copied. Instead, it permitted moving the file but not duplication of it.

And to think, it's my own software that's blocking me. Oh the irony, he thought. *Anyway what matters is making sure I make the decision for the right reasons.*

Near the end of the day Dr Engels said "Ivanov open the damn letter." This was his way of telling himself to make a decision or stop overlooking something. Dr Engels remembered that in Checkov's *The Cherry Orchard* a family keeps walking past a letter and never opens it. He'd spent the whole play thinking that when they did it would save the orchard from being sold. He'd also read another play by Checkov called *Ivanov* around the same time, and for a while had thought that Ivanov was the name of the play with the letter. It took years before he stopped and thought about it enough to correct the error. He had started saying his little mix up again as a reminder that memory is not perfect, but also that action was necessary for things to change.

Dr Engels phoned the prison and made an appointment to see Mathew the following morning. He spent the next fifteen minutes retrieving the Level Twelve file from the quarantine drive. It was a deliberately difficult procedure. Once he had the file, Dr Engels transferred it to an mp4 player. He said goodbye to Jenny and went through the hidden door to his penthouse residence. He spent the night in a fitful sleep. Twice he turned on the player to view Level Twelve for himself, but the passwords he tried did not work. When he dreamt, it was of a group of people that he couldn't join. When he finally got up he knew what he had to do.

Later that morning at the prison Dr Engels signed in and

had the mp4 player go through a scan. He was confident that they would it let it through.

"Really, that is the music you are bringing him?" one of the security guards joked, "hasn't he suffered enough?"

"I guess not," Dr Engels said with a smirk.

"Well he did do a bad thing. He's in cellblock F for Foucault, suite seven," the security guard continued with a laugh. "Follow that corridor to the end, turn left and take your second right and you will get to the meeting room. Prisoner Eight-One-Nine will meet you there. Remember he did a bad thing," the guard repeated jovially.

"Thanks," Dr Engels said as he set off.

Walking through the jail produced feelings of discomfort in Dr Engels and he knew that people like Mathew and him didn't belong in a place like this. For them, the prison would terminate their humanity. Dr Engels knew he was about to give Mathew the means to choose the way he left it. The thought did little to quell the concern that he was helping him commit euthanasia.

The meeting room was sparsely furnished. There were three tables with bench seats. All were bolted to the floor. After Dr Engels had sat down, a guard brought in Mathew and left them alone in the room. Dr Engels was shocked at the sight of him. Even though it had only been a month since the trial he had noticeably lost weight and aged considerably. He looked drawn. As he approached he tapped his ear. Dr Engels picked up on the clue that people would be listening. They would have to speak in coded messages.

"Thank you for coming. Did you bring what I asked?"

Mathew queried as he sat down.

"Cutting to the chase so soon?" Dr Engels said with wry smile.

"Touché," Mathew replied.

"Yes I did. I know you are aware of the consequences of listening to music like this?" Dr Engels questioned.

"Yes I am aware that my brain may shrivel from such trash, but I need that in here," Mathew replied, barely concealing the meaning of their dialogue. Dr Engels paused to give him a moment to refocus.

"You know I never figured out how to open the files on one of these things," Dr Engels said cautiously.

"I am sure I can do it for myself," Mathew replied confidently. He had thought about little else for the two months since his arrest.

"And if you can't?" asked Dr Engels.

"Then I will miss out. But at least I will have had the chance to experience it, there would be some comfort in that," Mathew said.

"You know I wish things could have worked out differently," Dr Engels said, suddenly nostalgic.

"Yes it would be nice to go back to our regular chats over coffee in those wonderful sling chairs of yours. They really are cosy," Mathew replied with an equal measure of nostalgia.

"Indeed they are. Jenny says hello by the way, and that she misses your flirting," Dr Engels said.

"I hardly believe that," Mathew replied.

"Ok, you caught me, I made that one up. I think she is secretly pleased that you won't harass her anymore," Dr Engels stated quietly.

"That's more like it," Mathew said, "You know you

really should let her show more of her wicked sense of humour and warm personality to outsiders you know."

"That would defeat the purpose. She behaves the way she does to reflect that Leviathan is clinical and efficient in what it does. Given that she is the first person people see when they come in, they see her as embodying the values of the organisation. Only those that are worthy get to see that other side of her," Dr Engels replied.

"You mean those tattooed folk you keep having round?" Mathew asked with a bitter laugh.

"I guess so… So what sort of things do they have you do around here?" Dr Engels asked.

"Well I have a job in what they say passes for a library. The range is woeful and the books are out of date. I mean their science section has nothing recent. It's like reading a history of science rather than about science," Mathew said disdainfully.

"Maybe I can get them some more books?" Dr Engels said trying to sound positive.

"If anyone could it would be you. But you miss the point. It's like being in Plato's cave. The whole place is so out of touch with what you and I know about the world that a few books would not change anything. It takes more than knowledge to transform thinking, as you know," Mathew said disdainfully.

"Indeed I do. So is there anything else I can get you?" Dr Engels asked sombrely.

"Maybe next time you could bring one of those coffees Jenny used to make? The swill they serve in here has made me give up coffee," Mathew said mournfully, in a tone that was rich with meaning. They both knew that there would not be a next time.

294

"I'll see what I can do," Dr Engels said with a tear in his eye. Mathew had been a good friend for the last few years and despite their falling out, he was genuinely missing their relationship. They both stood up and embraced each other.

"Until next time, Mathew," Dr Engels said, each syllable filled with emotion.

"Goodbye Carl," Mathew replied, "and thank you."

###

It had started nobly, as a quest for knowledge, but led to a quest for world domination. Where and when the shift had occurred, Mathew was not sure. Perhaps it was inevitable, like a perverse variant of Godwin's law. *If you study humanity for long enough eventually you'll want to take over the world.* Mathew smiled at the thought. He knew that the rush of having his world view change as he progressed through the levels of the program was addictive, and he wanted to keep that rush going by changing the world.

Mathew's plan was to make himself immensely wealthy and powerful. What he had not told Dr Engels was that his plan had changed in the weeks before he was arrested. It was no longer about taking the program to everyone and trying to bring about the age of the philosopher kings that way, but to take the program to the elite and use it to remove them from power. It was his intent to wipe out the top 'percenters' and for society to crumble. In the ensuing chaos he and others he'd been working with, would rise to positions of influence. They had bought numerous stocks via a 'short selling' strategy in many companies, knowing that if the program worked as expected amongst their targets, it would wipe out the value of the companies. The group could then take over the companies and repurpose them as they wished. Mathew and the others would then use their power and influence to alter the structure of society so that it could be ruled correctly. Mathew wished he could have shared his plan with Dr Engels, but feared that if he did, his friend would find a way to stop him. Dr Engels wouldn't understand that he was going to take the idea of a Philosopher King from an ideal to a reality and make it so Philosopher Kings ruled around the world.

Mathew had made a few changes to the program that meant that participants no longer needed to join FONT. They still had to solve the riddle of the Pansy image, but there was no Eliza or tattoo needed to make further progress, instead it was a straight continuation of opening password protected files containing the relevant level. He had been pleased to find out where the Dame had produced the powder and was happy to be able to include it in the program as he knew it was vital for its success and his new plan. It had been a simple matter of hacking the delivery company's database and finding the pick-up point for the delivery he'd received a couple of years previously. He'd been thrilled to discover that the plant was automated and that after the Professor and the Dame's deaths it had been closed. It was easy to surreptitiously reopen and restock it with enough material to produce a vast quantity of the powder for distribution. He had five full time workers who he paid to keep everything operational and keep things going in his absence. All the workers had to do was reload the bins when the raw ingredients ran out and make an occasional call for more of them to be delivered. The rest pretty much ran on its own. The powder was even boxed and labelled for delivery by the machinery.

Mathew had set a single date for delivery in a few months' time, once the production was complete. A rotating roster of delivery companies would send out packages to the selected targets. The shipments included the program up to Level Eleven, more than enough to keep the targets occupied while the powder did its work. Mathew had added a dose of dimethyl mercury to the powder. It would not kill those who took it for months, but death would be inevitable for them. *No point in assuming they would all make it to Level Twelve,* he'd thought; *Not that I had Level Twelve to send them.*

Mathew looked at the mp4 player Dr Engels had brought him. Its smooth aluminium surface was a triumph of design and it was no wonder the security guards would have let it through as they probably had similar ones themselves. What they couldn't have known was that this one had been reprogrammed by Dr Engels. Mathew pressed on the screen and the normal menu appeared as expected and the music files all played when selected. He had been expecting this – there was nothing better than having something have the surface appearance of doing one thing to conceal the fact that it did something else. Plus the contents had to be scrutinised by the prison before they would let him have the device. After playing with the device for a while without locating the file, Mathew began to feel angry. Had Dr Engels cheated him? There were no hidden files that he could find. Mathew paced around the room and wished it had thick carpet like his office used to. How was he meant to think in a place like this?

In his frustration he decided to turn off the device and as he did so realised that this was probably what he was meant to have done to begin with. After a reboot the device asked for a pin. Mathew thought back to his conversation with the Doctor and his deliberate reference to Jenny saying hello. He typed in Jenny but a wrong password image flashed on the screen. Mathew smiled, "fine, you and your numbers, doctor, but would you please learn that she is so much more than a number." He typed in 53669 and the device rebooted again. When it reloaded a new home screen came up. It was a simple graphical interface with one folder. Opening the folder revealed a file named 'onceonly.' Mathew was grateful for the reminder and resolved that if he did manage to open it, he would make sure he was well rested before viewing it.

Over the next few days Mathew tried every password he could think of to open the file. He tried various Latin phrases such as *cogito ergo sum, temet nosce* and even *caveat emptor* with and without spaces. He tried various ways of expressing the term 'the sum.' He tried more whimsical passwords such as 'open sesame' and 'squeamish ossifrage' but they were not the magic words. Mathew gave up.

A week later he was in the prison library restocking shelves. *I wish I were somewhere else,* he thought as he absently returned a book to its shelf. Mathew was in the 300's nonfiction section when he saw a book title that made him smile wryly, and think of the Doctor.

Even in here I cannot escape you Doctor, but then that seems somewhat appropriate given the content of this text.

He took the book off the shelf and brushed some dust off the cover before using his index finger to trace the title – *Leviathan.* As he skimmed through the book a Latin phrase caught his eye "*nosce te ipsum.*" As he read on he knew he had discovered the password as it fit with Level Eleven. It translated to "read thyself," and the author asserted that doing this would enable you to read and know the thoughts and passions of *all* other men. The adrenaline surge Mathew felt made him feel like he was about to pass out.

Level Eleven had indicated that memories were not stored in synapses – the gap between cells in the brain – as previously thought, but in the cells – the neurons themselves. Through stimulation the neurons could regrow or restore these connections and once lost memories be regenerated. This, combined with rest of the levels gave a way to link everything you ever knew. Mathew knew that Level Twelve was a means of initiating this process.

By the time his shift finished and he'd returned to his cell he realised that he was crashing. *Thank you evolution,* he thought sarcastically, annoyed that his parasympathetic nervous system was doing its job. Mathew went straight to bed and despite a fitful night's sleep, awoke refreshed in the morning.

Upon waking up, he immediately turned on the mp4 player and accessed the file. He typed in the password backwards and without spaces and the file opened. Mathew smiled to himself that his certainty that it would work meant that he hadn't even tried it the previous day.

He paused to consider what he was about to experience, knowing that it could end his life, but thrilled at the potential understanding it could bring. Mathew questioned if he was truly prepared for the consequences and eventually decided he was. He reasoned that the Professor had survived for a while after creating the level, so perhaps he could too.

As Mathew pressed play he experienced a shiver of apprehension. As the video loaded, he thought about how he had been stopped from distributing his version of the program. A wave of regret rippled through him. Mathew managed to regroup his thoughts just as the Professor's face appeared on the screen.

"Greetings, welcome to Level Twelve and congratulations on making it this far. Unification cannot lead to one knowledge, but it can lead to a way of understanding all things," the Professor said jovially. Mathew smiled and just had enough time to send a mental thank you to his friend, before the Professor's tone changed.

"Mystics are pictured with halos because they understood that breathing influenced their body's functioning. Much research has shown that behavioural practices can influence the physical structure of the brain. The mystics may not have known that glial cells in the brain are implicated in breath control, nor that the opposite is true, controlling your breath can make the glial cells function better. This allows these cells to perform their function to clean and maintain the brain at an optimal level. This is also a way of inducing neurogenesis and this is what caused the mystics to glow and have the halo, but the extent to which they could achieve neurogenesis and growth was limited by this method. In order to cause neurogenesis and repair at a whole new level, you need to appreciate five things."

The Professor then listed the activities needed and their simplicity meant that Mathew memorised them instantly, even before the Professor explained what each would involve. As he listened, Mathew felt a shift in his mind as though barriers were falling away, but then it stopped.

Hmm, I guess I will need to actually do the things the Professor said, Mathew thought with disappointment. *I was hoping this would be it.*

Two days later Mathew was alone in his cell when a random thought triggered the reaction he had been expecting. Mathew felt a rush of understanding and adrenaline unlike anything he had ever experienced before. He felt the heat generated by the surge in his neural activity. He had done it. He had opened the secret to all knowledge. The key was not in the common origin of all living things, nor was it in metaphysical thoughts or logic. The key was within himself and he should have known this all along. He knew everything. Mathew felt like he was experiencing the world directly. He had taken perception out of the equation and could just 'see' whatever he wanted to know from the quantum to the macro scales. The world was so beautiful…

Mathew died, his neurons had disintegrated and his brain turned to liquid. His last thought was one of horror that one of his friends might try to finish his plan.

Epilogue

The next morning Amy went to get the paper while Brad put their breakfast on the table. Brad watched her walk through their front door and admired the way her silk dressing gown showed her figure and revealed her ballet dancer legs. Amy did not notice the door as it shut behind her. A short moment later she flung it open and burst dramatically into the home. She ran straight to the kitchen.

"Look!" she cried as she placed the paper on their breakfast bar.

The headline read *The Return of the Melting Brain?*

"No!" Brad said in surprise.

They read the article side by side.

Mathew Arnold, who was famous for setting up an elaborate scheme to steal evidence from a police warehouse was found dead in his prison cell yesterday. Mathew was a former partner in Sci-Co and renowned for his creative and scientific solutions to corporate problems. "His manner of death is consistent with those from the "Melting Brain Affair"" said the Medical Examiner, Dr Samantha Westlake. The death has reopened interest in the so-called "Program" that was implicated in the original series of deaths and in the mysterious powder created by Dame Sagan, herself a victim of the melting brain. It is also known that Leviathan Enterprises' CEO, Dr Engels, had visited Mr Arnold while he was in prison. "Mathew was a friend of mine and that was why I visited him. Just because he was in prison does not mean he stopped being my friend," Dr Engels said in a press release yesterday. Dr Engels also reaffirmed that Leviathan Enterprises was not involved in the Program. For more on this developing story and the history of the affair turn to page 5...

"What does this mean?" Amy asked Brad.

"I'm not sure. But I would guess that Dr Engels gave Mathew Level Twelve. I'm not sure that I could arrest him for it though. Although, it would be interesting to argue that he used knowledge as a weapon to kill someone," Brad said absently as his phone began to vibrate on the bench. It was a blocked number. *Who would call me from a blocked number?*

"Hello Doctor," he said.

"Hello Detective," Dr Engels said sounding as though his throat was dry.

"That's Sergeant now," Brad responded instinctively.

"Indeed, congratulations again on your promotion... I just wanted to say that I had mortally wounded his soul, so letting him do what he did to his brain was my retribution. If our positions were reversed I would hope he would have done the same for me, despite the personal cost," Dr Engels said.

"Which in your case was?"

"The loss of Level Twelve, the loss of a friend and external scrutiny," Dr Engels said mournfully.

"That's quite a cost," replied Brad, realising that any one of those consequences would have seemed like a high price to pay for the Doctor.

"Yes. Until next time," Dr Engels said, his voice catching as he hung up. Brad was still wondering which loss affected him the most.

The day at the Police Station was mostly a blur for Brad. He was grateful that he could hide away in his office. The media had phoned him constantly, asking inane questions like "wasn't that the case that you made your name on?", "how does this make you feel?" and "will you arrest anyone?" Brad left the moment the clock said he was allowed.

That night he spent a sleepless night pondering the case all over again. Amy eventually kicked him out of their bed and sent him to the couch so that at least one of them could get some rest. After contemplating the entire caper, he had the sudden thought that there might be something else on the Professor's phone that could be of use. The Professor liked to record things so maybe there would be a voice memo on his phone. He hadn't looked at the memos as he was interested in the contacts list and phone call record.

Upon arriving in the office, he immediately made arrangements to see the boxes of evidence from the case. They had been moved from the previous storage facility to a more secure one. A couple of hours and a short car ride later and Brad had the evidence box in front of him. He found the Professor's phone at the bottom, underneath several folders of files. He took out the charger he had brought with him, plugged it in and turned on the phone. He quickly touched the microphone icon to bring up the Professor's voice memos. Three were listed, two from the morning the Professor had died. The first was a shopping list. Brad selected the newest and last recording. The Professor spoke rapidly; "It is too late for me, but here is Level Thirteen, you can control the reaction by…" Brad quickly stopped the recording, his heart pounding. He smiled and acknowledged the maturity he was about to display. It was as though the old him that lacked confidence, was poor at reasoning and found much of his life to be a struggle, had died.

I am happy, he thought. Brad decided he didn't want to know what was on the recording or in Level Twelve, and returned the phone to the box. Some things were better left unknown…

THE END

Acknowledgements

I would like to thank the people who read early drafts of the novel. I am grateful for your feedback, enthusiasm and encouragement.

Thank you to my editor, Meredith, whose suggestions and support were invaluable. I also thank Sylvia for her help and advice during the publishing process.

I would also like to thank you, the reader for choosing this book. I hope you enjoy reading it as much as I enjoyed writing it.

About The Author

According to his wife, Robert has spent too much of his life studying. She has a point as he recently completed a fifth university degree to go with two other tertiary qualifications. Robert has degrees in psychology, sociology, biology and education, all of which inspire his writing. He lives in Melbourne with his wife, two children and a dog. This is his second novel.

robertsnew.com
talepublishing.com